SOME

OF

THE

PARTS

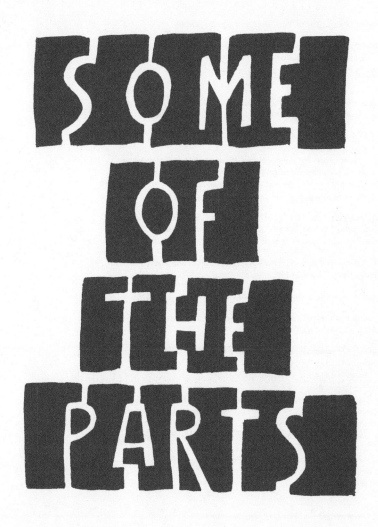

HANNAH BARNABY

Alfred A. Knopf 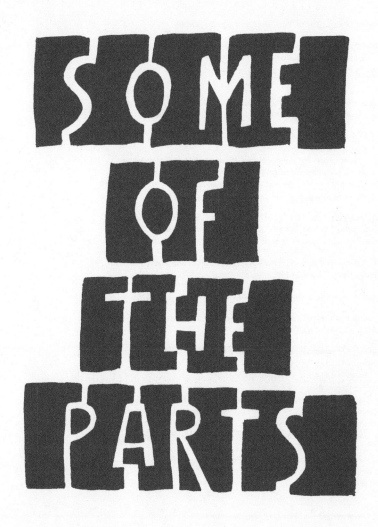 New York

THIS IS A BORZOI BOOK PUBLISHED BY ALFRED A. KNOPF

Visit us on the Web! randomhouseteens.com

Educators and librarians, for a variety of teaching tools, visit us at
RHTeachersLibrarians.com

Library of Congress Cataloging-in-Publication Data
Barnaby, Hannah Rodgers.
   Some of the parts / Hannah Barnaby.
      pages   cm.
   Summary: A devastated teenaged girl sets out on a quest to track
down transplant recipients after she discovers that her older brother was
an organ donor.
   ISBN 978-0-553-53963-9 (trade) — ISBN 978-0-553-53964-6 (lib. bdg.) —
ISBN 978-0-553-53965-3 (ebook)
[1. Grief—Fiction. 2. Brothers and sisters—Fiction.] I. Title.
   PZ7.B253So 2016
   [Fic]—dc23
                       2015012311

The text of this book is set in 12-point Fournier MT Std.

Printed in the United States of America

February 2016

10 9 8 7 6 5 4 3 2 1

First Edition

FOR JESSE

The whole is more than the sum of its parts.
—ARISTOTLE, *METAPHYSICS*

ONE

HOLD ON

saturday 9/20

We are driving around town in Mel's inherited Oldsmobile when we see the pig truck.

Mel and I first became friends when she was the only one in my comp class who liked my short story. It was called "The President Dreams of His Mother," and it was about how the president of the United States had a dream that he was talking to his mother and she was completely naked the whole time and he was so disturbed by the dream that he couldn't concentrate on his job, which resulted in the nuclear annihilation of the entire East Coast.

Truthfully, the story wasn't very good. But Mel called it "delightfully obtuse" and clapped for an inappropriately long time at the end of my reading. I'm never sure if Mel knows what she's talking about but I make a lot of effort to believe that she does, because it's nice to think that someone is (a) knowledgeable and (b) on my side.

Mel never knew my brother very well—we were more friends within the boundaries of the school building than friends who paint each other's toenails at sleepovers. Amy and Zoey and Fiona had filled that category, but they hadn't come over since the accident and I hadn't tried to call them. Maybe none of us knew who was supposed to call first. Then Mel showed up at my house, and when she did, she acted totally normal. Her visit was like the social equivalent of mouth-to-mouth resuscitation. For a week I had been holding my breath whenever I went anywhere because people were constantly coming up to me and hugging me, or pretending they hadn't seen me because they didn't know what to say. Mel just knocked on my front door and said, "Do you have any chocolate? I am *dying* for some chocolate." She even used the word *dying* without cringing or gasping or anything. So I let her in.

Hanging out with Mel makes it easy for me to be quiet. There's no pressure for me to talk because Mel is always working on something and she is fully focused on whatever that is. She doesn't care if I zone out when I see a pair of mittens that look like the ones my brother had when we were little, or a car that looks like the one he was saving up for when he died.

A black Mustang.

There are more of those around than you might think.

So it's a decent arrangement, even though Mel is not always easy. Her voice is like gravel under tires and her laugh is harsh and she makes jokes that aren't funny. And she drives like a maniac. I don't think it occurs to her that I might have a personal issue with reckless driving. At least, I hope it doesn't. I hope it's just ignorance and not cruelty. It is useful to have a friend with a car. We are in the same grade, but she is a year older because once upon a time her parents sent her to an expensive school that was called "progressive" and then turned out to be a front for a religious cult. Mel had to repeat third grade, and her mother has never gotten over it.

It is difficult to keep my composure when she drives like that. I am always waiting for the next crash, the sickening crunch of metal and glass, the pain, the sirens, the chaos.

For all her faults, Mel insulates me from the rest of the world, the world that looks so bright and sharp now, in the after. She talks and talks and fills my ears so I don't have to listen for those terrible sounds. She keeps a list of word combinations that would make great band names. Terminal Butterfly. Soapbox Evangelists. She makes up games for us to play so I don't have to think. Our favorite is Opposite.

"What's the opposite of bridge?" I ask.

"Burn," she tells me.

Today Mel is driving a bit more reasonably than usual because even she is not immune to the effect of the maple trees that line the highway, their leaves turning obscene shades of red and orange. I am holding my hand out the open window and letting it coast the invisible wave of air. And because my hand is pleasantly numbed by the chill-edged air, and because the leaves are rioting all around us, and because the sky is so blue, I am temporarily fooled into thinking that the world might be coming back online.

Mel has just said *burn* when the pig truck appears in the distance, like some strange mirage. We come up on it slowly. I recognize the sort of truck it is as we get closer, know to expect something alive inside of it by the ventilation holes all around the huge metal cargo container. It is not until we pull up alongside the truck that I see the shocking, dreadful pink of the pigs. Their bodies are pressed against the metal, bulging out of the holes like fleshy bubbles. I can't see their faces, can't make out their individual bodies, so it is as if there is just one endless mass of pig stuffed into the truck, as if they have all been mashed together into some kind of living, breathing, horrible pulp.

"Oh my god," I whisper.

Mel looks over. "Gross," she comments, but she says it so casually that I know she isn't having the same trouble breathing that I'm having. My chest is tight and my throat is, too, and I'm caught between wanting to retch and wanting to cry. This is how I am now. Unfeeling, numb, until something pierces my casing and I pour messily out into the world.

I try to gather myself back into place, but it's no use. The pigs are too pink, the sun deepening their color until they are almost as bright as the trees. All I can do is cover my eyes. It feels like cheating, but I do it anyway.

And Mel must see me do it because she says, "Hang on," and I hear the enormous engine of the Oldsmobile groan with the effort of accelerating. I peek out from between my fingers to see the front edge of the trailer recede past my window, and as we pass the truck's cab, the driver waggles his fingers at us and grins.

TWO

MISS MISERY

Mel and I head for Common Grounds and get there just in time for my shift. I try to avoid coming here on my days off—Cranky Andy doesn't like having to treat his employees like customers. It stretches the limits of his already limited social energy. He'd rather be practicing his foam-art technique or making a spreadsheet to chart sales trends in baked goods. So Mel likes to drive me to work because she can get a latte to go. The only other place to get coffee in town is Dunkin' Donuts and Mel says their coffee tastes "like industry," whatever that means.

Common Grounds used to be a drugstore, and when they converted it into a coffee shop, they decided to keep some of the old features, including the automatic doors. They swoosh open as if by magic. I mean, it's not magic, obviously. It's magnets or electric sensors or something. Anyway, the swoosh was accompanied by a *ding* until Cranky Andy said he couldn't stand it anymore and made them disconnect the dinger. Cranky Andy gets what he wants. No one else in this town can make a decent latte, especially not with decorative designs engraved in the foam.

I had just gotten used to the *ding* when it stopped. I had just stopped being startled by it and now I kind of miss it. But I'll adjust.

I have to, if I want normal again. I started working here two weeks after the accident. School wasn't out yet but it was clear to everyone that I wasn't going back. Nothing really hurt anymore, my cuts were healing into a map of pink scars threading across my hands and forearms, but I was still tired all the time. My teachers agreed (or were convinced) to give me incompletes on my report card and let me make up the final exams over the summer. So I had a jump on the rest of the summer-job scrabblers when I walked into Common Grounds and asked for an application.

Cranky Andy watched me fill it out. "You're that girl," he said after I handed it back to him. I had used my full name: Taliesin West McGovern. My parents named me after Frank Lloyd Wright's architecture school in the Arizona desert. They visited it on their honeymoon, and my mother even applied to go there but then she got pregnant with my brother.

Of course I knew exactly what he was talking about, but I made him say it anyway. I was still forcing people to acknowledge it. I wasn't letting anyone get away with less. "What girl?"

"The girl who . . ." He paused, but barely. "That accident on River Road. Your brother died?"

I nodded.

"That sucks," he said. It was just a fact, the way he said it. There was no disputing it.

"It does."

He looked down again at my application, like it was a picture of something interesting. Or distasteful. "You're hired."

"Because you feel sorry for me?" That was still important then. Less so, now.

Cranky Andy raised his eyes, set them on me. "No, because I can't stand chatty and you don't talk much. And because I don't feel like interviewing a hundred high school kids who don't have the attention span to take a coffee order."

I didn't need a job, really. I was only there because I couldn't stand it at home, where the air had turned to wet cement and all of us were choking on it. The automatic door swooshed and the not-yet-abolished dinger *ding*ed. I jumped.

"You okay?"

"I'm great," I said. "When do I start?"

"Right now, if you can."

I looked around. There were, like, three customers in the whole place.

"I don't know how to make anything," I told him.

"You don't need to. I make the drinks, you handle the register and the bakery stuff. It gets delivered in the morning, ready to go."

"What if it gets busy? Shouldn't I be able to help with—"

He put a possessive hand on the milk frother. "I work alone," he said darkly.

So that was my first day at work, standing at the register, knowledgeless, while Cranky Andy slipped into the back room to record a *Minecraft* tutorial on his phone. I realized later that we hadn't discussed how much I'd get paid. But it didn't really matter.

I would have paid *him* for getting me out of the house, for re-installing me in the outside world. School ended without me. Summer limped toward fall, and I forced it to carry me on its sweaty back. I was too tired to walk. I woke up in the morning and never felt like I had slept. I was mechanical and dazed, but I proceeded. I ate, I showered, I passed my final exams. I worked. I rode in Mel's car and braced myself for the crash that never came.

I kept on being the one who survived.

The job was like medicine: vaguely unpleasant but probably good for me. Dealing with customers during a rush was exhausting—the eye contact, the forced smiles, the small talk—but I liked it when it was quiet. I spent my time alphabetizing bags of coffee and arranging muffins under glass domes as if they were exhibits in a museum. And Cranky Andy turned out to be a pretty decent boss. He is not the owner of Common Grounds—that's some guy who used to live here and now lives elsewhere but couldn't be bothered to sell the place. Early on, I made the mistake of asking Andy if he was going to buy it. He snapped, "It's not for sale!" and then dumped a bag of beans into the huge industrial coffee grinder with a surprising show of upper-body strength.

I kept myself busy with small, simple tasks and tried to ignore how hollow and disjointed I felt. Sometimes watching the people in the coffee shop was like watching a room full of ghosts who didn't realize that they were in another dimension altogether. That nearby there was a tree ringed by flower arrangements, dried and bleached by the sun that relentlessly rises every day.

So I pretended I didn't know this either, tried to appear as if I was just like them, because that was what I wanted. I wanted to be like them again. Oblivious. Content. Caffeinated.

Unharmed.

Mel takes her coffee and oinks to me on her way out the door, her way of telling me that (a) I didn't imagine that truck and (b) life goes on. I oink back, still shaky but determined to hide it. Determined to act normal.

And then Amy comes in.

Amy and Zoey and Fiona.

The trio that used to be a foursome, when I was part of the club. The friends who used to star in the movie of my life. Until the movie jumped genres from comedy to tearjerker.

Of the three of them, Amy's the only one who reacts to the sight of me. Her eyes widen ever so slightly and she pauses a half step but keeps walking. Plants herself in front of me and says, "Large skim latte, please." And then, "Hi."

Before I can answer, she starts digging around in her bag, staring into its vast unseeable depths. She never could find anything in there. I'd given her a flashlight for her birthday as a joke. I think about mentioning it.

"Got it," Amy tells no one in particular. Someone other than me. She extracts a debit card and holds it out, pinched between two fingers, her eyes set on something behind me so she doesn't accidentally make eye contact.

I take the card, careful to keep our hands from touching.

Fiona and Zoey are hovering behind her. "Hurry up," Zoey whines. "We're already late for our pedis." School started three weeks ago but it's still warm enough outside, just barely, to wear flip-flops.

This is where Mel would jump in with a sarcastic warning about the dangers of foot infections from unsanitary salon tools. But Mel is not here. Mel is driving around with her latte, scouting the roads for freshly run-over animals.

Amy glares at Zoey and for a second I think she's going to

defend me—the slow cashier at the coffee shop—or herself—the one whose bag is too big. But she doesn't say anything, and as I hand her card back, I am weirdly aware of how close our fingertips are. Our fingerprints coexisting on the same plastic surface, our trace bits of DNA overlapping. We used to be this close all the time.

Now I am radioactive.

Maybe we would have reached the end of our road anyway, even without the accident. I read somewhere that you change friends every seven years, and we'd passed that milestone years ago. We were on borrowed time. We spent our seven years on preschool, ballet classes, soccer teams, birthday parties. Our mothers were friends, so we were friends, too. Little kids don't ask whether they have anything in common. That comes later.

And I don't blame Amy, or her vapid sidekicks, or the girls I played soccer with, or any of the others who avoid me now. Because I get it. I've been marked by this tragedy and the sight of me reminds them that life ends. Whether it's a heart attack or old age or an overdose or a car hitting a tree, there's an end in store for each of us.

It freaks them out.

I know, too, that Amy has her own reasons to hate me for what happened.

Hence my mission: to pay my penance, to get back to normal, back to before. So when they see me, it's not death they see, or the shadow of the boy who always used to be next to me. It's proof that life can be reconstructed, that the tree on River Road can be just a tree again, that the sun-bleached flowers can be swept away and forgotten.

I am convincing myself of this as Amy and Zoey and Fiona walk out the swooshing doors. They pause outside, and for a second I think Amy will walk back in and say something to me. Even something angry would be better than the silence we've shared for the last four months. Then I see that they have stopped to check out a boy who is walking toward them from across the street. Amy simply gapes at him, but Zoey and Fiona compose themselves in photo formation, hips turned and chins tucked down, as if he might take a mental picture of them as he passes. But he strides past them without a glance and displaces their footsteps with his own as he enters Common Grounds.

There are a few colleges in towns nearby, and sometimes professors decide they want to live a little farther away from where they work. When I see him for the first time, I think maybe that is his story—the son of a professor, or a university student—because he looks thoughtful and very sure of himself, and because he is carrying a thick book, one arm curled protectively around it. He doesn't balk at the swoosh of the doors (no more *ding*) or hesitate as he walks to the counter. He doesn't squint at the chalkboard menu over my head. He just looks me straight in the eye and orders an iced chai with whole milk, as if everything could be so simple.

His voice is deep and soothing. He sounds as if he will read audiobooks someday. Or meditation podcasts.

I notice his voice, and I notice these things, too: his hair, which is curly and dark and flops into place when he pushes his fingers through it; his fingers, which are long and would have been praised effusively by my piano teacher; his eyes, which are chocolate brown.

In short, everything he has in common with—

Everything that reminds me of—

I almost knock Cranky Andy to the floor as I sprint down the back hall, where I gasp for air and wait for the vise in my chest to release my heart.

So much for normal.

THREE

IN BETWEEN DAYS

I hide in the employee bathroom for an unmeasured amount of time. It feels good to be in a small space. I take comfort in the damp concrete walls, the rust on the metal door, the frayed-edge posters that have faded over the years, as if the effort to brighten up the room has exhausted their colors. The last things I need are sunshine and rainbows. I like things worn and weary these days.

Then Cranky Andy bangs on the door. Back to reality.

I occupy myself with filling little boxes with sweetener packets, carefully lining up their corners. Blue, pink, yellow. The colors of baby clothes. Meant to soothe you and make you forget that the packets are full of chemicals.

The boy is still here, sitting in a far corner, one hand curled around his cup. He glances at me for a few seconds and then goes back to reading his book, flipping the pages, a pile of rustling leaves. I load my tray with the sweeteners and deliver a box to each table, and when I am close enough to peek over his shoulder, I see that he is looking at a page of photographs bound into the middle of the book. The captions are too small for me to read without completely invading his personal space, and also I might accidentally find out what he smells like and if it's anything like—

The last box of packets slides off my tray and onto the floor, scattering its contents. I duck down to gather them up again, crush them in my hand, and throw the ruined collection back onto the tray. He turns his head just enough for me to see his profile and then stills like a portrait.

"You okay?" he asks quietly.

"I'm fine," I tell him. I should leave it at that—I've already displayed enough buffoonery—but curiosity gets the upper hand. And it feels good to test myself, make myself talk to someone who, even up close, resembles my brother. Not well enough to play him in a dramatic reenactment, maybe, but more than the average guy on the street. "What are you reading?"

He turns toward his table and looks down, as if he's forgotten what book he's holding. His hair curls around his ear like leaves on a vine. "A biography." He puts his finger in between the pages to mark his place, and closes the book so I can see the cover. A man with dark hair and hooded eyes is staring at us, his arms extended to show the handcuffs linking his wrists. *The Secret Life of Houdini*.

"The magician?" I ask.

"Among other things."

The book is rippled, worn at the corners. "How many times have you read it?"

"I don't know," he says. He looks up at me as he pulls his finger out of the book.

"You'll lose your place," I tell him.

He shrugs. "I'll find it again." Then he says, "I lied to you."

"What?"

"I know exactly how many times I've read it. See?" He flips the front cover open and shows me the marks, four straight vertical lines with a fifth diagonal slash across them. Three sets of them, plus two extra verticals.

"Seventeen?"

"I'm a creature of habit. Why sugarcoat it?" He grins. "It's been a while, though. We just moved here and I found this when I was putting my stuff away."

Sugarcoat would be a great band name, I think. I will try and remember to tell Mel this later. Emboldened by this thought, I step closer. "Do you read anything else?"

"Other biographies, mostly. It's interesting to see what a person's life adds up to. Don't you think?"

Remembering is practically all I do these days. It's such a relief that he can't see it written all over me that I almost laugh out loud. "I guess. But does a person have to be dead before you can do the math?"

He smiles, and it looks almost sad. "I like to know how the story ends."

The door swooshes then and more people walk in, and Cranky Andy bangs two milk steamers together to get my attention.

"Gotta go," I say lamely.

The boy nods, a single motion. "I'm Chase," he says.

I roll the name around, fitting it to him like a limb grafted to a tree. I should offer my name in return, but I don't like to say it anymore. The sound of it scrapes at my heart. It reminds me of my brother, the way our names were always spoken together as if they were one long sound.

"You should try one," Chase says, lifting the book as if he's toasting me with it. "There are some amazing stories out there."

I nod. *There are stories everywhere,* I think.

When he finally gathers his belongings and exits the automatic doors, he looks back at me—one second, two seconds, he turns away at three—and I envy his ability to look at another person like that, without wondering if he's breaking some unwritten rule. I wonder if I could read the story of someone else's life and forgive their faults so easily.

But I can't devote myself to nostalgia for people I never knew.

I have my own memories to deal with.

I live in limbo, between before and after. Before the accident, and after. And there's a sizable gap in the middle. Try as I might to ignore this, to act like I didn't lose a whole chunk of my personal timeline four months ago, I haven't really climbed out of the chasm yet. I'm still in between. Before is over, and after is going to happen whether I like it or not.

Before the accident, I saw the usual things in the usual way. My eyes communicated with my brain and there was no misunderstanding. Now, after, my heart keeps throwing itself into the conversation. Everything is scratched, tinged with a wash of blackened light. Nothing is clear. It is, I imagine, how a blind person would feel if someone snuck into their apartment and moved everything around. There is a lot of bumping into things. There is a lot of confusion and frustration and temptation to give up and sit down in one place for however much time is left.

The world is misaligned, uneasy in its balance.

But I have gotten very good at pretending otherwise.

At home, for instance, I can walk through the front door like I used to and I can act like the door is just a door, even though it looks (as everything does) a little bit wrong. A little crooked. Too sharp around its edges. I can keep my face perfectly still so that no one knows how much everything reminds me of—

Because I stop myself, you see? I don't let his name in.

I don't let myself remember how he always slammed the door too hard, how my mother called to him sharply and he had her laughing seconds later. How he got away with leaving his football gear and his backpack and everything else in a pile because none of us could stay mad at him.

I don't think of it.

After the accident, everyone was really nice. Too nice. People I barely knew came up to me in the drugstore and hugged me, clutched me too tight and whispered things like "Oh, you poor thing." Beyond that, they didn't really know what to say, which became apparent when I tried to go back for the last two weeks of school. Every time I walked down a hallway, the herd of bodies parted like the Red Sea around me. Amy avoided me—she'd duck into a bathroom or down a hallway when she saw me coming— and Zoey and Fiona were only too glad to follow her. I tried to make a joke out of it but no one laughed at my jokes anymore. Except in that nervous way that doesn't sound as much like happiness as it sounds like concern that someone in the room is unstable and might suddenly do something really inappropriate. And then, to everyone's relief, Principal Hunter sent me home again and got my teachers to delay my exams. So I could recover. Whatever that meant.

Everyone could see I was different. Of course I was, because what kind of person would I be if my brother died and I stayed exactly the same? But they still don't know what the real change is, that I can't make the words come out right, that I can't feel anything the way I used to. That my heart is twisted, a knot I can't unravel.

I keep hoping the rituals will fix me.

I call them rituals even though they're not religious and they don't involve voodoo dolls or magic spells—I like to think of them as things that are important to do, important in a way that's beyond my just wanting to do them. So, every day, usually after school, I spend five minutes looking at his high school yearbook. Not the pictures. The index. The list of numbers that signify which pages his pictures are on. I have it memorized by now, but I like seeing the digits printed on the page, always the same, preserved. I cover his name with my fingertip and stare at the numbers: 8, 11, 19, 33, 34, 35, 42, 56, 58, and 73. Senior picture, track picture, student government, photography club, newspaper. Candids in the cafeteria, the chem lab, the parking lot, the library. Best eyes. Best smile. Most likely to succeed.

Fat chance of that now.

But that's the kind of thing I'm not supposed to say. The joke that isn't funny.

Mom and Dad don't know about the rituals. They don't know much about what I do these days. I don't think this was ever their intention, this distance. It's more like a habit that formed over the summer. Right after the accident, there was a frenzy of attention and smothering care—my mother took me everywhere she went, either because she was afraid to let me out of her sight or because she was scared to be alone, and she chattered nonstop about meaningless stuff. But after a few weeks, the mania wore off and she settled into a quiet numbness. She withdrew and my dad did, too, and now we orbit each other like planets. Same solar system, different paths. Different rates of motion.

After the yearbook, I lie down on my bed and close my eyes and feel around for a memory, something with lots of details. Pick an image, bring it into focus until I can see it projected on my eyelids like a movie on a screen. I have my favorites. Swimming in the lake at the cabin when I was five. The day the geese chased us after we ran out of bread and he carried me on his back until we were safe. The first time I beat him at *Mario Kart*. The dinner we made for Mom and Dad's anniversary. Me and him in the kitchen, arguing about whether or not the chicken was done.

"Just cut it open," I told him.

"No way," he said, and then added, in a terrible French accent, "Eet will *ruin* zee presentation."

I go over it again and again, the cooking part. Not the dinner itself. I don't need to remember Mom and Dad. They're still here.

Sort of.

The remembering can take a long time or not, depending on how clearly I can get the picture to focus. I stay there until it's very sharp. It takes work, sometimes. Sometimes I can't remember exactly what he said after I said something, or what the tomato sauce smelled like after we put the anchovies in, or how it felt when he swung me up onto his back and hooked his arms around my legs. But I can usually get it. That's the point. To make sure it's still there.

I do this with one good memory, and then I find a bad one,

because I know he wasn't perfect and I want to be accurate. A fight we had. A bruise he gave me. The time he ripped my teddy bear's arm off because he was mad at me.

Two weeks before the accident, when I saw him kissing Amy behind the gym.

I try to avoid that one, but sometimes it pops up unannounced, and then I have to let it in. And it carries a potency that few other memories have, because it's one of the only things we argued about that never got to be okay. How he hadn't told me. How I was the last one to know. We ran out of time to make it okay. And Amy clearly doesn't want to discuss it.

After I'm done with the remembering, I go to my closet and take out the green flannel shirt I stole from his room. It still smells like him. But barely. I can't decide if it would be cheating to buy a new can of his deodorant and spray some on the shirt.

That's the problem with the rituals: There's no one else to tell me how to do them, whether I can make new rules or not. No one to tell me whether they're working. Because sometimes I'm really not sure.

It seems like he's fading anyway.

FOUR

I'M LOOKING THROUGH YOU

sunday 9/21

My parents have already left for church when I wake up. Everyone has their Sunday traditions. Brunch, football games, farmers' markets, bike rides, hiking, meditation, cleaning the house, washing the car, washing the dog. Ours used to be the early service at St. Anne's—me trying not to giggle as my brother drew muppety pictures of Father Paul on his leaflet—followed by bagels and hot chocolate at Roundabouts, and then the guys would spend the afternoon watching whatever sport was in season while Mom crafted things in her fabric sanctuary upstairs, and I would wander between them, checking scores and occasionally getting to hot-glue-gun something. It was completely boring. It was perfect.

I hated having to get up early for church. But I loved the windows, especially on sunny mornings, when all of the saints were lit up in crayon colors. They looked so bright and flawless that I was shocked when my grandmother gave me a copy of *The Lives of the Saints* and I learned about their grisly deaths. I shared it with my brother, the two of us poring over the gruesome pictures and choosing the best stories. My favorite was Lucy, patron saint of the blind. She was tortured, her eyes plucked out, her body covered in boiling oil and set on fire. And when even that didn't finish her off, they stabbed her through the heart with a sword. In her portrait, she was blond and pretty, her eyes downcast and bleeding elegantly, and she held a plate with her disembodied eyeballs on it.

Now I can't stand church, the dusty scent of the air, the shadows, the sunbeams that slice across the pews. I haven't been inside since the funeral. My parents have stopped asking if I want to go, which is a relief, but the silence when I'm home alone is like the ocean. It used to be soothing, and now it threatens to drown me.

I try to fill it with noise: the television, popcorn in the microwave, the sounds of my own feet walking across every creaky spot on the floor. Today it almost works, until this last method brings me to a loose floorboard that makes a particularly loud creak. In front of my brother's room, when I'm standing outside his door.

I've been in his room since the accident. I took a few of his things for myself, for the rituals. I even sat down on his bed once to see if it made anything happen inside of me. It didn't.

But now—maybe the rituals are finally working, or maybe it's just that I've worn a hole in myself somewhere and something is leaking out like a toxic gas—the sight of his door, closed like a tomb, makes me want to scream and scream until every corner of the house is filled with my voice.

I clap my hands over my mouth and run into my room. Grab my phone. Call Mel.

She sounds groggy and far away when she answers. "Whaddayawant?"

"I . . ."

I don't know. To not be alone. To feel something good for a change. I grab at an answer that will keep her on the phone. "Coffee."

Mel grunts.

"And I need to pick up my schedule at work."

This fact has just occurred to me, but it's true. Or true enough. And I tell myself that the relief that floods my body is all thanks to this, a simple reason to leave the house. I won't admit, at least not to the point of allowing the words to fully form in my brain, that it might have something to do with seeing a boy who looks a bit like my brother.

Every time I walk into Common Grounds, even though I've worked here for so long, it feels both familiar and foreign, as if things have shifted ever so slightly since the last time I was here. My house feels this way sometimes, too. Everywhere does.

Martha is behind the counter. She showed up a couple of weeks ago, and Cranky Andy let me know on the sly that she is the owner's sister and not to be trifled with. Her hair is like steel wool and she wears sweatshirts with cats on them. She looks soft and grandmotherly but underneath she is hard, like a pillow with an anvil hidden inside. I've seen her lift fifty-pound bags of coffee beans as if they were sleeping babies.

Cranky Andy is clearly afraid of her. I sort of want to *be* her.

I wait in line while Mel looks for seats. She is far better at finding the right people to intimidate into leaving. She stands next to their table, staring at them relentlessly until they become annoyed or unnerved enough to get up. Her method never fails. But this time she abandons her post to show me a flyer she ripped off the notice board.

"Check it out!" she crows, waving the goldenrod page over her head like a flag. "The supernatural has finally made it to Molton!"

Everyone, of course, turns to look. Which is Mel's general purpose in life.

I grab the paper. "Go find a table, would you?"

She hangs her head and whimpers, a scolded puppy. As she slinks away, still whimpering, I read the scratchy print on the flyer. It looks like it was written with a Sharpie, all caps, in a hurry. It must have been put up this morning, because it wasn't there when we closed last night.

SÉANCE

SUNDAY

8 P.M.

THE ELBOW ROOM

BRING $10 AND AN OPEN MIND

There's a poorly reproduced picture of a pair of hands at the bottom, open palms holding nothing.

This must be a joke, I think.

"Hello," Martha says brightly. Her smile is a blank line and she shows no signs of familiarity, as if we've never met before. As if I wasn't the one who trained her on the register. "What can I get you?" Then she lowers her voice and leans in a bit. "You know you're not supposed to take things off the bulletin board."

"I'll put it back, I promise." I cross my heart with my index finger.

Martha looks skeptical.

I order our lattes and wait patiently while she searches for the right button on the cash register. "It's that one," I offer, and start to reach around to show her, but she stops me in my tracks with a glare that would freeze the coffee I just ordered.

When Cranky Andy pushes the finished drinks toward me, I raise an eyebrow in what I hope is a nonaggressive, casual way and ask, "How's she doing?"

He hunches down a bit. "Fine," he says. Then, almost in the same breath, he adds, "She's taking over the day shift."

"Every day?"

He nods, intently focused on the milk frother.

Before I can ask what this means for my own schedule, Mel's voice rockets across the room.

"Are we going to the séance!"

It isn't even a question, the way she's shouting it. It's a declaration that happens to be in the form of a question. The way the answers on *Jeopardy!* are only technically questions. They're never said that way. The contestants' voices lack the proper inflection. That has always bothered me.

"Hold on!" I whisper-shout back.

Andy already has his back to me, working on the next round of orders, so I figure I'll talk to him about my schedule another time. I hustle our lattes over to the table and sit quickly, hunching over as if that will somehow deflect the number of eyes looking my way. I can feel them on me like spiders.

"Could you please?" I say.

"Sorry, sorry." Mel waves her hand over her coffee, diffusing the smell of the cinnamon that sits on top of the foam like fertilizer. "So, what do you say? Shall we attend this mysterious gathering?"

"Why would I want to do that?"

Mel rolls her eyes. "Why *wouldn't* you?"

Sometimes we dance around the subject, Mel and I. I won't ever say that I wish I could talk to my brother again, and she won't ever say that she understands what I wish for. Saying either of those things would put us uncomfortably close to sharing our feelings.

While I'm considering the question, Mel raises her phone between us and I hear the virtual click of the camera. She likes to take pictures of me at random moments, and I let her as long as she doesn't (a) show them to me or (b) use them in some depraved art installation.

"I don't know," I say. "I think those things are creepy." I say *creepy*, but I mean *sad*. I used to watch this show where a psychic picked people out of the audience and gave them messages from lost loved ones. And you could tell they were so happy to hear something, anything, about that person who wasn't there anymore. But I always imagined the moment right after the show was over, when the cameras shut off and the psychic pulled off his microphone, and whatever connection had been there between the living and the dead just . . . died all over again.

"True," Mel agrees, "but I seriously doubt the Elbow Room is capable of getting actually scary. It's probably like one of those haunted houses we went to in elementary school. I used to laugh my ass off in those things."

Mel is not afraid of anything. She is that kind of girl, a girl who dyes the tips of her curly hair black and wears costumes to school on days that aren't Halloween and does taxidermy in her spare time. Last Christmas she installed a roadkill Nativity scene in front of her house that got her in trouble with every church for fifty miles around. Casting a dead squirrel as the baby Jesus was too much for just about everyone, but Mel cited freedom of speech and eventually the protesters moved on. I think it was an added bonus that her mother refused to speak to her for more than a week.

I do not tell her—I can't—that I was terrified of those haunted houses. Goblins and skeletons leaping out from half-opened doors, hands grabbing for me in the darkness, the echoing voices, the stale air. The sense that I might never find my way out. But I don't say any of this.

What I say is "Pick me up at seven-thirty."

FIVE

BREAK ON THROUGH TO THE OTHER SIDE

My parents and I have our usual pizza-and-silence dinner, followed by Dad retreating to his study to watch home-improvement videos online. Our home does not need much improvement (structurally, at least) but Dad likes to be prepared in case of a spackling or drywall emergency. So he spends hours watching other dads discuss the proper tools for every possible job, watching them demonstrate various techniques for cutting tile, installing bathroom fans, and grouting.

I know this is what he does because I check his browser history on a regular basis. I also read the journal that my mother's therapist told her to start writing in. Just because my parents and I don't talk doesn't mean I don't care what they're up to.

This is also how I know that my dad wants us to move. Pages and pages of realty and location searches. Plus, I eavesdrop. Dad has been trying to talk Mom into moving and so far she hasn't let him pierce her bubble of solitude, but if he keeps wearing away at her, she'll probably change her mind. Before the accident, Mom was very opinionated and did not make any decisions without copious research and a town-wide opinion poll. Now . . . well, she seems to just want someone else to figure everything out.

Do I have my doubts about staying here? Of course.

But maybe that boy who looks like my brother is right. Remembering is vital. This is where we lost him, and this is where we should be. Maybe if I can make contact tonight, I can get N—my brother to help me.

Once Dad is safely ensconced in the study and Mom is occupied with some work-related matter upstairs, I write a quick note: *Going out with Mel—back by 10.* It's partly a test, to see whether they'll accept so little explanation. They wouldn't have last spring.

Before.

I open the kitchen door as quietly as I can. Opened too quickly, the door will squeak. My parents might come looking for me, spin out of their orbits. They can't totally shake that sense of obligation. Leaving a note and sneaking out is much less awkward. For all of us.

The air is crisp and the lack of streetlights makes the night denser, the stars more garish. A crescent moon hangs in the sky like the ghost of a banana. I stand at the end of the driveway and listen to my own breathing. I trace my favorite scar, the one that crosses my left hand like a fledgling river.

I am immensely relieved when I see Mel's car turn the corner and head my way.

"Hey." I say it out loud, even though she is still a few houses away, to warm up my voice a little. It is amazing how quickly you forget the sound of your own voice if you don't use it enough. I sound really weird to myself. I make a mental note to talk to myself more when I am home alone. Maybe start reading Mom's journal out loud. Although there's nothing very interesting in it yet.

Mel pulls up fast and hits the brakes so her car jolts to a stop with the passenger door directly in front of me. "Nice," I tell her as I get in. "You're getting better at that." She usually overshoots and has—once or twice—come dangerously close to running down our mailbox.

"I know, right?" she says. "It drives my mother crazy, but I think it's important to challenge one's depth perception now and then."

"Where did you tell her we were going?" I ask as we pull away from the curb.

"Library."

"At eight o'clock on a Sunday? Is the library even open on Sunday night?"

Mel shrugs. "Who knows? She didn't ask for further details."

This is something Mel and I have in common: parents who don't want to know. Mel's mother is a bank manager, a job that suits her perfectly because it enables her to find out how much money everyone else has compared to her. Mel's dad has one of those financial jobs with a hollow title and frequent travel to countries I couldn't identify on a map. All of which means Mel has as much freedom as I do, with a much bigger allowance.

With Molton being about the size of a Monopoly board, it doesn't take us long to get to the Elbow Room, about a song and a half. My brother measured trips that way, by song length, and made playlists that fit our family road trips perfectly. When we drove cross-country three summers ago, he managed to find a whole bunch of songs that mentioned cities by name and he put them in geographical order: "Via Chicago," "Wichita Skyline," "Leaving Las Vegas." He made a customized playlist for every one of his college visits. They're still on his MP3 player.

A song and a half does not a road trip make. But it's enough to get a decent distance from home. The same moon hangs above us and the same cold air presses on the windows, but I feel calmer. Until I remember why we're here.

Mel has to park at the far end of the lot because all the good spaces are taken. She laments her lack of a handicapped sign to hang from her rearview mirror, and I refrain from pointing out that the Elbow Room doesn't even have handicapped parking. It's a New Age bookstore that used to be a dive bar. The original owner died a few years ago and left the place to his son Steve. Steve quickly decided he didn't want to keep a possum's hours and the Elbow Room was reinvented. Only Steve didn't have much of a budget for renovations, so the place looks exactly the same as it did before. And he still serves drinks. And doesn't card. Which makes the Elbow Room one of Mel's favorite places.

However, neither Mel nor I want to mix alcohol and the super-natural. We pay our ten-dollar cover charge and order sodas and stake out a couple of barstools so we can check out the scene. It isn't difficult to tell which customers are here for the séance—they look a little nervous, and they thumb through esoteric books that they would likely never buy. One woman, older than my mother and draped in a number of multicolored scarves, glances furtively from side to side every minute or so, as if there might be ghosts strolling around the store, waiting like we are for the séance to begin. I am wondering if there is a specific ghost she is looking for when Mel elbows me and clears her throat. I follow her eyes to a far corner of the room, where one of Steve's ancient, too-soft couches is nearly swallowing someone.

A boy.

Dark curly hair.

Long piano-player fingers combing through it.

He doesn't seem to know what to do with his hands now that he's not holding his Houdini biography. They flutter around a bit before he sticks them into the pockets of his jacket. And he looks straight at us, and he smiles crookedly.

"Not that I doubt my own allure," Mel says, "but I think that kid is looking at you."

I hear myself suck in my breath and then try to sound casual as I say, "He might be."

"Friend of yours?" she asks.

"Not really."

Mel cackles softly. "You need to work on your subtlety, my dear."

I force myself to look back to Scarf Lady and mumble, "Forget it."

"I'm just messing with you," Mel says. "He's in my calculus class."

I'm surprised to hear this. I know I've been in a fog at school, but new kids are usually high-profile, since most of us have known each other since our diaper days.

"His name is . . . like . . . It's a verb. Trot or Sprint or . . ."

"Chase," I tell her. "It's Chase."

"He looks like your brother, doesn't he?"

The answer, as she already knows, is yes. He does. Although not as much as he did when I first saw him. I can see even more clearly now the ways in which Chase and my brother are different. My brother's jaw was stronger, and his hair was really dark, almost black. Chase's is melted brown with strands of gold.

I am just about to articulate this when a mustachioed man in a cape emerges from the Self-Help and Actualization section and announces, "I am Absalom!"

"Good lord," Mel replies.

Absalom is undeterred by her tone. "Come, sisters and brothers! Let us form a circle of truth!"

The two of us and Scarf Lady and a few other sheepish folks approach Absalom as one might approach a land mine. Chase quietly does the same—we step forward in unison, in time with the same silent music. Just a regular guy, running into a perfectly normal girl. At a séance.

"Join hands!" Absalom crows. "We will be united in our call to the other side!"

Mel mutters, "Like anyone wants to be united with this lunatic." Sure enough, the other séance attendees have all bunched to one side of the circle, to avoid having to hold either of Absalom's oddly tiny hands. Finally, Chase takes pity on him and steps to Absalom's left side, putting himself just a few people away from me.

I keep my eyes to myself, though I can feel him looking in my direction. I feel something like an electric current traveling from hand to hand, trying to get my attention. We already had what could be considered a playful conversation at Common Grounds. Attending the same séance could be mistaken for a whole new level of connection.

Lucky for me, Absalom continues to bellow platitudes, encouraging us to "visualize the lost souls" and "call forth our heart mates." The circle of us shuffles uneasily, unable to stand still in the midst of so much that is strange. I am more accustomed than most people to this kind of discomfort, but somehow this circle seems to magnify every nervous movement. Finally, Absalom stops talking and begins to sway from side to side, dragging Chase and Scarf Lady—who has wedged her purse between her feet, in case the Elbow Room is invaded by marauding thieves—with him.

"Dear departed," Absalom calls out, "bring us word from the other side!"

Mel can't help herself. "What's the weather like over there?"

Absalom stops swaying and glares at her. "Unbelievers may exit out the back."

Mel smiles sweetly. "I would never leave my friend here alone. I am here to support her in her time of need."

Now Absalom looks torn. He turns his beady gaze my way. "Is there someone you would like to speak with? Someone to whom I can reach out on your behalf?"

Words choke me, as usual. I am suddenly mortified that I let Mel talk me into this, ashamed to be here with this motley crew of desperate people when I could be safely encased in the quiet denial of my family. This is my limbo, trapped between wanting to escape the house and wanting to never leave it again. I cough.

"Her brother," Mel says.

Don't say his name.

"What's his name?" Absalom asks.

Don't say his name.

I can feel the panic mounting like a science-class baking-soda volcano in my gut. I shake my head, hop on the balls of my feet, try to break it down. Then Chase saves the day.

"My turn!" he yells, suddenly animated, as if someone flipped a switch in his back. "I was here first!"

Absalom glances sideways. "This isn't the deli counter," he remarks. "There aren't any numbers."

"I was here first," Chase says again.

Absalom rolls his eyes. "Fine. Who do you want to contact?"

"Harry Houdini."

"I beg your pardon?"

"Harry Houdini," Chase announces. "He was my great-great-grandfather."

"That seems unlikely," Absalom tells him, "since Houdini never had children."

"Ha!" Mel shouts. "He's got you there. Now what?"

The other members of the circle, most of whom have stopped holding hands, are noticeably unhappy. "Excuse me," says Scarf Lady, her feet still clutching her purse as if it might run away. "But are the rest of us going to get a turn?"

Absalom points to the entrance. "Not until the unbelievers have left us."

"I thought you said unbelievers had to go out the back way," Mel says.

"You can leave any way you like," Absalom tells her.

"How very democratic. Do I get my ten dollars back?"

"No refunds," Absalom barks.

Mel grabs my hand again and tugs me toward the door. My feet feel strangely flat, like after you've been roller-skating and then go back to regular walking. But I follow her.

Before we've taken three steps, though, she turns back to the circle and jabs a finger at Chase. "You coming?" she asks him.

"Uh—" he starts to say, and then Absalom loses what's left of his composure and shoves Chase in our direction.

"He's right behind you," Absalom says.

"All right, Absalom." Chase bows to him, and walks to where Mel and I are waiting. Then he turns and begins to walk backward, saying, "Oh my son Absalom, my son, my son Absalom! Would God I had died for thee, oh Absalom, my son, my son!"

The rest of the séance attendees, still standing in a sloppy circle (now with three holes in it), watch him, slack-jawed.

"Very funny," Absalom mutters.

"Well, then," Chase says before we exit, "pick a better stage name. May I suggest Erik Weisz?"

"You may not," Absalom snaps, and he disappears behind the front door of the Elbow Room as it closes with us on the other side of it.

Mel looks at Chase quizzically. "Erik Weisz?"

He tucks his hands into his back pockets and shrugs. "Harry Houdini's real name," he says. Then he slopes off toward Aspect Avenue, and calls over his shoulder, "See ya, Tallie."

SIX

ALWAYS SOMETHING
THERE TO REMIND ME

I am shaking when I get home. Being Mel's passenger produces that effect from time to time, but I am pretty sure this particular set of tremors is the result of my latest encounter with Chase, of hearing him say my name out loud. Very few people say it anymore. Cranky Andy hollers it across the coffee shop once in a while, but that's entirely different from the sound it made in Chase's voice, so easy and deep, like a low note on a piano.

Mom and Dad are talking in the kitchen. Normally, I would sneak quietly up the stairs to spare us all the agony of questions and answers, but something about the tone of their voices makes me pause. They sound intense, like hissing snakes.

"Don't do this," Dad says.

"I'm not *doing* anything."

"You're thinking about doing something."

"The agency called and said that one of them wants to write to us, and I said we would be open to receiving a letter. That's all."

"These people can't offer you anything," Dad says. "It's not going to bring him back."

My knotted heart pulls even tighter.

They are talking about him.

They *never* talk about him.

"They want to thank us, that's all," Mom says. "What's so wrong about them wanting to thank us?"

"Don't do this," Dad says again.

"It's not up to you, Gene," Mom snaps. "I can do this with or without your blessing." It's as if Mom has been reanimated, like Sleeping Beauty awakened from her hundred years' nap. She's fighting for something again. Better this, whatever it is, than Dad's campaign to leave Molton forever.

I can't see Dad's face, but his silence says that he didn't expect this either.

More quietly Mom adds, "I know I can't bring him back. But I'm also not going to erase him. He lived. He was here. He was *real*."

"He *was* here," Dad says. "*Was.* Tallie still *is,* and if Dr. Blankenbaker thinks that we should move—just remember that we agreed to consider her recommendation. You've got three and a half weeks until the appointment. Do whatever you want until then."

My shaking gets worse. I run upstairs before either of them gets angry enough to say his name out loud, fire it like a bullet.

When things get bad like this, the yearbook and the memories aren't enough. I need my secret weapon. I use it sparingly, as one must do with something small and powerful, or else the power will disperse like smoke.

I keep it in an old cookie tin on my bookshelf, tucked in with seashells from family trips and movie ticket stubs and junk jewelry.

His MP3 player.

He called it Matthew Pendergrass the Third. Matty, for short.

My parents don't know I still have it. They think it was destroyed in the accident, or lost in the aftermath, but it wasn't. It came to the hospital with us because it was in his pocket, and when they cut his clothes off his body, it fell out and a nurse picked it up and later she brought it to my room. I know this because the nurse told me when she handed it to me. She was perceptive enough to realize I might want it, but not enough to leave out the part about them cutting my brother's clothes off.

I keep my eyes closed when I turn it on because it has his name on the screen when it first lights up, and run my fingers across the places where the blue coating is chipped and dented. I know by now how to get the songs to shuffle without looking: 793 songs. That sounds like a lot, but it isn't really, it won't last very long. So I have to be careful. I have it on shuffle and I let myself listen to two songs at a time. Three, if it's getting really bad. It would be so easy to lie back and let the music play and play and play, play for hours, play until I was dried up like a raisin, petrified like wood. Preserved. Motionless.

But my parents would come looking for me, eventually, and they'd see my secret weapon and they'd probably take it away. They would want it for themselves, wouldn't they? Because it is a vital thing, to have someone's handpicked collection of songs in your grasp. It's the soundtrack of that person, and everyone knows the soundtrack is the most important part. There would be no mood without it, no impact. Even silent movies had soundtracks.

The soundtrack is the key.

Part of my brain wants to make sense of what I heard in the

kitchen, what my parents could possibly have been talking about. But every time I let the conversation scratch at the door, too many other thoughts threaten to flood in along with it. So I lock it up again and retreat. I am allowed to do that.

No excuses are required of me.

I have the earbuds in now, I have the first song beginning to flow, and even though it's loud and frenetic-sounding, I feel myself calming down. Until I'm calm enough to picture Chase, the shape of his shoulders as he half turned around and said my name. I'm not upset with him. He doesn't know I don't like people to say my name anymore. He doesn't know that I can't feel enough to connect with him, can't construct a bridge out of the metal shards and splinters I've got left. I'm dragging myself back to normal, but I'm not there yet.

But it's not his fault for trying.

I decide I will forgive him.

I fall asleep before I figure out what that means.

SEVEN

WOULDN'T MAMA BE PROUD?

monday 9/22

In that way the universe has of taunting you with what you least want to think about or deal with, Chase is the first person I see the next morning. Sometimes Mel sleeps late, so I walk to school, and it's a long enough journey that I go into a kind of trance state, which is not unpleasant. But it is hard to come out of, and I am almost past the Star Students display before I see him, leaning slouchily against the edge of the glass case. He is wearing a dark blue T-shirt that says, simply, BOOM.

Along with the detritus of others' achievements, the display holds a memorial to my brother. I loathe the Star Students display. I usually walk past it with my eyes closed but I'm startled into for-getting to do it, so I accidentally catch a glimpse of my brother's preserved image—the particular color of his hair, a fleeting sense that he is trying to get my attention—because Chase is there. Does he realize his proximity to the picture? It seems an unlikely coincidence, but I kind of hope it is. Because—my stomach sinks at the thought—if he's heard about me, if he's been told and he's standing there on purpose, that makes him just a bit of an asshole. Which would make it harder to be around him. Not impossible. Just harder.

On the other hand, it would be the perfect reason, should I need to give myself one, for never talking to him again. I'll keep that in my proverbial pocket for later.

I stride past the display case, willing my eyes forward, and Chase launches himself into rhythm next to me, following me down the hall, and says, "Some scene last night, huh?"

For a moment, I hear my parents arguing and wonder how he knows. Then I realize that he is talking about the séance.

"Sure was," I say, trying to match his casual-cool tone. And failing.

"Did it surprise you that I knew your name?" he asks. "You looked surprised."

"Um—um," I stammer, "a little, maybe, I guess . . ."

"I believe in honest emotional exchange," he tells me.

"Right," I say. "Well, that doesn't mean you have to use it like a hammer."

We are nearing my locker, so I slow down. His locker must be in a different hall, which could explain why I haven't seen him in school before now, but he matches my waning pace and stops when I stop, hovering behind me as I subject my ancient combination lock to the usual series of twists and turns. It often takes at least three tries to open the thing, but the gods are obliging today, benevolent. First try and I'm in.

The door swings open and I am greeted by a chipmunk perched

on the edge of the locker's shelf, one paw raised in greeting, a tiny bowler hat on his head. Pinned to his chest is a wee sign that says CECI N'EST PAS UN TAMIA.

I successfully swallow a scream, but Chase yells, "What the hell?!"

"This is not a chipmunk," I translate for him. Mel is a fan of both taxidermy and Magritte, and never misses a chance to combine the two.

"But it *is* a chipmunk, isn't it?"

"No," I say. "It's not a chipmunk anymore. Now it's the representation of a chipmunk. It's something that signifies a chipmunk."

"It's dead," he says.

"Yes. The chipmunk is dead."

We both look at it intently so we don't look at each other.

Chase says, "Long live the chipmunk."

And then the bell rings, and we part. This time, he doesn't say my name as he walks away. I wonder if this was too weird for him. I wonder if I'm disappointed if it was.

I whisper my own name to myself one time, twice, and it actually feels okay. Then I start to say my brother's. "Na—" But I stop because my stomach flips at the sound.

Maybe I can work up to the other letters. Maybe it could be like any other word again.

Over the summer, I developed what you could call an odd habit. At least once a day, usually more, I imagined I was talking to a therapist. Just a guy I made up, no one too specific. And then that escalated into imagining that Dr. Imaginary was with me in my house. Sort of like a sidekick. But one who was a really good listener and endlessly fascinated with everything I had to say. I talked for hours, in my head, about my life and my parents and how I felt about everything. Or how I would have felt if I wasn't numb from the inside out, as if my heart had fallen asleep like an errant appendage.

The only problem was that when Mom decided, in those early postaccident days, that I should actually talk to someone, I had nothing left to say. I had told Dr. I. all about it and I was done. The therapist my mother brought me to—Dr. Blankenbaker—was not so receptive to this logic. But she was no Dr. I., let me tell you. I think she was just jealous.

We sat in her professionally furnished office, which looked exactly like the set of a TV show about a therapist counseling a girl who had lost her brother in a car accident, and she delivered her lines with clipped, clean, perfect diction while I said nothing at all.

"I can't tell," she finally admitted, "if you're trying to antagonize me."

"I'm not," I assured her.

"Okay," she said. She set her notepad and pen on her flawlessly organized desk, called my mother into the room, and told her that our time was up.

My mother said there was no point in continuing the sessions if I wasn't going to say anything, but Dad disagreed—I think he wanted a diagnostic checklist that showed I was okay, like the paper they give you when you take your car for an oil change. Dr. Blankenbaker agreed that there wasn't much point in forcing things, but before she released us from her office, she made us schedule a follow-up appointment for an in-depth evaluation. That's what she called it.

"I am sympathetic to Tallie's reluctance to talk about what happened," she told my parents. And me, but only because I was eavesdropping. (Someone should really tell Dr. Blankenbaker that the heating vent in her waiting room makes it very easy to hear what's being said in her office.) "But if she doesn't face what happened, it could be crippling for her future."

Use the word *future* with anyone's parents and they'll do whatever you say.

So an appointment was made. October fifteenth. It's on our calendar at home, circled in red so none of us forget about it. Red Circle Day. On that day I will be escorted back to Dr. Blankenbaker's office and asked many probing questions, and my father made it clear (before he entered into his silent orbit) that I *will* answer those questions, and if Dr. Blankenbaker believes I should change schools or take pills or spend three afternoons a week with her, that is what will happen. Because she is the expert.

And this is what we must do after life knocks the wind out of us so thoroughly. We must follow the advice of those who know better. Lucky for me, school is also full of well-meaning professionals just chomping at the bit to tell me what to do. Specifically:

dr. elias hunter, principal

ms. stephanie doberskiff, guidance counselor/cheerleading coach

In light of my failed attempt to come back to school after the accident as if nothing had happened, Principal Hunter and Ms. Doberskiff corralled me on the first day this year and laid out the Plan (approved, they said, by my parents), wherein I was presented with some rules. The first one was that I would attend weekly support-group meetings.

The group at my school operates under the laborious name Bridges Through Grief to New Beginnings. Obviously, we all just refer to it as Bridges, for efficiency as well as to avoid sounding like a cult. Many other names were proposed for the group when it first started, but they all sounded too sad or too weird or marginally perverse. And then someone suggested it was discriminatory to have a group just for kids with families in which someone had died, so the group was expanded to include any student "grappling with a life-altering change or loss of any kind."

This covers a lot of territory. *Loss* is an entirely relative term.

Ms. Doberskiff sadistically scheduled our Bridges meetings for Monday afternoons, claiming it was the only day she was free. Seeing as how she is also the cheerleading coach, a school counselor, and the faculty advisor for the literary magazine, it is true that her schedule is chock-full of angst-producing activities.

Mel is highly suspicious of Ms. Doberskiff, as she is of anyone who would voluntarily spend so much time listening to high school students talk about themselves.

"Maybe she just cares a lot about other people," I suggested once.

"Maybe she's avoiding her own problems," Mel retorted. "Maybe she's collecting material for a tell-all exposé on the modern American teenager. Maybe she's a sociopath, studying emotional patterns to learn how to act like a normal person."

"Sometimes I think you're a sociopath," I offered.

Mel shrugged. "I just don't happen to think *caring* is a good enough reason to wallow in the pity pool week after week."

She probably doesn't think "because the principal told me to" is a very good reason either. But she doesn't give me a hard time about it. She even walks me to the meetings and pretends she's dropping me off at something distinctly more fun than Bridges. "Have fun!" she trills, and nudges me through the door.

"Let's get started," Ms. Doberskiff says. Everyone is in their usual place. Toby and Jackson have already annihilated the snack table. Margaret nibbles conspicuously at a donut hole, which will take her fifteen minutes to finish. Bethany is texting, getting in a few more vital messages before Ms. Doberskiff makes everyone turn their phones off and put them away. Jackson sits closest to the door, I guess in case he might suddenly have to run out of the room. He never has, but he always seems right on the verge of fleeing. Bethany sits on my other side, then Margaret, then Toby. We sit this way every time. We like our routines.

"Who has something to share?" asks Ms. Doberskiff.

A hand shoots up. Margaret. "I do!" she yelps. Margaret always has something to share. Margaret is an oversharer. But at least half of anything she says is a lie, and the other half isn't entirely true. No one knows whether Margaret has ever actually experienced a personal tragedy of any kind. I think she was sent to Bridges as a last-ditch effort, as if everyone got together and said, *We can't get her to admit she's a compulsive liar, so we'll pretend she's telling the truth and see how far it goes.*

Ms. Doberskiff smiles, a pained but tolerant smile that comes from being freshly trained in grief counseling. "Why don't we let someone else go first this time, Margaret?"

Ignoring her, Margaret tells us that her grandmother is gravely ill. "She may not survive the week."

Ms. Doberskiff forces herself to say, "That must be very difficult for you, Margaret." And this is all Margaret needs to hear, really. She's a sympathy addict, a junkie for pity. Which is what makes me think that probably nothing bad has ever really happened to her. The truly traumatized don't like this kind of attention. Jackson, for instance, has a mother with stage #4 brain cancer and all he wants to talk about is old movies. Now Ms. Doberskiff will ask how he's doing and he'll try to change the subject. Observe:

"And how is your mother, Jackson? Any change?"

Jackson's foot starts tapping like a woodpecker. "No," he says, and in the same breath he adds, "I watched *Blade Runner* last night. I really think the whole human-android dichotomy says a lot about social strata in our—"

Ms. Doberskiff cuts in. "Did your mother watch the movie with you?"

Jackson's foot slows, stops. "She mostly just sleeps. The hospital gave us a bed. It's in the living room."

I can almost feel the air in the room drawing away from me, like a vacuum.

"I see," says Ms. Doberskiff. "That must be"—she is about to say *very difficult,* but she knows she can't use the same words for Jackson's real dying mother as she did for Margaret's probably fake dying grandmother—"incredibly painful."

Jackson shrugs. "They keep saying she can't feel anything."

Toby nods. He has been told the same thing about his father. That it was fast. Mercifully fast.

There's a hierarchy of sorts in Bridges. Dead or dying parents are at the top, then brothers and sisters, then grandparents, then pets. But it's hard to say whether slow death trumps sudden. Like, is Jackson higher up than Toby because his mother is dying slowly, in the living room, day after day? Toby's father hit a roadside bomb somewhere in Afghanistan, out of the blue, and Toby didn't see it or hear it or anything. Does that count for less? Or is it worse for Toby because he didn't get to say goodbye?

These are the questions we'd like to ask Ms. Doberskiff, or whoever. At least, these are the questions *I* would ask. I would like to know where I stand on the spectrum of sadness. I would like someone to tell me exactly who has it worse than me, or better.

But Ms. Doberskiff would never let us talk about that. It's too raw, too difficult. She must protect us from our own tragic events, convince us that we are still ourselves, despite what has happened.

"Bethany?" Ms. Doberskiff keeps just the right volume to her voice, soft but clear, so as not to startle us. She would make an excellent wild-animal trainer, if this whole shaping-young-minds gig doesn't work out. "Do you have anything you want to share with the group?"

Bethany has her notebook open in front of her, pen in hand, and has been drawing spirals, swirling loops across the page. She speaks without looking at us. "Not really," she says. "My dog is still dead. Frank still doesn't care that he killed him."

"I'm sure that's not true," Ms. Doberskiff assures her. "Maybe your stepfather just doesn't know what to say. Sometimes it's hard for us to articulate what we're feeling."

"How about *I'm sorry I ran over your dog*?" Jackson suggests.

Ms. Doberskiff glares at him, then corrects herself. Bethany's pen continues swooping. The sound of it, the soft rushing hum, wants to put me to sleep. But I don't think Principal Hunter will give me credit for attending the meeting if I lose consciousness.

Try to focus on something else, I tell myself.

The room where we have our Bridges meetings looks out over the athletic fields at the back of the school. As I wait for my inquiry from Ms. Doberskiff, my eyes trace the white lines painted on the fields, following their angles through the grass and dust over and over again. I like their regularity, how solid they appear from here, even though I know that, close up, they are patchy and wavering and even slightly crooked in spots. I know that they are like the lines painted on every road and every highway—deceptively reliable, incapable of actually keeping us in our places.

The door opens one more time, and Chase walks in.

This is not good, I think. The last thing I want is for Chase to hear my story like this, in a room where all the air has been replaced with sadness and self-pity. But Ms. Doberskiff's reaction is very different.

"Welcome!" she gasps. "Please, take a seat. You're just in time!"

"Unless you wanted something to eat," Bethany mutters.

Chase crosses the room and pulls up a chair between Bethany and Margaret, so he's one seat away from me. I look intently at his right shoe. I will look no higher.

"I'm Chase," he says.

"And why are you here?" Ms. Doberskiff asks gently.

"Because while I believe in honesty, I have not been completely honest with . . . certain people." His bravado is wavering. Bridges has that effect on people.

Margaret snorts.

Chase's shoes turn toward me. "I should have said something when we first met at the coffee shop, or at the séance—"

"The what?" Ms. Doberskiff says.

"—but I chickened out both times, and then when I saw how well you handled that dead chipmunk in your locker—"

Ms. Doberskiff holds up a hand, though it is clear Chase is not finished. I think we are all relieved. "Do I need to . . . alert someone?" she asks me. "Like the health department? Or the police? Is this a stalking situation?"

"The chipmunk wasn't from me," Chase starts, but Ms. Doberskiff's hand remains firmly raised.

"It's fine," I assure her. "I'm fine." And I am pleasantly surprised to find that it's true. The knot that my stomach tied itself into when Chase walked in has vanished. Whether or not it was his intention, he distracted me with his confession, drowned out the noise in my head with something else. Something interesting.

But he doesn't get to finish because Margaret starts to choke on the powdered sugar from her donut hole, and Ms. Doberskiff leaps to her rescue and then adjourns the meeting in order to take her to the nurse.

Mel is right outside the door when we're done, waiting to retrieve me. She cocks her head and raises one eyebrow when she sees Chase coming out behind me. "New member of the Sadness Club?" she inquires.

"I came for the snacks," he tells her.

I spin around, startling him. "What were you going to say?"

"Uh—I . . ." He glances at Mel, who is only too happy to chime in.

"You need to have a problem to be here. That's how it works. So?" She puts her arm around me. It feels like a chain.

"I'd rather not talk about it in the hallway," he says, with surprising composure. "Can you—would you come by sometime? To my house? To hang out?"

Mel guffaws and bumps her hip into mine, knocking me off balance. "Like we haven't heard that one before." Then she begins to steer me down the hallway, pulling me like a stiff puppet.

"I admire your moxie," she calls back to Chase. "But we've got carnival work to do."

Much of what Mel says is coded, so *carnival work* could refer to just about anything. This time, though, she means what she says. The school carnival is in four days and Mel is in charge of set design. She normally rejects school activities, but this time her love of power tools and ordering people around overruled her disdain for sanctioned events.

"Come with me," she says to me. "I'll let you drill holes in things. You'll feel better."

"You're probably right," I concede, "but I'll take a rain check. I'm working today." This may or may not be true. I haven't gotten a straight answer from Cranky Andy about whether I still have a job now that Martha's working so many hours. But it's as good an excuse as any.

Mel holds me for another few seconds, then releases me. I can feel her imprint on my body as I walk away. She lets me take five or six steps before she calls, "Are you okay?"

I don't turn around, just raise my hand and wave it a little. She doesn't need more than that. Doesn't want more than that. It's our arrangement.

Five more steps and then I call back, "What's the opposite of happiness?"

"Plastic," she shouts.

EIGHT

KILLING THE BLUES

I walk home, trying not to think about what Chase said at Bridges. Trying to figure out whether his invitation meant anything more. Before, I would have laughed it off, or taken the bait, but either way I would have felt every part of it. The elation, the anticipation. The disappointment, the damage. Feelings used to be like the vinegar in my baking-soda-volcano gut. They came along and made a mess and died down again and left me with the memory of that brief, gorgeous thrill. Buzzing. Waiting for the next time.

But we're in the after now. Now I can't think of the last time anything *felt* like anything. I am accustomed to being broken, lurching along like an old machine. The rituals stir something up, sometimes, but it's more like a dull and distant itch than any actual emotion.

Everything I see as I walk is far away, too. My house comes into sight and seems to be just a painting of itself, flat, impossible to enter. My reflection in the hallway mirror is missing some dimension that would make it look real—I stare into my own eyes, seeing myself there, shrunken and receding.

All I feel is mild fascination. Am I protecting myself? Can I choose to stop, force my way out of limbo and back into the world? The back-to-normal quest—I still believe in it, but it seems impossible sometimes.

We had a globe when I was little, the kind with topographical bumps and ridges, and my brother and I spent a lot of time tracing them with our fingertips and trying to match them to parts of our faces. Occasionally our fingers would collide and we would become territorial, arguing over who had feeling rights to which mountain ranges. The bridge of his nose was more defined than mine, so he claimed the Andes and I got stuck with the Catskills. But they were solid, real. There was no questioning them.

Now I trace my scars from the accident the same way, small white lines that crisscross my arms. I reach down to the one on my hand that I touch when I'm nervous. A different kind of ritual, not for remembering as much as . . . wondering. About what really happened, because my memories are so fragmented, like the shards of a mirror that don't make a whole mirror when they're glued back together.

My parents don't offer to discuss it, and my doctors talked to them, not to me. So all I know is what I remember from before the accident happened, and what I was able to gather from the newspaper before terrible things happened to other people and replaced our story in print.

It was May twenty-fifth. Three weeks left of school. We had both been working on papers, but we couldn't concentrate anymore, so we went to the Sip'N'Dip for ice cream. We took my mother's car, the station wagon we called the Green Goblin. He drove there, but I wanted to drive us home. I had just turned sixteen, and had practiced in the simulator. I had my permit but my parents hadn't taken me out for many driving lessons yet because they were too busy. My brother was only a year older than me, not old enough to teach me, but he still had ice cream in his cone and I was finished with mine, so I begged. I begged until he gave in. And I didn't care that it made him nervous, didn't listen to his objections.

So I was driving. For real, for the first time. And I was doing fine.

He was instructing me between mouthfuls of ice cream. "Light on the brakes, good, check your mirrors." He turned the radio on and found a song we both liked. And it was good. Better than that. It was great.

But it had rained a lot that morning, and for two days before that.

I got us almost all the way home. The last thing I remember was my brother cheering me on, the sound of his teeth biting into his ice cream cone, the crunch merging perfectly with the sound of our tires splashing through puddles on the road.

And then I drove straight into a huge one, deeper than it looked, and the tires hit the water and seized up.

We hydroplaned off the side of the road and into a tree.

The car hooked left at the last second. The impact was almost entirely on the passenger side. Where my brother was sitting. Where I would have been sitting if he had just finished his ice cream—the vanilla fudge dip cone he always, always ordered—at the Sip'N'Dip instead of slowly eating the rest in the car. If I hadn't begged so much. If he hadn't given in. If we had followed the rules.

I was lucky, they said.

But whatever part of me made it out of that car, whatever

shell-self I have become now, is nothing like the girl who was driving. And the red circle around October fifteenth screams at me every day, reminding me that if I can't find my way out of this limbo soon, I may lose my chance to make my own choices. I will be counseled, medicated, moved away. My parents may be in their own orbits for now but I am all they have left, and Dad is poised and ready to move somewhere else and start over. Which would mean leaving my brother's room behind, leaving the spaces he used to inhabit, leaving our only connection to where he used to be. Losing him all over again.

Hence, my mission: to prove that I can be who I was before. Or at least that I can convincingly act like it.

I text Cranky Andy to ask about my schedule, and he replies almost immediately:

martha has us covered for now. will let you know

I search myself for a reaction to this. I can't tell how I feel. So I tell myself that I am relieved, and maybe a bit offended. Put some anger in the mix. Make a recipe for what a normal reaction would be. I'm debating about what to write back when a message pops up from a number I don't recognize:

sorry about the ambush. if you change your mind: 844 linden place

His address jumps out like the numbers in the yearbook index, numbers on a calendar, a code.

How did he find me? My own voice whispers in my head.

I tell myself that it doesn't matter. I am standing at the edge. I cannot afford to go backward.

I haven't taken my bike out in a long time. It's been waiting for me in the garage, a dusty companion with endless patience. I brush it off with my bare hands, then wipe my hands on my jeans, leaving brown trails that look like ineffective camouflage. My helmet watches me accusingly from its hook on the wall, knowing that I want to leave it behind. It's too tight, and it has a purple cat on it. Humiliating. But I put it on. I will do that much for my mother.

Curse her for making me protect her this way.

Riding the bike, at least, is easy. The burning in my thighs is welcome, familiar, and I push harder and harder to keep it going, to get to a speed where sheer momentum keeps me upright and moving. It's different from riding in a car. I'm in control. The roads are blessedly dry. And I know exactly where I'm going.

Chase only lives a couple of miles away from me, but those miles contain a universe of their own. Each house is larger than the next, newer, with a manicured lawn and stone driveway, and even the asphalt beneath my wheels seems smoother.

He is surprised to see me when I ring the bell. I have been thinking about what to say on the way over, but I'm so stunned by the size of his house and the scale of everything around it that I am struck silent as a doll.

"Martha gave me your number," he offers.

"Ah," I say. "She's awfully helpful." She must really want Cranky Andy all to herself. I decide that she can have him.

"Come in," Chase says, and then quickly adds, "If you want to."

"Well, I didn't ride all this way to stand on the porch." It sounds harsher than I meant it to, so I throw a smile on it. I step into the house and at the same time he takes a step back to let me through. It's like choreography. But much more awkward.

"You, um . . . Can I take that for you?" He points at my head and I realize that I am still wearing my helmet. The rush of blood to my face feels good, dizzying and fast. *Act normal,* I tell myself. And then, as a consolation, *You can leave whenever you want to.* But first I want to see what this mysterious show-and-tell is all about.

I hand him the helmet. "What's on the agenda?"

"I have, um . . ." He runs his fingers through his hair, and I grant myself a moment to enjoy his discomfort. It's a nice change from my own.

"I have something to show you. Upstairs," he says, but I hesitate and he sees it and says, "Actually, wait here. I'll go get it." He sets my helmet on an empty hall table and springs up the staircase.

I look around and listen to the rhythm of his footsteps on the marble floor. Photographs cling to the walls, fighting gravity in identical black frames. A mountainous landscape, a portrait of Chase's parents on their wedding day, a smiling baby swathed in blankets. I assume it's Chase, although the baby's eyes are lighter than his are now.

He comes back, carrying a thick black binder.

I follow him into the living room, full of oversized couches and chairs. I wonder how many people live here, if there's some secret tribe of brothers and sisters that Chase hasn't mentioned yet. We haven't talked about our families.

He sets the binder down on the enormous coffee table and flips the front cover open. "Here," he tells me.

I lower myself carefully and the page comes into focus. It's a newspaper article, cut out and pasted onto beige paper. The headline says HOUSE FIRE CLAIMS LIVES OF SIX. Without speaking, Chase slowly turns the page and reveals another clipping: FATHER OF THREE KILLS FAMILY, SELF. And then another: HUMAN REMAINS FOUND ON ABANDONED FARM.

"What . . ." I don't even know what question to ask, don't

even know what it is that I'm feeling. Horror. Fascination. It's like his own version of *The Lives of the Saints*, but with regular people. Real ones.

"It's a memorial," he says quietly. "The stories of people who will never have a biography written about them."

He flips all the way to the back. "This was the first one."

It's an obituary.

ELEANOR AND AVERY ABBOTT. A photograph of a woman and a baby. The same baby as in the photograph in the hallway.

"My father's first wife and son," Chase says.

I look at the dates. They died years ago, before Chase and I were born.

"I didn't know about them for a long time, not until I was ten or eleven. He never talks about them. He would never tell me what happened. So I went online and I found them myself."

I run my finger across the baby's face. "He's really cute," I say lamely. My voice sounds far away, like I'm talking into a tunnel.

"He'd be out of college by now. He'd have a job somewhere. He'd have a past. And I'd have . . ." *An older brother.* He doesn't say it. Doesn't need to.

It's absurd that we're missing the same thing. But not the same thing. He never knew this boy. It's not the same. But he's still talking and I want to act normal, so I listen. I make myself focus and listen.

"And it made me think about other people who died, people I never knew—but that I could find out about, with these."

"Like little biographies," I say.

Remembering. It seems like such a simple thing, an involuntary process, like breathing. And then we complicate it, mess it up, force it into dark corners and rip it back out. We punish ourselves. We pay.

This is his fascination, and I get it, and I'm just about to tell him when he flips the pages one more time.

NATHANIEL MCGOVERN.

No, I think.

"When my dad told me we were moving here, I did what I always do. I got online, I looked for stories. And then we got here, and I came to Common Grounds—"

"Stop," I say, but he's talking so fast that he can't.

"I didn't tell you when we first met, and I'm sorry," he says. "I knew about you. I knew before we moved here. But I didn't know I'd meet you that day, I didn't know I'd—"

"No," I say. I don't want to hear what comes next. "I can't."

It's a dream, the kind where you can't move because there's thickness everywhere, the kind where it takes superhuman effort to get off the couch and walk to the front door and open it and drag your bike off the ground.

It's a dream as I ride away.

And I don't notice until I'm almost home that I'm not wearing my helmet.

NINE

MAKE SOMETHING GOOD

tuesday 9/23–wednesday 9/24

Chase keeps his distance for the next couple of days but he leaves my bike helmet in my mailbox and repeatedly texts.

i'm sorry

I delete every message. Mel must sense that something is off, because I find offerings in my locker. An eraser shaped like a piece of sushi; a postcard from Bismarck, North Dakota, with a picture of a UFO drawn on the back; a small bag of what claims to be chocolate-covered ants. They are strange, these things, and they provide the perfect distraction.

After school, she lures me to the gym and puts me to work painting signs for the carnival's game booths, directing me to "marry kitsch and readability." I nod as if I understand, and paint block letters while eavesdropping on Zoey telling Fiona that they should start a new slang term. Much to my relief, Amy is nowhere to be seen.

"How do we do that?" Fiona asks.

"We just start using it," Zoey says. "And everyone else will pick it up."

"Oh," Fiona says. "Like, what do we say?"

"How about instead of *lame* we say *scud*? Like, *This carnival is totally scud.*"

"I don't know." Fiona sounds skeptical.

"Oh, whatever," Zoey snaps. "I'll do it myself."

I am sorely tempted to get Mel in on this, but she is currently harassing some unfortunate kid about his lack of attention to detail, and I am having trouble remembering whether *beanbag* is one word or two. I have painted BEAN in huge letters and suddenly the question of where to put the next *B* is deeply important. I feel the beginnings of a sweat storm brewing across the small of my back. I set my brush down carefully, stand up to stretch, and force my eyes to look somewhere else. Straight ahead. Which creates the illusion for Principal Hunter, who is striding purposefully toward me, that his timing couldn't be more perfect.

"Tallie," he says solemnly. He speaks this way to most students, but especially to me. He is a large man whose clothes seem always on the verge of giving up trying to hold him in, and his booming voice is being amplified by the gym acoustics even as he tries to keep it low.

"Hello," I say, gripping my paintbrush.

"Just checking in," Hunter says. He tries to cross his arms but they are too short to breach his belly and he succeeds only in gripping his forearms.

"We're in good shape, I think. The signs are being painted and the construction on the booths—"

"Yes, yes." He waves a plump hand at the other kids and then nestles it back into the crook of his arm. "Looks fine. I'm more interested"—he turns to face me—"in how *you* are doing."

I will let you in on a little secret:

There is a delicate balance at this moment, at any time when people ask the how-are-you-doing question. I cannot seem too stable or happy, but I cannot give them more cause for concern or the *how are you doing*s will multiply until it's the only question I ever get. "As well as can be expected, I guess." I say this slowly, with gravity. I say it so I sound tired but brave. That is what people seem to want from me, most days.

"We are all so *proud* of you, Tallie," Principal Hunter says. "I have assured your parents that you've been attending Bridges meetings, as we agreed you should, and they have brought me up to speed, as it were, about their plans for"—he lowers his voice— "*reevaluation*. In a few weeks."

Apparently, like me, my parents have messy bursts of emotion punctuating their days. And apparently, when the bursts happen, they sometimes call Hunter to check on me.

"That is good to know," I tell him. I mean it, in a way. It *is* good to know that my parents still have a sense of purpose. And that they're checking up on me.

"Of course, we would hate to see you transfer to another school. But we would understand if it was just too . . . painful for you to be here."

It probably should be, I think. More confirmation that I'm not feeling things properly.

"Well"—Hunter frees his arms and claps once—"back to it! Excellent work, everyone!"

Mel salutes him as he exits.

Suddenly the smell of all the paint joins the haze of Principal Hunter's cologne and I have to close my eyes. And then I feel Mel jab me in the arm with her finger.

"Remind me to never volunteer for anything ever again."

"You got it."

"Are you okay?" Mel asks.

"Sure." It's the best I can offer right now. Because I really don't know. But I recognize that I am acting strange, and even with Mel it's vital to keep things as normal as possible. "I can't remember if it's *beanbag* or *bean*-space-*bag*."

"Spacebag?"

"No, I mean, is *beanbag* one word or two words?"

Mel pats my shoulder. "My little perfectionist. Make it one word. If it's wrong, we'll post a retraction in the school paper."

I force myself to smile. I am my own marionette.

Mel cocks her head, pulls out her phone, and takes my picture. Then she says, "I'm starving." It's a statement, pure fact. No emotion involved, just a basic physical need that must be served. This I can handle.

So after a full afternoon of carnival work, we head to Common Grounds. We walk straight to the counter and order croissants and cappuccinos. Mel pays and I ignore Martha's smug looks and Cranky Andy's limp attempts at conversation as I wait. They think I'm sad not to be working here anymore, but they're wrong. Being among the customers is better than observing them from a distance. I can blend. They're my camouflage.

I pick up the tray, careful to keep it balanced, and turn to see that Mel has selected a table next to Chase. I was so determined to approach Martha without flinching that I completely missed the fact that he was here. *Sloppy*, I chide myself.

Mel widens her eyes at me as I approach, all fake innocence. "Look who I found," she says. "Just sitting here. Almost as if he was expecting us." She draws out *expecting* and glances at Chase, who shrugs one shoulder, unruffled.

"I've been texting you," he says.

"I am aware of that," I tell him.

"But you haven't texted back," he says.

"I am aware of that, too."

"Naughty Tallie," Mel says, stirring one foamy finger around and around in her mug. "She's so self-absorbed sometimes. On account of"—she lowers her voice to a whisper—"the *accident*."

Chase can't help but react to this, grimacing at the whispered word.

"Mel," I warn.

"What? I'm just dealing you your get-out-of-acting-weird-free card. You never use it, and I'm pretty sure it expires at some point."

I glare at her.

"Okay, okay." She stands up, gathering her cappuccino and croissant. "I'll be over there. Scud. So sensitive."

Chase waits until she's out of earshot before saying, "That was kind of awful. I have to admit, I'm not totally seeing why you're friends with her."

I sit, the chair still warm from Mel's body. "She's not careful with me."

"I can see that."

"No, I mean, it's a good thing. I think. Everyone else is afraid to say certain words around me. Mel doesn't try to stop herself. She doesn't treat me like I'm breakable."

"Is that what you want?" Chase asks. "For people to be tougher on you?"

What do you want? is a very different question than *How are you?* It wants a real answer.

"Not tough," I tell him. "Just normal."

He smiles. "What's that?"

"I'm working on a definition," I say. "I'll let you know."

Then. Silence. So.

"I didn't handle that very well," Chase says. "Showing you the binder. I guess I thought showing you would be easier than telling you."

"Easier for who?" I ask pointedly.

He nods. "That's fair."

"Are you planning to ambush anyone else in Molton, now that you're here? I think the cafeteria lady's husband died in a boating accident a few years ago."

He shakes his head.

"So the honor is all mine."

Fingers through the hair. I bet he's a terrible poker player.

"I've never shown it to anyone," he says. "I'm not even sure why I keep adding to it anymore. But there was something about your story—your brother—my brother—"

"It's not the same," I say.

But in a strange way, it's a relief, to sit here and know that I'm not the only one who is trying to remember. The rituals have lost much of their power since the summer. I've all but given up on them, at least on doing them with any sustained focus. They're too formless, too indirect. Maybe the binder—knowing that it exists and that it has him in it—means I can replace them with something better.

"It's okay," I tell him.

Chase reaches into his pocket and extracts something. It looks like a tiny basket but it's shaped like a cylinder, with holes on either end. Like a tunnel. He holds it out to me, and I take it. The pattern of thin wooden strips woven together, the straight lines and perfect corners, is mesmerizing.

"Thank you," I say. And I roll it over in my hands as he tells me about a secret museum in Las Vegas where David Copperfield has Houdini's best tricks and devices set up. The museum is hidden behind a replica of the men's clothing store that Copperfield's father owned when he was young, and you can only get inside by special invitation or if you're an apprentice magician or you're researching a book or something. As Chase is saying that he would like to write a book about Houdini someday, I feel something strange, and when I look down, my index fingers are stuck in either end of the tiny tunnel.

"Oh," I say. I pull my fingers apart. The tunnel tightens around them.

"No," Chase tells me, "you have to . . ."

But there's a kind of roaring in my ears and my heart is racing as I'm pulling, pulling, and it feels like my fingers are being suffocated, like they're choking and I can't see how to get them out. The panic, it's like being packed in snow. It's all around me.

Chase reaches over, grabs my fingers and forces them closer together. And they are released.

"It's a Chinese finger trap," I hear him say, but he sounds really far away, even though I can see him right in front of me. "Haven't you ever seen one before?"

I shake my head. I can still feel the grip on my fingers, and my heart is slowing but still beating fast. I feel like laughing.

I feel.

I feel.

"Are you okay?" Chase asks, because I am rubbing my fingers but also grinning crazily. I can feel the smile on my face, stretching my cheeks, pushing against my eyes. It's like a mask I used to wear. It feels strange and excellent.

"I'm good," I tell him. "You were saying?"

"I forget."

I press my throbbing finger onto my plate, gathering croissant flakes. I bring my finger to my mouth, scrape them off with my teeth, and say, "Something else, then."

"Did you know Houdini wanted to be a movie star?"

"You know a lot about Houdini."

"Biographies. I'm addicted."

Then he tells me about Harry Houdini's movies, in which he played a series of characters with *H*-names. "Harvey Handford, Harry Harper, Howard Hillary. You get the idea. I guess he could never really let go of being himself even when he was supposed to be acting like someone else."

I let him talk, his voice floating around me like a cloud, and I think about how I wished so much, in the early days of after, that my brother would send me some kind of sign. A sign that he forgave me, or at least that things were going to be okay. Could this be it? A boy who looks like him, who is a bottomless well of words about magic and possibility? Not a reincarnation of my brother, of course, but maybe a representative.

Then Mel scoots her chair noisily up to our table and shatters the calm. And before I can even register feeling silly about such hopeful thoughts, she says loudly, "Hate to interrupt, but it's about time I get this little lady home. Can't worry the parentals, y'know?"

Chase smiles stiffly. "I do."

I stand, sling my bag over my shoulder, and turn to go. I know I should say something but I'm afraid of what will come out, so I just reach down and roll the finger trap toward him.

"Keep it," he says.

"Are you sure?"

He smiles, for real this time. "You obviously need to work on your escape technique."

I pick it up carefully—keeping my fingers away from the ends, as if it might grab on to me by itself—and tuck it into my pocket. Stand there, shift my weight.

"Ohfergodsake," Mel mutters. "Let's go."

But something won't let me move. Now that my brain has brought me the idea that Chase has been sent, I'm afraid that he'll disappear as suddenly as he arrived. What if I walk out of Common Grounds and never see him again? What if there's something I'm supposed to do or say and I miss my chance?

He knows something. He has to, because he stands up, too, and says, "I'll walk you out." And then a miracle happens. Chase waves to Cranky Andy and calls, "G'night, man," and Cranky Andy actually lifts his hand and waves back.

Mel gasps. "Unprecedented," she whispers.

I stroke the finger trap in my pocket.

"Indeed," I say.

Mel drops me off and roars away, revving her engine to show her disdain for people who go to bed before eleven. I watch her taillights shrink into the darkness and turn the corner, and then I stand in the black for a moment, letting it envelop me. Darkness was one of my trials after the accident, a penance I tried to pay. I blocked all the light from my room and imagined I was buried, trying to scare myself. It never worked. Now I can see a perfect square of light at the base of my house, a sign that my father is in his basement workshop, sorting his nails and screws into tiny labeled drawers.

I stop to get the mail before I go inside. The mailbox has been my domain for the last few years—my dad pays all the bills online and my mother does her shopping the same way, so neither one of them cares anymore about what shows up in our green plastic receptacle. Even my report cards are delivered by email, though the last one was all screwed up because of our arrangement with the school. I imagine I'll have to explain that someday, if I'm applying to colleges. But that particular someday seems impossibly distant. The depth of one dark mailbox is about as far as I can reach right now.

Awaiting me is the usual assortment of junk: shiny postcards from various politicians and real estate agencies, coupons for lawn care and gutter cleaning, catalogs. But then I notice a large manila envelope with a white label on the front. TO THE FAMILY OF, it says, and then my brother's name and our address. The return label in the upper left corner says LIFE CHOICE.

They're a little late, I think. I tuck the envelope under my jacket so my father won't see it if he comes upstairs when he hears me in the kitchen. It is one of my unspoken tasks, making sure my parents don't have to see my brother's name in print.

There is a note on the kitchen table, something about Mom going to her office in the morning and bagels in the freezer, which I crumple up and toss into the recycling bin along with all of the mail except the manila envelope. That comes with me to my room and waits patiently on my bed while I wash my face and brush my teeth. And it is still waiting after I jam my clothes into the hamper and put on my favorite black T-shirt and a clean pair of under-pants.

My desk drawer is full of mail addressed to him that I can't read but won't throw away. I opened the first thing that came for him after the accident, and it turned out to be a bill for the ambulance ride. As if he could have paid it. As if anyone should have to. *You didn't save him,* I thought. I couldn't bear to give it to my parents, so I stuck it in the drawer. Now it's under a pile of other envelopes: college brochures, magazine subscription notices, offers he can't accept or reject anymore.

I lay the Life Choice envelope across the top of the pile, like a blanket, and close the drawer slowly. I retrieve Matty from his hiding place, hoping the music will do something for me, but this time I go to the playlists. I need something more than shuffle, more than Matty's random selections. I need a design. I need my brother's thought process.

Most of the lists aren't titled, they're just numbered with dates, but there's one that's different: FOR AMY.

It's a family of songs, all sad and sweet. I've heard them all before but not together, not this way—I've been listening to them on their own, separate links of a chain I didn't know existed.

FOR AMY.

No wonder she won't come near me. All this time I thought she just didn't know what to say to me. I thought if I got normal again, we'd be okay. But it wasn't about me at all.

He really liked her. He might have even loved her.

And I took him away.

I fall asleep stroking my river scar.

If I dream, I don't know it.

TEN

SILVER LINING

thursday 9/25

Mom is already gone when I wake up. She has an interior-design company with her friends Susan and Michelle—the three of them always liked to shop together, and while my father maintains that their business is just an excuse to flash their business cards at fabric stores, my mother insists that there's "more to it than that." Of course, she never actually explains what the "more" is. Maybe she can't remember now. She stopped going for a while after the accident, and I had started to wonder if she felt the same way about Susan and Michelle that I did about Amy. But a month ago, on the first day of school, I came into the kitchen and found Mom showered, dressed, and ready to go. She's been working two or three days a week since then.

Dad leaves while I'm eating breakfast. I still have some time before I need to get ready for school, so I walk into Dad's study and wake up his computer. He never totally shuts it down—no matter how many times my brother lectured him about backing up his files and program updates and all that, Dad just can't be bothered. So all it takes is a shake of the mouse, and the screen lights up. It's not even password-protected.

Poor Dad. Does he really trust everyone so much?

The browser history, of course, has never been cleared. There's the usual list of sites and links to videos about electrical wiring and shower tile installation, and I'm just about to quit out when something new catches my eye. A search.

COMPASSIONATE COMPANIONS

A little bell rings inside my head. I know a grief-group name when I see one. If there's anything I've learned from Bridges, it's that talking endlessly about how sad you are, how much you miss the person who's gone, doesn't change anything. It might give you a good feeling for a little while, like you're doing something about your unhappiness, but it's really just the illusion of action. There is nothing to show for it at the end of the meeting.

I don't want Dad to get sucked into that vortex. He needs real results, he needs materials and supplies, tangible achievements. I make a mental note to tell him that I would like crown molding in my bedroom. If I can keep him working on *this* house, maybe he'll forget he wants a different one.

I take a quick detour on my way to the shower to check Mom's journal for new entries. Like Dad, she doesn't make any effort to hide it—it lives in her nightstand drawer, waiting to be written in. And then to be read. I know how wrong it seems that I do this, but I think of it this way: My parents have become like mannequins of themselves, like characters flattened in a book, and I need to follow their story. Sometimes I even need to direct it a little, push it in the right direction, because there's one thing we all agree on: None of us like surprises anymore.

And I'll admit there's a slightly more selfish motivation, too. I want to know if Mom and Dr. B. are talking about me.

Only one new installment since the last time I looked. Naughty Mom. She's supposed to write in it every day. (I know this because the first entry says, *Dr. Blankenbaker wants me to write in this book every day.*)

Drove past the Victorian on Sycamore Street today, it says. *They painted the trim a new shade of blue again. It seems as if they can't decide on what color would be best. I could tell them. I know exactly what blue they should have there, and exactly what flowers should go in the planters. All they have in there is trailing ivy. It's such a waste. Everything seems like such a waste.*

I close the book and set my hand on its cover for a moment, like a blessing. Then I tuck it away again, leaving it in its dark drawer home.

School proceeds in its pleasantly predictable way. I think I see Chase a few times among the sea of faces, but I don't allow myself to actually look for him. Now that the door to feeling has opened a crack, I'm not as insulated as I was before. A riot of noise and color hits me when I walk into the gym to help with the carnival prep. I manage to get Mel's attention with a wave.

"You are my only hope," she says as she walks toward me. She is wielding a hammer in a vaguely threatening way. "No one here respects my authority."

"That's because they've never seen you handle a chipmunk," I hear myself tell her.

She taps her chin thoughtfully with the clawed side of the hammer's head. "Maybe I should suggest a taxidermy exhibit for the carnival. That'd shut them up."

I nod, though we both know that displaying Mel's skills would probably cause more social harm than anything else. It wouldn't help me renormalize, that's for sure.

"Oh well. At least, I can order you around." She winks elaborately, then yells, "Back to work, lackey!"

Her instructions are forceful, but not very specific. I look around for something to work on, something that doesn't require excessive risk or noise. There's a group of kids arguing about paint colors for the game booths, and I'm about to walk over and offer my services when I see Amy.

She's using a nail gun to put the booths together, the staccato shots ringing off the gym walls in a way that both excites and terrifies me. The fluorescent lights cast a glare on her safety goggles, so I can't see her eyes, but her jaw is set in a way that I recognize. She is squatting, and her whole body is tense, like she's an animal ready to take off running. There is nothing about her posture that says, *This would be a good time to come talk to me.* But I see her so rarely that I decide to chance it. I wait until she pauses between nail shots and cautiously walk over to her. My heart is hammering in my chest, but I won't let it show in my voice.

"Hey."

It seems that I've been a bit *too* cautious, because she jumps back on her heels and then falls on her butt. The nail gun wobbles in her hand and threatens to hit the floor, but Amy grabs hold of it with both hands and sets it down carefully before she stands up and pushes her goggles onto the top of her head.

She squints at me for a second and then says, "Something I can do for you?"

Talk to me, I think. *Tell me how you're doing.*

Instead, I say, "I found the playlist."

Amy crosses her arms, a shield. "What playlist?"

"The one that—the one he made for you."

"I don't know what you're talking about." But I know she's lying, because whenever Amy lies, she twirls her hair, and as she says this, her right hand creeps up over her shoulder and entwines itself in her ponytail and starts flipping strands around and around.

She sees me watching, and stops. "Just leave me alone," she hisses, and yanks her safety goggles back down, to hide her eyes, to close the door.

I back away slowly, my heart still pounding, and peer around the gym to make sure no one else was listening, to search for some task that I can perform. My eyes skid across the collection of bodies in the bleachers and settle on a single figure at the top. A boy. He looks back at me.

This has happened to me before, seeing someone who looks so much like him that I am stunned into a kind of reeling panic. It's just like one of those dreams where something terrible is about to grab you and you think, frantically, *How do I wake myself up?* But you've forgotten how to walk or run or do anything but stare at the beautiful, menacing thing that is going to be the end of you. Closing your eyes is the only recourse you have. But this time, because Amy's voice is still ringing in my ears and I want so much to be able to undo what I did, and that boy up there looks *so* much like—I want *so* badly for it to be—

I don't close my eyes. And even though I know that the boy I'm seeing isn't my brother, I make myself believe for just a second, just long enough to say his name.

"Nate," I whisper to myself, just to myself. I say it, and it stings, but it doesn't unravel me. I say it a little louder. "Nate."

There's a crash from across the gym, and I look toward it by reflex.

"Scud!" hollers Mel.

When I look at the bleachers again, the boy is gone. New loss washes over me.

Act normal. I find a paintbrush. I find a wooden board with outlined letters waiting to be filled in. I do what I am supposed to do.

That empty space in the bleachers looms over me as I paint.

ELEVEN

FIX YOU

I get all the way home before I can breathe without feeling like there's a snake tightening itself around my neck.

I'm caught between wanting to forget how Amy sounded and wanting to get another jolt of the anxious energy her anger shot through me. I'm becoming an addict, a junkie for feelings. It doesn't even matter if they're good feelings or not.

Maybe this is what everyone likes so much about doing drugs. But it's all a matter of finding the right one.

What can I do to make myself feel something again, right now? Everything in the house has been sanitized, reminders removed, pictures and trophies carefully boxed up by my father to "give us some time." There's nothing here that will shock me. I think about throwing myself into Nate's room, going through all of his stuff in the hopes of finding more secrets.

Then I remember the mail in my desk drawer.

My hands are shaking with doubt by the time I get to my room, but I don't care. I take the whole pile out and flip it over. Start from the bottom and work my way up. It's all mass-produced, there's nothing of him in it, but I open everything and stare at his name on every piece of paper. I hear myself breathing too quickly but I keep going, opening everything, until I get to the Life Choice envelope.

It looks so much more official, somehow, than the other mail and for a split second I start to tell myself that I've gone far enough for one day.

Then I rip it open anyway.

There are two letters inside. One is in a plain sealed envelope, and the other is loose, just folded up like all letters are—the bottom edge folded up to the middle and pressed, the top edge folded down over it. It's just regular white printer paper. I pick it up even though my arm feels suddenly like lead, as if the rest of my body is conspiring to paralyze it. I lift the top edge and see words, but they jumble as I read them, as if my eyes, too, are trying to keep this secret.

Dear Mr. and Mrs. McGovern:

I look at the envelope that holds the other letter. Handwritten on its smooth paper skin is simply *To the family*. The letters are shaky, tremulous, and the same writing is all over the lined paper I withdraw from the envelope. Words swimming in place, pushing against the confines of their wide-ruled lanes.

Dear friends,
I do not know your names. I do not know the name of the son
you lost, but I know that your tragedy enabled me to live a
new life, and for that, I thank you.

My doctors said that my chances of survival without a lung transplant were basically nonexistent. I would certainly be dead by now if it were not for the sacrifice that your son made by donating his organs to people like me, people in desperate need.

There are no words strong enough to express my gratitude, but I hope that the knowledge that your son did not die without purpose will bring you some small measure of comfort.

Sincerely,

Gerald R.

I go back to the other letter, the typed one, with LIFE CHOICE printed in blue at the top. Underneath that, in a smaller font but still in blue, it says TRANSPLANT SERVICES DIVISION.

Because your son was in excellent health, the letter says, *and possessed type O-negative blood—the universally compatible blood type—we are honored to report that we found recipients for the following organs.* Then comes a list:

heart
liver
lungs
kidneys
corneas

There is more, but my eyes won't move from the list. I whisper the words to myself over and over again. There's a certain rhythm to them, like a poem or a song. As I say them, I start to see them, shapes extracted from the body. The heart like a fist. The liver like the head of an ax. The kidneys, a pair of quiet creatures, rounded toward each other. I loved the map of the human body in my biology textbook. Now all I can see in my mind is a butcher's diagram, dotted lines directing where the different cuts of meat begin and end.

Waves of nausea push at me. This is the other side of feeling again. It can't all be smiles and sunshine and happiness. There's messiness, there are dark edges and hurt. There's a toll to pay on the bridge out of limbo. And here it is.

My parents donated Nate's organs.

They gave him away.

This is what they were talking about in the kitchen. My mother said these people could write letters to her. These people for whom the doctors divided my brother up and took the parts they wanted. It's in the letter.

The nausea subsides and then rises again. I throw myself at the cookie tin, grabbing for Matty, but my fingers brush something softer. His wallet. I let them close around the leather, pull it out, and open it before I lose my nerve.

His driver's license is there, held behind clear plastic. I haven't looked at it in a long time. After he first got it, I used to stare at it through the plastic but he never let me take it out. Now I break that rule, too. I pinch my fingernails underneath the plastic and draw it out of its pocket. Flip it over and there it is.

A tiny red heart, in the bottom right corner. Tiny white letters. DONOR.

So he wanted this, I think. But did he really think about what that meant, checking that perfect little box at the RMV? Surely, he never imagined that anyone would take him up on this particular offer.

My parents did, though.

Cross my heart.

He taught me that when we were younger, how to make a promise that way. *Cross my heart and hope to die, stick a needle in my eye.* We had to do it quietly so my mother wouldn't hear. It always bothered her, even though it never meant that much to us. Now, though. Now it means something entirely new.

His heart is still alive, in someone else's body.

I wanted to feel. Now I feel too much. It's a jumble, anger mixed with aching sadness mixed with . . . relief.

I thought I had to let him go, but now I know that he isn't really gone.

I tuck the letters back into their envelope cave, slide it under my pillow, and start the music.

TWELVE

CARNIVAL

friday 9/26

I am bursting with secrets. I carry them with me to the carnival like a collection of breakable and precious artifacts. I do not want to show them to anyone—I am already a novelty in my school and would rather not become known as a lunatic on top of everything else. *Act normal.* My mission. Still, it seems a shame to keep these things all to myself.

I navigate between the bodies, floating, buoyant. So many heartbeats in one place that I can almost feel them synchronizing with each other like a chorus of bass drums. Everyone seems vulnerable now.

Be careful, I want to tell them. *Anything can happen. You are the key to someone else's survival.* I see their pieces, their eyes and openings, their precious bones holding everything together. They have no idea.

Mel is a tornado, marking a path of angry instruction from booth to booth. "Wake up!" she hollers at her inattentive volunteers. "Haven't you ever been to a carnival before? You're not supposed to let everyone win *every time.*"

I look for Amy, wanting and not wanting to see her in equal measure. Maybe she's at home, listening to the playlist I tortured myself with for hours last night. The one she claimed not to know about.

Chase appears, another solitary ship on the sea. Other, cooler girls—accustomed to having first dibs on any boy who is new to Molton and at least passably attractive—track him with eyes as hard as stone and whisper to each other when he stops next to me. I feel like all sorts of people are staring at us, but he is oblivious, focusing instead on Mel.

"Wow," he says, watching her.

"I know," I say. "She is really in her element, isn't she?"

Even though she is yelling, she has a huge grin on her face. She spins around, stopping every few feet to take a picture with her phone. She points it at me and Chase for a half second but then turns away and tucks the phone into her back pocket.

"Having fun?" Chase asks.

I nod. Can he see the secrets? Are they writing themselves on my skin? It feels like it. He takes my silence as a chance to say something else.

"I just wanted to tell you—" But I cut him off, grabbing his hand. I can't let this elation go to waste, can't let even a hint of serious conversation take it away.

"Chase," I tell him. "Life is short. This is a carnival. And it has a truly excellent beanbag toss."

"Is *beanbag* one word or two?" he asks me.

"Exactly! Let's go." I drag him farther into the gym, weaving through the crowd at breakneck speed.

"Whoa, Nellie!" Chase grabs our joined hands with his free

one and pulls us to a stop. "You passed the beanbag toss, like, three booths ago."

Sure enough, we are parked in front of Fiona and Zoey's kissing booth. CHEEKS ONLY says a sign. Zachary Burlie is threatening to lower his pants. "I've got two cheeks right here," he crows.

Fiona and Zoey roll their eyes. "Ew," they protest halfheartedly. "Don't."

Ms. Doberskiff arrives to rescue her cheerleaders. "Zachary," she says, "if I see even a hint of your underclothes, I will personally escort you out of the school. Or better yet, I will install you in the dunking booth and let the girls' softball team have their way with you."

Zachary slinks away, pants in place, and Ms. Doberskiff notices me and Chase standing there.

"Tallie, Chase, I am sorry you had to witness that." Ms. Doberskiff seems to think that once you've been traumatized, just about any little thing can send you spinning off the rails. "I'm not sure this booth was even sanctioned by Principal Hunter. . . ."

"We're fine," Chase assures her. "But I think it would do us some good to release our unexpressed emotions at the beanbag toss."

"Very constructive," Ms. Doberskiff says. "Tallie, are you all right?"

She probably asks this because I am craning my neck to see over the carnival booths and into the bleachers, in case that boy I envisioned is there again and I can get another feelings fix. I reassume a normal stance and assure her that I am. But after Ms. Doberskiff walks away, Chase takes my hand again.

"Are you?"

"What?"

"All right? You're acting kind of strange."

"I'm *fine*," I tell him, and then, before he can ask any follow-up questions, I ask him to get me some popcorn.

"Um, okay," he says. "I'll be right back."

"I'll be here!" I sound ridiculous, like Martha when she lays that false cheer over her real voice like frosting. But it works, he believes me, and I actually do a little spin to celebrate, or maybe just to see what it feels like. And of course, Amy is right behind me and I knock her cotton candy to the floor.

"Hey!" she yells. Then she seems to realize that it was louder than necessary and says "Dammit" just as I say "Sorry."

A few kids have stopped to see what's going on and I am acutely aware of their eyes on us, both of us. The girl with the dead brother and the dead brother's girlfriend. Like some kind of performance-art piece.

"Sorry," I say again, in case Amy didn't hear me.

She looks around and laughs, again too loud. "Oh, *no*, don't *worry* about it, Tallie. It was an *accident*. No big *deal*."

She keeps talking, keeps saying it's okay, but she won't make eye contact with me, and as I'm looking at her, I can see the girl who used to be my friend, like a phantom blotted out by this new version of Amy. I hate this new Amy, and more than that, I hate how much she hates me. I don't know what to say to her, but if she would just—

"Amy!"

She stops, surprised that I would interrupt her.

But before I can say anything else, Chase reappears with the popcorn. And Mel. "What the hell is going on?" she barks, and I'm about to yell at her, too, because why not? But then the anger evaporates just as quickly as it hit. I feel it draining out of me like water and I don't say anything when Amy slips away through the crowd.

"Nothing," I mumble.

"That did not look like nothing," Mel says.

"Sorry." I'm really tired now. "I think I need to sit down."

Chase and Mel walk me over to the bleachers and I let them steer me while I concentrate intently on the floor so I don't have to see all the weird looks I'm getting. I let them plop me down on the lowest bleacher, and when Mel asks if I need anything, for some reason I tell her that I want cotton candy. I don't even like cotton candy. She looks skeptical but she doesn't argue. She says to Chase, "You'll stay with her?" and he nods.

We watch her walk away.

We sit.

"Are you . . ." Chase starts to ask me if I'm okay. I can hear the whole question in those two words.

"I'm okay," I tell him. "It's just . . . There's some stuff going on."

"Do you want to talk about it?" His voice is very quiet, like I'm a wild animal and he's afraid of startling me.

The truth is, I hate secrets. They're everywhere—whispered in the hallways at school, hidden in closets at home, waiting in your mailbox. They're like extra molecules in the air, clogging my nose, humming in my ears and my brain, making me itch. *Tell us,* they hiss. And Chase is sitting here, asking about them, and they're getting louder and itchier.

"I . . . can't," I tell him.

"You can if you want to," he says.

I look at him. His eyes are the color of melted chocolate. I can see that he's really listening to me, and I'm pretty sure he wouldn't think I was completely crazy if I said, *I killed my brother and my parents donated his body and I have to make it up to Amy but I don't know how.*

And I'm just about to try and explain it, or some version of it, when I remember the maps.

Nate used to draw elaborate treasure maps and send me hunting for hidden items all over the house and the backyard. I got really good at reading the maps and pretty soon the game was over too quickly, so he switched to rhyming clues to slow me down. It wasn't finding the things that made it great—those were just toys he'd taken from my room. It was decoding the puzzle.

Maybe this is the ultimate puzzle. Maybe, knowing there are pieces of Nate still in the world, I can find a way to fix what I did.

"Tallie?" Chase is staring back at me. "What is it?"

It's the perfect chance to tell him, to say something like *How do you feel about scavenger hunts?* But the secrets are mine, still. The burning weight of them is the first original thing I've felt since the accident. Everything else has been so predictable. The stages of grief were laid out a long time ago, and my reactions to the binder, to the finger trap, weren't breaking any emotional ground. Those moments woke me up, but they weren't my choice. This is different. This is something entirely new.

"Nothing," I tell him. "I'm fine."

Then Mel comes back with the cotton candy and the three of us sit there, watching the mad choreography of the crowd, while I eat it. It melts in my mouth and goes down like medicine, and we don't say a word.

THIRTEEN

BLACKBIRD

saturday 9/27–sunday 9/28

The next morning Mel picks me up and we drive to the barn.
She is wearing her taxidermy clothes: an old flannel shirt
that reeks of formaldehyde and a pair of blue Dickies work pants
with the cuffs rolled up. If she cut her hair short and dyed it brown,
she would look like a carbon copy of her uncle Enoch (minus the
deep wrinkles and soulless gaze). I have only met Enoch once, but
his is not a face you forget. Mel's tool belt is curled up beside her,
cradling its wire cutters, assortment of knives, and supply of glass
eyes. There's a large cardboard box in the backseat.

"What's that?" I hook my thumb toward the box after putting
my seat belt on.

"Forms," Mel tells me, screeching backward out of the
driveway.

We drive the rest of the way in silence, a continuation of last
night's contract. After I finished my cotton candy, Chase offered
me a ride home but Mel asserted her friendship rights and claimed
custody of me. I had to stay until the carnival was over, but it

broke up pretty fast after someone circulated word that Amy was having a party at her house. Mel's anti-Amy sentiment dovetailed nicely with my desire to absolve myself of any guilt about the scene I caused, so she drove me straight home and retrieved me again this morning before my parents had time to intervene. My strange savior.

The barn is about half an hour outside of town, on what's left of Mel's family farm. Her father grew up here, but when her parents got married, her mother wanted to live "in civilization." And to not be a farmer's wife. And to pretend that Mel's dad's relatives weren't actually related to him. He gave in to most of her demands but he wanted Mel to know his family, so he brought her out here a lot when she was little, and Uncle Enoch started teaching her the family hobby. Which, as Mel's mother has pointed out more than once, is proof that they should have moved a lot farther away.

Taxidermy makes Mel happy in a way that nothing else does. She has other pursuits, like welding old pieces of farm equipment into dangerous sculptures. Last year she made a series of abstract paintings named after punctuation marks. But when she's working on a taxidermy project, she's different. She is utterly precise in everything she does. The entire process takes days, sometimes weeks, so I've only seen bits of it. But I've seen enough to know that it requires quiet and patience, and Mel doesn't generally have those qualities. Except when she's here.

Enoch built the workshop along the back wall of the barn and enclosed it with walls and a door. Then he added some windows because the room had become too dark to see anything and a ventilation system so he didn't gas himself with chemicals. It's almost totally silent, except for the humming of an ancient refrigerator and the occasional comment from one of the cows who live in the rest of the barn. It's cozy, and it's the same every time we come. And it's seriously creepy.

Enoch's work is installed all over the barn so that every edge and corner is inhabited by some motionless creature staring intently at you. I've gotten used to it, but the first time I came, Mel had to push me through the door. I still didn't know her very well and I half thought that she might have brought me here to murder me. Which wasn't a totally unpleasant notion, with Nate newly gone.

I wish I could bring him here.

Just as a precaution against something leaping out at me, I cough loudly as I walk in behind Mel.

She turns and her tool belt slides off the box she's carrying. I lean down to pick it up and take a deep breath, drawing in the scent of hay and animals and dusky air. Mel looks at me intently as I hand her the belt, worried (maybe) about another outburst.

"Come on," I tell her, doing my best to sound calm. "Show me what you're working on."

It turns out that "forms" does not mean paperwork. It means an assortment of molded shapes, bald suggestions of animals. Mel chooses one that looks like an unfinished sculpture, five smooth lumps for legs and tail, and a head shaped like a sideways egg. She sets it down on the table and opens the refrigerator. It is full of unmarked brown paper packages.

"I found the perfect cat the other day," Mel says, selecting a bundle.

She unwraps the cat and holds it up. It hangs there like a furry handbag.

"Very handsome," I say, even though I'm starting to feel a little sick looking at it.

"My uncle helped me skin it."

"What happens to the rest of it?" I ask. The words stick in my throat like cotton candy that won't melt.

She shrugs. "We throw it away. Uncle Enoch has a dumping ground in the woods. You should see all the turkey vultures that show up there. It's like a buffet or something."

I'm dizzy, thinking of the cat and so many other animals, stripped of their insides and thrown away like garbage. Is that what was left of Nate? His skin? His bones? The carcass that remained after they took what they could use?

"Jeez, are you okay?" Mel asks. She is holding the cat skin in one hand and the naked form in the other. The plaid on her shirt swirls like a lava lamp.

"I need some air." I lurch out the workshop door, drag myself past the startled cows, and throw myself outside, gasping. It's cold for late September. The air has teeth and I let it bite me because it feels good. Anything is better than the tight noose of panic and the heavy, sickening beat of my heart.

There is very little to see from the barn. The white clapboard house where Mel's grandparents live with Uncle Enoch, the roof of a cow shelter in the distance, the thread of road that comes here from town. Everything else is clear and level, open fields and blue sky scarred with streaks of cloud, framed on three sides by trees that are too old to notice me. I walk to the nearest crowd, the edge of a forest that Mel says never scared her but I know did because she wouldn't have bothered to say it otherwise. The trees huddle together like soldiers and it is so black under their canopy that the blue sky all around me can't compete. It draws me, the darkness. The dark at the end of the tunnel.

But then I step on a dry stick and it cracks like gunfire. And in the same moment, the darkness lifts off the trees in sharp little pieces and takes to the sky. Blackbirds. Hundreds of them, and the flapping of their wings sounds like someone whispering my name.

Blackbird singing in the dead of night. Nate's favorite Beatles song.

Mel comes running. "Oh my god, did you *see* that?"

She stops next to me, breathing hard, and we watch the birds become specks, like glitter tossed into the wind.

"Did you do that?" she asks.

I shake my head. *Nate did,* I want to tell her. I want that to be true.

"Come back inside," Mel says. "The worst is over."

I follow her, and hope she's right.

Come, sit down to dinner. It goes like this: We fill our chairs, we eat without enthusiasm, we make small talk until it's over. It's simple. It's reliable.

It has occurred to me that my parents might be in possession of useful information about their decision, about the organ donation agency and how to find the other people who got pieces of Nate. It has also occurred to me that my mother will start to wonder what happened if the letter she's expecting never shows up. I may not have much time. So I try something new, shake the snow globe ever so slightly.

"How was your day, Mom?"

She looks startled. "It was—well—fine. I guess."

A few more minutes of silence, and it's my father's turn. "Dad? How was your day?"

He is very focused on cutting his steak into uniform pieces. He does this now, cuts all of his food ahead of time, and then he barely eats any of it. My dad has lost a lot of weight in the last few months. Sometimes I don't recognize him right away when he walks into a room.

"Gene? Tallie asked you a question."

"What?" Dad looks up and seems surprised to see us.

"How was your day, Dad?"

"Oh," he says. "Okay."

I'm not sure if he means that his day was okay or that he's okay with being asked the question. Either way, it's another conversational dead end.

It's not that our dinners were so scintillating and exciting before my brother died. But he could at least keep a conversation going. He could look convincingly interested when my father went on and on about budgeting spreadsheets, had an arsenal of things to say when my mother brought up fabric swatches and furniture sales. A few times he helped move the heavy stuff around when Mom was on a decorating job, and they'd laugh about Susan and Michelle arguing over couch placement.

"Not *there*," Nate would shriek in a perfect imitation of Michelle, and Mom would laugh until she got the hiccups.

Other nights, the work talk was too boring even for him and I could tell that he wasn't really listening, but they couldn't stop, and so he was like a bottomless bowl that could hold all of their chatter. I'm more like a dessert plate. Small. Fragile. Not often used.

Where to go from here? I want to know what they know, but I can't ask directly about him. We don't even say his name in the house. I've been saying it to myself, but I can't say it to them. Not yet.

Dad pushes his plate back, most of his food still on it, and stands up to announce, "I'm going for a walk."

It is not an invitation.

Alone with Mom, who is staring out the window again, I try the only other approach I can think of. "I saw Ms. Appleton at school the other day. She said to say hello."

Ms. Appleton, Academic Olympiad coach and my brother's biggest fan, said no such thing. Ms. Appleton cannot even make eye contact with me anymore.

"Oh," Mom says vacantly. "That's nice."

I follow her gaze out the window, to the stand of oak trees in the side yard. They have been so overtaken with ivy that they look like huge upright serpents, leafy green scales layered thickly from bottom to top. They were one of the reasons that my parents bought this house, she used to tell me. The trees. The front porch. The charm. My mother loves old houses—she regularly drives around town to visit her favorites, parks outside them and watches, hoping (according to her journal) to catch a glimpse of some other version of herself living another life.

And seeing her like this, as if she's the ghost who's haunting me, I wish for her sake that there *was* some parallel world in which she hadn't lost anything, in which she and my dad traded up for that Victorian on Sycamore Street and rescued a greyhound and vacationed on the Cape. If any of that was possible, I would gladly let her go. Because being here without her would be better than being here with this version of her, hollowed out and staring at trees.

It is what I knew it to be.

I am on my own.

I clear the table, to show her that I understand.

As soon as my parents leave for church the next morning, I get online. I'm supposed to be researching mollusks for my biology essay, but I have plenty of time for that. Mr. Cunningham is one of my most forgiving teachers and he's already made it clear that the assignment is fluff, something for extra credit so he can excuse me from the upcoming unit on dissection. I didn't ask him to do this, but it's possible that the look on my face when he said "fetal pig" convinced him to save us all the trouble.

Mollusks can wait. I have a more pressing research topic now.

I start with the simplest search I can think of: *organ donation*. Which, of course, is far from simple. There are pages for networks like Life Choice, pages of information from the government and *Wikipedia*, pages hoping to dispel common myths about the donation process. News stories about the sacrifices people have made to save the lives of others. All very factual and feel-good. But nothing about what to do when you find out that your parents have donated your brother's body without telling you.

I click on the link for Life Choice and scan the tabs at the top of the page. BEFORE THE TRANSPLANT. AFTER THE TRANSPLANT. LIVING DONATION. PEDIATRIC. COMMUNITY. Each one has subheadings that drop down when I roll my mouse over them, but none of them sound like what I'm looking for. I stare at the screen, the home page scrolling through images of smiling families, husbands and wives walking on the beach. I wonder if Gerald R. is married. If he has kids. If they waited in the hospital for Nate's lungs to fix their father, if they were praying to God to save him at the same time that I was praying for Nate to live.

We couldn't both get what we asked for.

I close the search window and log in to Nate's iTunes account, which is still current because I have been adding music to it for the last few months. I debated about doing this but decided that it was okay if I limited myself to adding new tracks from only his favorite bands. And if I kept Matty disconnected from the computer so he didn't upload the new music. This way, Matty is like a true time capsule. Sealed. Accurate.

I pull a few of the newer songs into a playlist I started over the summer. UNTITLED, I called it, because I didn't know what to name it when it wasn't finished yet. But now I see how useless that is, calling something UNTITLED. It lacks intention.

I delete the name and watch the cursor blink, blink, blink, waiting for me.

I think about Phantom Amy, the false face she wears now. I want to tell her what I know about Nate, that he isn't completely gone anymore, that he never was. We won't ever be friends again like we were when we were little, but maybe if I give her this gift, she can forgive me. Maybe then I won't have to carry the blame for taking him away from her.

FOR AMY, I type. Then I add 2.

I drag and drop song after song into the playlist, only the most beautiful songs, only the ones that make me want to dance or cry or smile with their first few words. *If they can make* me *feel this way,* I think, *imagine what they can do for her.*

When I'm done, I send the playlist to my phone and tell myself that I'll figure out a way to get it to her. But just so I have him in my own way, too, I take a pen off my desk and I write his name on the inside of my wrist. The ballpoint tip tugs at my skin, makes the letters skip and stutter, so I trace it over again, and then one more time to be sure.

FOURTEEN

COMMUNICATION

monday 9/29

When I wake up in the morning, I hover as long as I can in the half awareness that waking brings, a kind of mental haze that shields me from knowing that he is gone. It's the best part of the day. But it doesn't last long. And today is different, because the knowing is followed by something else, a knot in my gut that is made of a twisted rope of happy and sick.

I have the first two periods free on Mondays, so Mom doesn't expect me to leave the house early. As soon as I see her car back out of the driveway, I start counting. I count to five hundred in case she forgot something and comes back.

I open my desk drawer just far enough to reach in and find the edge of the Life Choice envelope. Pull it out carefully, as if it might explode.

And maybe it will. Maybe this will blow what's left of my family to high heaven.

I read the first letter again, the one from Gerald R., who is now walking around with my brother's lungs in his body. No address or specific information, just those few details about his health, that name at the bottom. Just the shaky words of a deeply thankful person with a "new life." Which is nice. For him.

The other letter is from Life Choice—in addition to the list of successful transplants, there are the paragraphs I couldn't read the first time, which explain the rules. "Protocols," they call them. They contacted the next of kin to verify willingness to receive this letter, which is what my parents were arguing about. They forwarded this letter and will forward others like it, but it's all done anonymously until such time as both parties agree to personal communication. If personal communication is undertaken, both parties will be counseled on the risks and rewards of said communication, and asked to sign a waiver that says they won't sue the pants off Life Choice if they don't like each other after all (I'm paraphrasing, of course).

Please feel free to contact Life Choice with any questions or concerns, the letter tells me.

Don't mind if I do.

The phone rings several times and a woman's voice breaks in and says, "Life Choice, can you hold, please?" Tinny classical music fills my left ear before I can say yes or no. So much for choices.

"Life Choice, how may I direct your call?"

Suddenly I have no idea who or what to ask for. "Uh—uh," I stammer, "I got a letter from someone?"

"Yes," the woman says.

"And I was wondering if you can help me . . . find out who it's from?"

"Yes," the woman says.

"You can?"

"Well, that depends," the woman says. Her voice is gentle but utterly neutral, like she's an automated sympathy machine. "Are you the recipient or the donor?"

"I'm not—I mean, my brother is the donor. *Was* the donor."

"Okay," she says. "Are you the legal next of kin?"

I know that I'm not, but I decide to play innocent. "I'm not sure."

She sighs. The limits of her sympathy programming are being tested. "Are you over eighteen? Are you the executor of your brother's estate?"

Nate's only worldly possessions were his clothes and his athletic gear, all of which is still in his room, and Matty. He had money from his summer jobs—his car fund—but it's just sitting in the bank. After the funeral, I heard my uncle say that my parents should put it into a college fund for me, but then my aunt hit him on the arm and that was the end of the discussion.

So unless one of the books left in his room contains a secret treasure map or a coded message about a cache of stolen goods, there's no "estate" to speak of.

"No. And no."

"Then your parent or parents are likely the legal next of kin. Any communication on this matter has to involve them."

Crap. This isn't unexpected, but I was hoping for an easier road. I try another tack.

"I think, though, that this is really too painful for them right now. I don't want to upset them any more than they already are, y'know? It's just been so hard. . . ." I let my voice break a little and snuffle like I might be crying.

The sympathy robot is very well programmed. Her voice gets softer, slower. "I understand," she says. "Sometimes we work with a representative of the family, someone the family has chosen to handle things for them. But it still has to be a legal adult. How old are you now?"

"Sixteen," I tell her.

"Well, if you can wait a couple of years, we'll be able to do more."

I can do a lot of things, I want to tell her, *but waiting two years is not one of them.* "Thank you," I say instead. "I will consider that."

"You're welcome," she says, and then, "Thank you for calling Life Choice."

And she's gone. Her words ring in my ears like an echo. *Life choice, choice, choice.* What choice do I have now? I can't ask my parents. If they wanted me to know anything about this, they would have told me about donating his organs. But they didn't. So they have their secrets and I have mine, and that's how it's going to stay.

I hear a strange sound, and when I look down, I see that I have crunched the letters up into a ball in my fist. I set my phone down and use both hands to smooth the paper out again. Of course, you can never get a crumpled piece of paper back the way it was. It's just one of those things that can't be undone.

I decide to cut school and stay home for the rest of the day. If the school calls, I'll tell them I was traumatized by the kissing booth at the carnival on Friday. Ms. Doberskiff will back me up.

There's plenty to keep me busy. Checking up on Dad, reading Mom's journal (in which she has recently confessed to a habit of shoplifting lipsticks in her younger days), thinking about how to find the rest of Nate's parts. I conduct Internet searches for everything I can think of, and elaborate schemes keep forming in my head—hacking pharmaceutical databases to see who is taking suppression drugs so their bodies won't reject their new organs, visiting random hospitals and striking up conversations with possible transplant patients, putting up a Facebook page to lure the recipients into contacting me. But as soon as these plans start to take shape in my head, I realize how absurd they are.

I take a nap, I wake up, I heat soup in the microwave and burn my fingers on the edge of the bowl. I wonder what Chase and Mel are doing. I listen to Matty for a while, but every song is familiar and I realize that I have listened to all of them. I've used them all up and I can't add anything new because that would be my own choice, not Nate's. It would ruin the time capsule.

The house starts to feel like it's contracting, shrinking to fit me like I'm Alice in Wonderland.

I'm tired of waiting, and I'm losing what little equilibrium I have. So I decide to ride my bike into town.

I ride past St. Anne's, past gas stations and convenience stores, past the garage where Dad took the cars for oil changes and bought us packs of gum that we chewed all at once. I remember the way Nate made his eyes as big as moons as he folded each piece into his mouth. Blowing bubbles bigger than our faces and jabbing them into each other. The time mine got stuck to his and exploded, the hours we spent picking gum out of his hair and his eyebrows.

"Argh!" he kept yelling. "How did you *do* that?"

And me, trying not to giggle, desperate not to make him angry with me.

I try to see Nate in these places, try to make him appear, but I see only stone and gravel and the hard, unsympathetic surfaces of the roads and sidewalks. I used to be brave enough to ride with my eyes closed but now I am careful, so I have to watch everything as it slides away behind me.

Then everything is moving, not just front to back but sideways, too. My hands grip the bike's hard plastic handlebars, molded to receive my fingers but slipping underneath them. My helmet grips my head but it's too much—it's too tight and I can't breathe and I'm dizzy—so I stop.

I let the bike fall away from me as I fumble with the clip under my chin, releasing myself from the helmet's care. The sound of the bike clattering against a tree echoes like a distress call that I can only hope no one has heard. I do not want to be rescued. I just want to do the things I did before: ride a bike, wear a helmet, listen to music. I want there to be less meaning in everything. I want it all to signify nothing.

I don't want to know what I know.

I can think of nothing more simple than walking, so that is what I do. But even that betrays me, because before I realize where I'm going, I find myself standing across the street from the Sip'N'Dip, staring at the only other person there: Amy.

She doesn't see me right away. She is holding an ice cream cone and crying. She is not eating it, just letting it melt down her hand and her arm, and crying. She is sitting on one of the splintery picnic tables, sitting on the table itself instead of the bench, sitting with her legs tucked into each other. *Crisscross applesauce*, I think, or maybe I whisper it. Or maybe I even say it out loud, because she looks up at me in the same instant that I see that her cone is a vanilla fudge dip.

She looks up at me, and her face is not soft and sweet like ice cream. Her face is contorted with sadness and something that looks like anger. She throws the cone on the ground and takes a step toward me.

I run.

I run all the way home, past my bike and helmet, past the garage, the church, past all of the other houses that hold people who know me. People who don't know me anymore. I run until I think my head will explode and I almost hope that it will and I stand in the front hall waiting for it to happen, but it doesn't. *I ruined her,* I think. *I broke her.* There's no way a playlist will make up for that, not even accompanied by the news that Nate isn't wholly gone. And then finally, through some miraculous alchemy of exhaustion and panic, I know what to do.

I've been forging my mother's signature for years. I even signed off on Nate's teachers' notes, and stuff from school he didn't want my parents to see, because I had perfected Mom's handwriting better than he ever could. I liked that he needed me for something.

It didn't start out as anything intentional. Mostly, I just wanted to see how well I could copy her signature, and then one day she was too busy to sign a permission slip for my field trip to the apple orchard, so I signed it myself and got away with it. It made me feel grown-up to do it, to write her name in her fancy script with the lowercase *c* in our last name swooping up into the capital *G*. I have kept my own signature simple, for contrast. My writing is small and deliberate, tightly packed on the page. Mom's is airy and attention-seeking. At least, it used to be.

Still out of breath, I climb the stairs and lurch to my room. I sit at my desk, flip to a clean page in my notebook. I'm out of practice, so I start carefully.

Dear Sir, I write. *I am so pleased and grateful to hear from you.*

I try to channel Mom when I do this so I don't hesitate as I'm writing. I have to really pretend I'm her to keep the flow going. It would be easier to type, of course, but Gerald's letter was handwritten and I want to return the favor, establish a personal connection.

> *You can imagine how difficult this time has been for me and my family. Especially my daughter, who lost her brother so suddenly and tragically. It is so gratifying to know that my son's death was, in this way, not the end of his life. We wish you all the best.*

I want to ask for more, ask who he is and where I can find him, if we can email each other instead of writing these letters. But I know that my mother would show more restraint. And I can't sound desperate, or like a kid in any way. So I write a couple of paragraphs, just a few sentences each, about what a kind, talented boy Nate was, beloved in our community, an inspiration to his friends and neighbors. As if I'm writing a college recommendation, except it's in the past tense. Then I add one last thing.

> *I do hope you'll write again.*

I take an envelope and a stamp from the desk in the kitchen, and write the Life Choice address on the outside.

There is a mailbox up the street, not far from where my

abandoned bike rests in the shade. The door creaks when I open it, as all doors on all mailboxes seem to do, and then I drop the letter into the darkness before I lose my nerve. It feels like making a wish, throwing a penny into the well. I stand there, hands pressed to my chest, feeling my heart beat. I wonder if the heart recipient does this, too. I wonder if he thinks about Nate, where that heart came from, or if he tries not to.

Cross my heart.

A bird lands on the tree above me then. Its black feathers swallow the sunlight.

Confirmation.

I nod to the bird, and retrieve my bicycle and my helmet. I put them back in the garage so they are safe.

Then I listen to Matty's playlists until dinner.

FIFTEEN

FALLING SLOWLY

tuesday 9/30

There is a note from my mother in the kitchen the next morning, telling me that she will pick me up after school. Doctor's appointment. I panic, briefly, but then I check the calendar and see *t to dr balder* written in my mother's newly careful lettering, kept so neatly in the box that this day was given.

I had considered staying home again, but this clinches it. I have to go to school. Plus, if I don't show up for school two days in a row, Mel might come looking for me (if only out of curiosity), and I'm not sure if I want to tell her about this new plot twist. On the one hand, matters of organ donation are right up her alley. The removal of the essential parts, the surgical precision, the reanimation of something. Mel would find it poetic. I just don't know if I'm ready for this to be a metaphor.

We haven't been friends long enough for me to say that we don't keep secrets from each other. For all I know, Mel has warehouses full of secrets. So keeping one from her doesn't feel wrong. It doesn't feel like anything other than a necessity.

For some reason, though, as soon as I see Chase slouching in what has become his usual waiting-for-Tallie place, I have this compulsion to tell him everything. I fight it, of course.

"Hey, sicko," he says.

I am perplexed by this greeting, until I realize he must think I was home with an actual illness, a legitimate reason. He thinks I'm a girl who follows the rules. And he's not wrong. The threat of Red Circle Day has been keeping me in line for a while now.

My mission is to act normal. "Hey," I reply. "What'd I miss?"

"Nothing of import," he says, matching my pace as I walk down the hall. "Those girls from the kissing booth are in my history class, and they got chewed out by Ms. Appleton for calling World War II 'totally scud.' She went on this whole rampage about trying to force the evolution of language and disrespecting veterans. It was pretty intense."

"Poor Ms. Appleton," I say.

"She's usually so quiet."

"I know. She really hasn't been the same since—" I stop myself from saying *the accident*. This is going to be a day of stopping myself from saying things, I guess.

"I heard Absalom is having another event at the Elbow Room this weekend," Chase tells me. "Wanna go?"

"I don't think he would be very happy to see us. And I don't think he has any actual psychic abilities."

Chase snorts. "Of course he doesn't. You'd have better luck with half a Ouija board than with that guy. If you were trying to contact someone, I mean."

"Which I'm not." His lost brother might be fully on the other side, but mine isn't. At least, that's my hope.

A look passes across his face like an eclipse, and he says, "I always wanted to try when I was a kid, see if I could actually get through to Houdini. His wife tried for years, y'know? He told her to before he died. He told her he'd come back."

We're at my locker now, so I have the numbers to focus on to keep myself from looking at Chase when I ask, "Did he?"

"Nope. She tried for ten years. She had séances every year on Halloween because that was the anniversary of his death, and after ten years she announced that he wasn't coming back, and that proved it was impossible. Because if anyone could escape from the other side, it would be Houdini."

"But how did she know he didn't? What if she just missed something?"

"They had worked out a coded message. It never came through. People are still trying, though. Every Halloween since 1927. If he's out there, he's probably wishing they'd just give up."

What if that's what Nate wants, too? What if he wants us to just move on and I'm doing the wrong thing? I push the thought away and look at Chase.

"Do you really think it's impossible for someone to come back?"

He shrugs. "I doubt anything's impossible. Maybe Houdini was just being stubborn. He never believed in séances when he was alive, so coming back would have been kind of hypocritical anyway."

"Well, they're together now, right?"

Chase shakes his head. "His wife's family wouldn't put her in a Jewish cemetery, so they're not buried together."

"Oh." I can't say much more without saying too much. It feels like there's a dam at the back of my throat, and the more I talk, the more likely it is to burst and let everything rush out.

"Yeah," Chase says. "Hey, we missed you at Bridges yesterday."

"You went?"

He shrugs again. "I've been trying out some different things. So far, Bridges has the best snacks. Margaret had some kind of breakthrough, apparently. Confessed to lying about all kinds of stuff. Bethany wanted to kick her out of the club or whatever, but Ms. Doberskiff said she could stay and 'mourn her loss of truth' or something."

"Yuck." I can just picture it, the whole morbid scene. "I'm thinking of quitting." In fact, this thought has not occurred to me until just now, but it seems obvious that I should follow through on it. Even at the risk of getting in trouble with Principal Hunter, who will get me in trouble with my parents, who could get me in trouble with Dr. Blankenbaker. The fact is, I can hardly sit there and talk about Nate without this new secret bursting out of me like confetti. It's as if my tragedy has been rewound and redirected somehow. It wouldn't be right, acting like nothing has changed. Even if that's kind of what I have to do with Mel and Chase and my parents—to lie to the Bridges kids would be on a karmic par with repeatedly kicking a puppy.

"Yeah," Chase says.

"So," I reply, the words I will not say still hammering at the wall in my throat.

He cocks his head and squints a little, and he seems about to say something, but doesn't. He just points down the hall and then follows his own finger until the crowd swallows him whole.

. . .

Mel finds me eventually, as she always does, and it's round two of acting normal. We are walking down one of the many hallways toward one of the many, many stairwells of our school. Sometimes I wonder if the architectural plans for this building were inadvertently swapped with an Escher drawing.

"Hey," Mel says. "Want to help me drive Zoey and Fiona completely insane?"

"What now?"

"I'm starting a band called Scud. I need a bass player."

"I don't know how to play bass."

"Who cares? It's not like we're ever going to play any gigs. I just need people to be in a picture so I can set up a Tumblr page."

"Scud is a terrible name for a band," I tell her.

Mel looks at me with an expression of deep pity. "Obviously," she says. "If I was *actually* starting a band, it would be called Muskrocket."

"Um," I say. "That is also kind of terrible."

"Yes," says Mel. "But in a totally different way."

"What about your project at the barn?"

"That's a weekend thing. Uncle Enoch has dibs on the workshop during the week. And anyway, the cat's done. I just have to finish the cape and the hat for the raccoon's costume. And find a raccoon."

We stop at the bottom of the stairs and allow ourselves to be brushed against by the passing hordes. It is not unpleasant. Every once in a while, I realize how little human contact I have, physically. They've done studies with rats that are socially isolated, and the rats get all sad and their immune systems fall apart. I know this because we read about it in biology last year, and Mr. Cunningham felt compelled to remind us that humans are much more resilient and even if someone has, for instance, just gone through a painful divorce and only sees his children twice a month, he would still be okay. (Mr. Cunningham is now dating Ms. Pace, the fiber-arts teacher. They park next to each other in the faculty lot, and their vanity plates read, respectively, ORGNC MTR and SEWIN LOV.)

I see that Mel is looking at me and that she appears concerned, in her way, and I realize that she is waiting for me to answer a question I didn't hear.

"What?" I ask.

She hikes her backpack up onto her shoulder. "Go to the Grounds after school? I want to ask Cranky Andy if I can post a flyer for my band."

"Can't. I have a doctor's appointment."

Mel smirks. "Head doctor or regular doctor?"

"Regular." I've never talked to Mel about Red Circle Day or about Dr. Blankenbaker, but somehow she figured out that I'd been to a therapist. I guess that's just standard practice for trauma these days. Another layer in the tragedy cake.

Mel starts to say something but someone bumps into her, pushing her into me, and our bodies are touching for just a second before she recoils as if she's been electrocuted. I have this sudden urge to hug her, to make her uncomfortable, as uncomfortable as I am in my own skin.

"I could pick you up after," she offers. "Your new fanboy might be there."

Something crackles between us.

The bell rings.

"Whatever," Mel says, and disappears down the next flight of stairs while I stand there, watching everyone disperse like birds.

SIXTEEN

DOCTOR MY EYES

Dr. Balder is my pediatrician. He was also Nate's pediatrician, of course, and he is one of the only people who didn't say anything trite or hollow the first time I saw him after the accident. I had come to get my stitches taken out of the cuts on my arms, where the windshield had spit its broken glass into my flesh, and Dr. Balder was so patient and gentle and did not mind that I cried the entire time. At the end, he put his hand on my shoulder and said, "It's a damn shame, my girl. You both deserved better than that."

I felt, in that moment, like Dr. Balder and I were soldiers in the same platoon and had just lost an important battle. I felt fortified and, at the same time, really sad. For both of us.

My mother picks me up outside the school's front door. I'm still not used to seeing the silver SUV she got after the accident. I still look for the green station wagon and I have to remind myself that it's gone, too. We drive to Dr. Balder's office in nearly perfect silence, which is broken by only a few words: *hi how are you fine.*

She signs me in, like she always has, even though I've been able to write my own name for a while now. The waiting room is meant to look warm and comfortable, but no number of couches or floral prints can hide the fact that it's a doctor's office. The smell of antiseptic cleanliness, the surgical masks and hand sanitizer offered to protect you, the promises made by a wall full of brochures. I wish there was one that would be relevant to my circumstances. I wish it was as simple as chicken pox and personal hygiene.

I look at a magazine and listen to the music threading itself through the tiny wall-mounted speakers, a dramatic orchestral arrangement of a Billy Joel song my parents used to like. I keep my breathing very regular, and then the nurse calls my name. My mother looks at me, eyebrows raised, asking without asking if I want her to come with me. I shake my head and follow the nurse down the hall.

Dr. Balder is, in fact, bald. He often makes a joke about it, as if he feels it necessary to remind me that he has not forgotten about his baldness and the cruel irony of his name.

"Good thing my parents didn't name me Harry, hmm?" He guffaws and pats his stethoscope.

This comment makes me think of Harry Houdini, which makes me think of Chase, which is rather inconvenient right now because Dr. Balder notices me blushing and thinks I'm embarrassed for him. "Well," he mumbles. "How have you been?"

I trace my river scar with my finger.

"Fine. I mean, I've been kind of distracted lately," I tell him. And then quickly add, "It's probably just . . . stress." I pause before the word *stress* because I want to give it some gravity. I have read that almost every human ailment is caused by stress and that doctors are very receptive to this word.

"I see," says Dr. Balder. He looks down at my chart and rubs his head. I wonder if he did that when he had hair. "Can I give you some advice?"

"Okay." Maybe this will be like the verbal version of the brochure I wish I had.

"You've been through a lot, my girl. Your body and your mind are catching back up to each other. It might help to step back and give them a chance to do that work."

"Meaning?"

"Have you tried meditation?"

The rituals. "Sort of."

"Good, good. It can be scary sometimes to let yourself be open to what's happening, but the only way to get past something like this is to go straight through it. No shortcuts. You understand?"

I nod. Because I do understand. Or at least, I'm beginning to. I can't *think* my way out of this, or meditate out, or *will* something to happen. Finding out about Nate has derailed my back-to-normal mission. Can I have both? Can I move on, knowing that he's still around, or do I have to choose?

I found out the truth because I broke a rule. I can do it again. I can make something happen. It feels like trying to let go of the handlebars on a bike that's going seventy-five miles an hour. Against my instincts. Almost impossible.

Almost.

"Thank you, Dr. Balder," I say, and then, surprising both of us, I throw my arms around him. He smells like Old Spice and coffee, and his doctor's coat is softened from years of wear.

"You've been through a lot, my girl," Dr. Balder says again quietly, and before I let go, I tell him, "We all have."

As I'm walking out the door, something else occurs to me. Another way he might be able to help.

"I'm writing an article for the school paper on organ donation. You know, trying to get the kids to sign up to be an organ donor when they get their driver's license. Anyway, do you know anyone I could talk to? About how it works?"

Dr. Balder taps his pen against the manila folder with my name on the tab. Upside down it looks like hieroglyphics, something written in a lost language. "There's a new doctor at the hospital who might be able to help. Came from Boston. Dr. Abbott. I think his son may go to school with you. Jason, is it?" *Tap, tap, tap.* "No, Chase! That's it. Chase."

You've got to be kidding me.

"Yes," I say. "I think I may know him."

"Wonderful! Let me know if you have any trouble getting in touch with him. And I'd love to read the piece when it comes out."

"The what?"

Dr. Balder chuckles. "Your article. Bring a copy by the office, would you? We can put it up on the bulletin board."

"Absolutely," I tell him. "I will."

Another lie on my to-do list. And now I have to figure out a way to ask Chase for help without asking him for help. He shared his secret hobby with me, inducted me into the Society of the Memorial Binder. I could play into that, even though I know the truth: No one can really preserve anything. There are too many variables. The minute you dodge the speeding bus, a piano falls from the sky. This used to bother me, the unpredictability of things, but now, well, I think it can be very motivating to know you've only got so much time to do what you want.

And what I want is to find my brother.

SEVENTEEN

NIGHTSWIMMING

wednesday 10/1

At the YMCA, there's an indoor pool under a huge glass atrium, and you can stand on a balcony above it and watch the kids take their swimming lessons. It's like a human aquarium, small creatures in brightly colored swimsuits, oblivious to my presence. Suspended in the water, arms and legs spread in all directions, the children look like they're parachuting from a great height. They are unafraid. They are free.

We used to take lessons in that pool, and Nate would stand on the balcony after his were over and sometimes I would wave to him as I floated around on my back. So trusting. So sure he would be there when I looked up.

After the accident, I went there a few times when my mother wanted to walk around the indoor track but wouldn't leave me home alone. No one ever asked me what I was doing. I guess they assumed I had a little brother or sister in the pool. If they had asked, that's what I would have told them.

Now—hoping for another boy-in-the-bleachers moment—

I catch myself looking for him again: through store windows as I walk by, in passing cars, behind trees in the park. Despite the lump in my throat, the jumpy heart locked in my chest. I want to make it work, find a way to keep him and get over it at the same time. *Can I have both?* I ask myself again.

Mr. Cunningham says there is no randomness in the universe, only the illusion of randomness. Patterns that we cannot detect because they are too large, or too small.

He reminds me of this when he hands back my mollusk essay after class.

"Sometimes nature fools us," Mr. Cunningham says. "Sometimes we convince ourselves that nature needs our help, when all along nature has a bigger plan that we can't see."

"Sounds like what people say about God. That there's this big master plan and we're just too small or too stupid to understand it."

Mr. Cunningham shrugs. "I'm not a religious man. But I do believe there are forces at work on a scale that I cannot fully understand. Maybe biology is my religion."

"You should write Ms. Pace a song about that," I tell him. Mr. Cunningham pinkens. Mel told me that Mr. Cunningham uses his free periods to practice medieval love chants on the guitar. She also told me that Mr. Cunningham has a terrible singing voice. I don't want to seem cruel.

"Or a poem, maybe," I offer.

"Yes, well," he says. "In any case, I'm going to ask you to rewrite your essay. There's no rush, take your time. But the assignment was about shared characteristics of freshwater and terrestrial mollusks." He dips his head to the side a little as he says this, as if he's apologizing for trying to teach me. "I like what you wrote very much. But it's a bit . . . philosophical."

I tell him that I understand, and politely decline his offer of a late pass for my next class. There isn't a teacher in this school who will give me detention. I'm not as squeamish about their pity as I used to be. I'll take any kind of advantage I can get, especially now.

Dad flipped the calendar page this morning. It's October first.

Red Circle Day is on full display. If I want Chase's father to help me, I can't put this off any longer. *It doesn't have to be weird*, I tell myself. *Just keep it simple.*

I happen to know that Chase has calculus this period, so I saunter casually past his classroom and linger for a moment in the door's tall rectangular window. It takes about ten seconds for him to look up. Mel sees me, too. I shake my head and point at Chase, who quickly raises his hand and asks for a bathroom break. Dr. Monroe is about five hundred years old and probably spends most of his day in the bathroom. He will not deny any of his students the same privilege.

"What's up?" Chase asks after closing the classroom door behind him. He is wearing his BOOM shirt again. Mel scowls at us through the window, so I take a few steps backward and Chase follows. As we huddle against the water fountain, my keep-it-simple plan suddenly seems all wrong, and instead I say, "Do you believe there are universal forces that operate according to natural laws we cannot comprehend?"

His brown eyes widen. "Just a casual inquiry?"

"I'll rephrase. If Harry Houdini wanted to come back, do you think he could choose how he appeared, or who he could talk to? Are there operational rules for the afterlife?"

Chase strokes an invisible beard. "My best guess is that the connection between our realm and that one would be subject to some kind of structure, yes. But it might not be constant. It might not be the same for everyone."

"That's not a whole lot of help," I tell him.

"Sorry," he says. "I'm just a guy who's supposed to be going to the bathroom."

I can't for the life of me figure out how to steer the conversation properly, and even Dr. Monroe has limits on how long he'll let a student disappear. Then I notice that Chase is looking at my mouth. Either I have something on my face or I have just discovered that even this strange boy with the binder is not immune to hormones. My various inner voices can debate this discovery later. "What are you doing after school?" I ask.

"You tell me."

"Can I come over?"

He looks startled, and then pleased. "Sure," he says.

I see tiny Tallies in his pupils, like the angel and the devil on the shoulders of a cartoon hero. "I'll ride over later," I tell him. Whatever he is about to say in return is cut short by a set of sharp staccato taps on the door. Dr. Monroe is glaring at us through the glass.

"Later," I repeat.

And Chase echoes me. "Later."

I take out my phone as the door closes behind him and compose a text to Mel:

walking home

My thumb hovers over the send button. I have never lied to her before. I have never needed to. Is this what happens to secrets?

They split like atoms and create lies as their offspring? Mel doesn't expect me to tell her what I do or where I go, and yet I feel like I owe her an explanation for why I just pulled Chase out of class instead of her. A reason, even if it's an untrue one. Because I am starting to realize that, all this time, I've been expecting her to leave on her own, for our strange friendship arrangement to run its course, for her to move on to some other cause or passing attachment. And now I think it is not going to happen that way. Our moment in the stairwell yesterday taps me on the shoulder and whispers, *I can't tell her, not yet. She'll take it. She'll turn it into something else.*

Mel has been my companion in limbo.

But I'm climbing out of limbo, or trying to.

I send the text, and then I start for home. I walk through the empty halls, my footsteps calling out through the endless air, daring someone—anyone—to find me.

The Invasion of the Mollusk: An Essay
by Tallie McGovern

The pearl begins as a parasite, a microscopic invader, irritating a mollusk's slippery mechanisms like a deep itch so that the mollusk must cover it up. Layers upon layers of calcium carbonate trap the offending particle, held together with an organic compound called conchiolin, until whatever it was that snuck into the mollusk's shell— probably when it opened up to eat, or breathe—is contained, and made beautiful.

A pearl rarely forms spontaneously, or naturally. Most come from "farms," where thousands of mollusks are implanted with tissue from other mollusks, tiny transplanted pieces that are foreign and therefore biologically objected to by the recipients. Often a small bead is added to the donor tissue, to ensure the spherical shape of the pearl in its final form. The bead assists the unwitting clam or mussel in making something valuable out of what must be a rather unpleasant experience.

But does the mussel mind? Does the clam have the capacity to think, "This bead is driving me crazy"? The whole idea of irritation, discomfort, pain—it's really just a problem for us humans, isn't it? A mollusk does not feel loss, or regret. It does not bemoan its fate. It accepts the bit of tissue from its fellow mollusk because it has no choice, and that bit is given its own mineral compartment and is more or less fully assimilated until someone, some pearl farmer, comes along and removes it. And then what? Does the mollusk *miss* the pearl? Does it feel empty, somehow?

Does it want the pearl back?

EIGHTEEN

WAY DOWN

The bike ride to Chase's house feels shorter this time. The first time you go anywhere, it feels like it takes a while, even in your own town, even if it's not a long trip. The second time is always quicker than you remember, and this time I have Matty feeding music into my ears. Three songs. That's all it takes to get there.

I'm wearing the same clothes I wore to school this morning. The thought of Chase's rods and cones having recorded the shape of my mouth almost caused me to change, but then I decided against it. Chase seems like a guy who notices things like that and I don't want to give him the wrong idea. This is just business, research. At least for now.

I'm not put back together yet.

So I play it casual, tell him "Hey" when he opens the door, as if I wasn't half thinking all the way here about what to say. What not to say. And he says it back, easy as can be, and I walk into his house like I've done it a hundred times before. And it feels so normal, until he asks the question I should have seen coming, the one I didn't prepare for.

"What are you doing here?"

I can think just fast enough to throw him an answer he'll catch.

"I wanted to see it again. The binder."

Chase looks mildly surprised. "Really? Um, okay. Sure." He leads me into the den, where overstuffed couches laden with throw pillows and cashmere blankets wait patiently to embrace us. My mother would love this room—the books shelved by color, assorted sculptural objects arranged to look like someone just set them there. It looks like a room that Mom and Susan and Michelle would have decorated. Maybe they did.

And on the massive coffee table, the binder awaits. "It's so weird you came over when you did," Chase says. "I was just about to put it away."

"Then I'm glad I caught you."

"I'll be right back," Chase says. "I've got some new pages to put in."

It feels like a secret even though I've seen it before. I lean over and touch it gently, as if it might object or raise a voice I didn't know it had. But it remains a silent thing, even as I draw it closer, even as I open the cover and look inside.

In the front are the pages I have already seen. I flip past those, trying to discern whether there's a system or an order to their placement in the book. But it seems to be random, and there are too many for me to look at them all. Then I think about what the binder is, what it means. That it contains the ends of all of these lives, that the end is where the meaning lies.

I flip to the very back, then let the pages fly forward again, their plastic edges caressing my thumb. Until I see him.

He's still there.

Nate.

His name. His picture. And I am surprised to see that he doesn't look exactly as I remember him, that without the intrusion of actual photographs of him, my memory has made him different. I tell myself that pictures can be deceiving, inaccurate. I'm sure the images of me on Mel's phone don't look anything like me. But I know, too, how unreliable memory can be—like eyewitness testimony, colored and recast by new experiences. I turn the pages, wondering what made Chase deem these stories binder-worthy, how these families have gone on, whether they're even remotely the same.

Chase thinks it's vital to remember the ones who died, but I think of the people left in the wake of each death. The survivors.

There are always survivors.

A man appears in the doorway. "You must be Tallie," he says. His face is friendly, his voice deep and warm. It's like looking at a future projection of Chase, which comforts me. The idea of Chase's future, that he will have one despite his fixation on the past.

"I must be," I tell Dr. Abbott. "Nobody else wants the job."

"What have you got there?" he asks, not moving from the door but thrusting his eyes at the binder. I slam it closed, the cover almost whistling as it slices through the air.

"Just a school project," I tell him.

"History?" he asks.

"Mortality," I say.

"That sounds like a dark subject."

I shrug, putting my hand protectively on the binder. "That's why it's black."

He laughs, a single perfect burst of sound. "Stay for dinner," he says, and leaves before I can answer. It wasn't a question anyway.

Chase comes in a moment later, looking panicked. I pass him the binder, carefully, and say, "You owe me." And then, "What kind of music do you like?"

The ensuing grunge retrospective—delivered through conjoined sets of earbuds plugged into Chase's phone—is interrupted precisely at six o'clock, when we are summoned to the table by an actual bell. Chase's mother emerges from some other part of the house, comes to the table paint-spattered and sulky. Chase's father ignores her, instead asking me many questions about myself and my interests. Since I am not yet ready to reveal what my real interests are (organ recipients, subterfuge), I distract him with talk of journalism, field hockey, and aspirations to attend an East Coast college. Total bull. He loves it. Chase does his best to keep a straight face while I mimic things I heard Nate saying during his college-interview prep sessions with my father. Things like "I feel strongly that a small liberal arts college is the best place to develop my understanding of larger ethical issues."

Mrs. Abbott interjects. "College is overrated. I think every high school graduate should be sent to a foreign country for a year. Just dropped out of a helicopter with a backpack and forced to live by their wits."

Dr. Abbott rolls his eyes. "As I recall, darling, you said your year abroad was spent in a four-star hotel in Paris."

Mrs. Abbott sniffs and takes a sip of her wine. "Well, if I had it to do over again, I would like a more authentic experience."

"By all means!" Dr. Abbott declares. "Just say the word and I will have a helicopter and a parachute ready for you."

"Oh, you'd love that, wouldn't you," Mrs. Abbott mutters. She stabs a piece of steak with surprising ferocity and stares at her husband while she chews. The tension between them probably makes a lot of people uncomfortable, but I kind of like it. I can feel this energy in the room, crackling and snapping like burning twigs. It buoys me just enough to step closer to why I'm really here.

"Dr. Abbott," I say, "I wonder if I could ask you some questions. For an article I'm working on."

He sits back in his chair and folds his arms. "What kind of article?"

Chase is across the table from me, hovering in my peripheral vision. I hold him there, not looking at him but not blocking him out either, as I repeat what I told Dr. Balder about the school paper and wanting to encourage new drivers to check off the organ donor box on their license application. This is a higher level of pretense than the talk about private colleges and field hockey. I sound even more false to myself, and I'm sure Chase can hear the difference in my voice.

"A worthy cause," Dr. Abbott says. "I'd be happy to help. Shall we continue our conversation in the library?"

I nod just as Mrs. Abbott pushes herself away from the table and refills her wineglass. "I'll be in my studio," she announces, and, glass in hand, swoops out of the room and down a hallway to some hidden refuge. One, presumably, that Dr. Abbott never visits.

Chase and I follow his father down a different path, into a room with floor-to-ceiling shelves full of books that are so perfectly aligned it seems impossible that anyone has ever touched them. I pause in the doorway to survey the factory effect and Chase stops, too.

"Since when are you on the paper?" he asks.

"Oh, I'm full of surprises," I say lightly.

He looks at me and I can see myself, tiny and doubled, in his eyes again.

"I don't think you are, actually," he says. "I think you hate surprises."

He's right, of course. And suddenly I have the sinking feeling that I am going to ruin a perfectly good chance to like a boy, a boy who would like me back, by piling secrets on the two of us until we collapse. But here's the thing: There are only so many variations on a story, aren't there? A plot is a line connecting the dots, and it moves ever forward, and it is logical and so is life, most of the time. Short of running naked through a church or setting something important on fire, how many truly unpredictable things can a person do? Mel certainly tries, but even her fits of outsider performance art fizzle out most of the time. And I find this comforting, somehow, the sense that even if I am making a huge mistake right now, I cannot get irretrievably far from where I started. I cannot get totally lost.

But Dr. Abbott is not, as it turns out, a huge amount of help. We start off talking about the importance of organ donors in general, and then I steer him toward the politics of donor-recipient relationships, like, just for instance, if a donor's family member wanted to talk to the recipients, or meet them. For closure.

Every utterance of the word *recipient* is a cold wave crashing over me.

Most of the answers he gives me are not the ones I want to hear. It is nearly impossible for a minor to do anything without the consent or involvement of her parents when it comes to medical matters, and even if the hypothetical girl I present to him was able to ascertain the identities of the organ recipients, they are probably spread out all over the country. Medical information is highly confidential and only the people who work at the various organ procurement agencies would know who got what.

The bottom line is this: I have a single letter to work from, a letter I'm not supposed to have. A letter I was *definitely* not supposed to answer. Even if I can eventually meet this one man in person, he is unlikely to lead me to the others. Not to mention the dilemma of how I would explain why I am not actually a forty-two-year-old interior decorator named Sarah.

Just when I am starting to think that I have made my way to an impassable brick wall, Dr. Abbott gives me one tiny pearl of hope. "It is possible, of course," he says, "that a donor who dies in a major metropolitan area, with several hospitals or transplant centers nearby, would provide organs to a few people in the same general location. It's unusual, but it's not unheard of."

Like Boston, I think. They took Nate to Boston after the accident, airlifted him for emergency surgery. Which turned out to be futile, of course. My parents had fought about which one of them should make the trip and which one should stay with me. And then Nate died before the helicopter landed and the whole argument vaporized, vanished into the already toxic atmosphere. And then the doctor came to tell me and . . .

I shake my head to clear the memories and try to focus on what Dr. Abbott is saying. "I could put you in touch with a colleague at Brigham and Women's, if you'd like. Although I'm not sure how much detail you need for a school newspaper article."

It will start to look suspicious, the more specific my questions get. Someone is bound to guess why I'm digging for more. Given the way he's looking at me, Chase already has some idea.

"It might, um, be useful to compare how different hospitals handle these things," I say.

"Good point." Dr. Abbott nods. "Very well. Let me speak to my friend and see if she's amenable to being interviewed. If she is, Chase can pass along her contact information. Sound fair?"

Fair has very little to do with anything, I think. But I tell him that it does, and after thanking him for dinner (and refusing an offer of crème brûlée for dessert, which I don't think my nervous, dishonest stomach could handle), I let Chase walk me to the door. He has been very quiet, and I feel even guiltier for keeping so many secrets. I am tempted to spill them all, to throw them like pennies onto the glossy marble floor and watch them roll into every little hidden corner. If only I could leave them here for someone else to sort through. Chase hands me my bike helmet and I hug it, pressing it against my stomach. He opens the front door and I step onto the porch. The air feels like chilled liquid on my skin, tickling my bare arms. I loop my helmet straps over one hand and pull my sleeves down to cover the map of scars. I wait for one of us to speak.

"Well," he finally says, "this was . . . interesting."

"Very informative," I offer lamely.

"Why didn't you just tell me that you wanted to interview my father? How did you even know he was a surgeon?"

"My pediatrician told me." This is hands down the craziest-sounding thing I've ever said, and I smile in spite of myself. "I'm sorry," I tell Chase. "I should have run it by you first."

He is standing in the doorway, the massive front door of his house poised to receive him back inside. He drums his fingers along its face. "You don't owe me any explanations," he says. And then he adds, "I don't require total disclosure. Only honesty."

"Meaning?"

"You don't have to tell me everything. Just don't tell me anything that isn't true."

"You don't believe in lying by omission?" I ask.

He shrugs. "There's usually a good reason to leave out certain parts of the story. Just remember the story won't make sense with holes in it."

I flash on an image of Nate, holes all over his body where his missing parts used to be. I don't know whether to tell Chase what is happening, or how I would explain it. So many things make sense until you try to put them into words, and I'm not ready for this to unravel.

"I should go," I say. It's weak, but Chase doesn't call me on it.

"Later, gator," he replies.

He closes the door and I turn to go. Then I hear a raucous, grating cry from the tree above me. A blackbird.

"But I'm not ready," I whisper.

And the bird takes off, disgusted.

NINETEEN

A QUESTION MARK

thursday 10/2

I am in the library, the letter from Gerald laid out before me. I have read it so many times that I could recite it like a Shakespearean soliloquy, but I keep hoping it will tell me something new. Give me a clue. It has been eight days since I found it in the mailbox, three since I wrote back, and Red Circle Day is less than two weeks away. I let my pen wander on my open notebook, making lazy loops and curves like an infinite roller coaster, watching for patterns that refuse to appear. Trying to keep Dr. Abbott's words from coming back to me.

Doubt whispers in my ear. Even if Gerald writes again and I can intercept the letter and continue the correspondence, it could take time to extract information from him. And time is dangerous. Time means more chances for mistakes, tripping up, getting caught. Time runs out.

My life feels like a puzzle in which every piece is moving. Every piece has its own trajectory and none of them will stay still. Mel is occupied with band rehearsals after school. She wasn't quite content, in the end, with an imaginary group.

"This town needs more of a cultural scene than séances and lame poetry readings," she insisted. "And I'll be damned if I miss a chance to drive Zoey and Fiona over the edge."

Posting recruitment flyers for Scud all over town actually paid off, drawing a handful of somewhat talented guys who play instruments and have been rejected by Zoey and/or Fiona. They were totally on board with Mel's mission statement, and lo, the band was formed just in time for Battle of the Bands next month. For the last couple of days, Mel has been texting me samples of their lyrics—which are oddly sweet, almost reminiscent of the songs on my Amy playlist—but I haven't seen her since I pulled Chase out of calculus yesterday. I check the clock—creative writing starts in twenty minutes and I know she will be waiting for me in the doorway, out of some twisted kind of responsibility.

And Amy. I keep trying to find a way to talk to her, assure her that I won't tell anyone that she cries into her ice cream at the Sip'N'Dip, but now whenever she sees me, it's as if she's about to be attacked and she all but runs in the opposite direction.

Maybe we're all just like magnets facing the wrong way, repelling each other when we want to attract.

Ms. Huff, the librarian, is looking at me suspiciously, and when I check the clock again, I see that five minutes has passed, which is not a very long time if you're, say, running a marathon but is quite a long time to be sitting in a library and staring at absolutely nothing. I wave to her, smiling, and she smiles back because that is what people do.

"I'm revising an essay for Mr. Cunningham," I tell her. "Where would I find the books about mollusks?" I ask this question even though I know perfectly well where the books are, because I have been spending a lot of time in this library.

She directs me to the section on marine life and I congratulate myself on giving her a way to feel useful. Maybe that's all Mel is looking for, too. Maybe I'll ask her to teach me some guitar chords, give her an excuse to boss me around again now that the carnival is over.

I gather what I think is an impressive stack of books and carry them back to my desk.

"That's going to be some essay," Ms. Huff remarks. "How long does it have to be?"

"Two to three pages," I tell her. "But I want to be well informed."

I pull my school-issued laptop out of my backpack and set it on the desk, setting Gerald's letter and my notebook aside. I fish Matty out of my sweatshirt pocket and start up the Amy playlist. Mine, not Nate's. I broke my own rule and added it to the time capsule, and it may be sacrilege to say so, but I think mine is better. I really want to send it to her but I know I have to wait for the right time, so for now I listen to it myself. A lot.

I log in to the school network and watch the little white arrow hover over the *W* icon before it flies instead to the lowercase *e* and opens an Internet window. As if the computer is a Ouija board and I'm not controlling the keystrokes, I watch as the URL for the organ donor website appears in the address bar and the list of support groups pops up on the screen.

There are a few in Boston, some specific to the kind of transplant people have had, others more generic-sounding. Each one gives a street address and an email address for a contact person. The one at the top of the list is a woman named Sandra Goldman. My little white arrow floats around her name, wanting to click on her email and say something.

Don't lie, someone says, and it takes a second or two for me to realize that it was Matty, a lyric snaking through the earbuds. But I take the advice and close the browser.

Then I pull out my phone and, hiding it from Ms. Huff in case she's checking on my progress, send a text to Chase:

in library. can we talk?

He replies:

later

I stare at the word, willing it to say more.

By the time Chase gets to the library, I have gathered an offering. I hand him a thin stack of pages.

"What are these?" he asks.

"For the binder," I say. "Sorry they're just printouts."

I couldn't risk looking through recent obituaries, of course, and I still don't know what the criteria are for inclusion in the binder. But it was a simple thing to visit the website for the Molton Historical Society and gather some of the more interesting death records from past generations. After a while it stopped feeling morbid and started to feel . . . good. Like I was honoring these deaths, ever so briefly, by connecting them back to the lives that came first. Some of the records even had pictures of the deceased before they had earned that designation, so I printed those, too. Something about the stern black-and-white faces reminded me of Chase's house, of the gallery hanging in the hallway. These are definitely people who aren't getting remembered on a regular basis.

Chase accepts my payment with a mix of suspicion and delight, and quickly tucks the pages into his bag.

"Thanks," he says. "Anything else?"

Don't lie, I hear again, in my own voice this time.

And then just, *Don't*.

I push the word away, and begin to answer the questions that hang in the air between us. What surprises me most is how relieved I feel to tell him everything, even though it truly does sound like some insane fairy tale. *Once upon a time there was a girl whose brother died and her parents donated his organs so she went on a quest to find his missing parts and . . .* Well, even I don't know what comes next. I can only tell Chase what's already happened.

Chase is masterfully cool about it, not asking any questions, just letting me speak until I'm finished. Only then does he clear his throat and, tapping his fingers on the desk, say, "That is . . . Wow."

I try to discern the notes in his voice, like separating the layers in a song. Do I hear sympathy? Fear?

"I don't think I can help you," he says.

I expected maybe he'd be angry that I used him to get to his father. But not this. Not indifference.

My shock must show. "No," he says quickly, "it's not that I don't want to. It's just, well, even my dad probably doesn't know where your brother's . . . where everything went. He was pretty high up in the food chain at Brigham and Women's, but then he left to come here. And I'm pretty sure all of the organ donation stuff is, like, fully confidential."

"He did say he would send me his contact in Boston, didn't he?"

"My dad says a lot of things. He usually doesn't follow through unless it involves making money or getting his name in a medical journal. So you probably shouldn't wait around for him to get back to you."

"What if you can get back to me on his behalf?" I ask, trying to sound playful despite the anxiety radiating across my body.

"What do you mean?"

"I don't know. Find out who he's talking about? Get me a phone number?"

The rhythm of his fingers on the desk pauses, then picks up again. "I like a secret mission as much as the next guy," he assures me. "But what you're asking—it feels like lies on top of lies. I don't exactly *like* my dad, but I still love him. Pretty much. And you know how I feel about honesty."

"Fine. You're not obligated to help me." I stand up. "I should go."

Chase sighs. Sets his fingers into his hair and pulls his own head back, raising his eyes to mine. I want to step closer, see what I look like reflected in them, but I hold my position. Wait.

"Don't do that. I didn't say I *wouldn't* help. I'm just thinking it through out loud. It's my process."

"Is that part of your process, too?" I point at his fingers, rapidly tapping again.

"Apparently." He stills his hand. "Okay," he says. "Let me see what I can find without getting anyone in trouble. Especially us."

"How?"

"By searching my dad's email account for contacts at Brigham and Women's."

"You know his password?"

"It's the date he was appointed chief of surgery. It took me about ten seconds to figure it out."

"So, you've done this before."

"I don't make a habit of it, if that's what you're implying."

"Of course not," I say. "You pretty much love him after all."

The bell rings.

"I gotta go," Chase says. "I'll be in touch."

I gather my things as if I, too, have to get to class. As if I am not going to walk out the front door of the school and take the long way home, as if I have any energy left to talk to Mel or Amy or walk the halls full of people who don't know the story I just told Chase. They think they know what happened to me. They think the accident was the end of something.

They could never understand, as I do now, that it was only the beginning.

TWENTY

ASHES TO ASHES

friday 10/3

I don't really decide to skip school. It's just what happens. I text Mel to sign me in on the clipboard in the school office—Molton has an automated system that calls your parents if you're missing from homeroom, but the secretaries cross-check it against the list in the office, so your parents won't get a call if your name is there. It matters more that it's on the clipboard than who put it there.

She texts back:

y?

I respond:

mental health day

Then, to placate her:

making list of covers for scud

After my parents leave for work like they're supposed to, I ride my bike to Common Grounds and order an overly complicated coffee and two kinds of muffins, all of which I consume very slowly while watching Cranky Andy and Martha bicker about how much to charge for the new T-shirts they're selling. Then I ride to the

Elbow Room and, sitting on the couch where I saw Chase at the séance, flip slowly through a huge book that contains full-color diagrams of the human body, trying to imagine the lines that would be drawn on people as if they were pigs about to be butchered. Some of the diagrams indicate things other than organs, things that can't be seen, like chakras and auras and vestigial energy fields, and I wonder what happens to those when organs are traded from one person to another. Does the heart have its own aura? Does the liver? The lungs? Do the energies get mixed up like paint colors, muddying the recipient's aura until it looks like the water that's left in the cup after you rinse your brushes out?

I stop at the Sip'N'Dip for an ice cream cone (mocha almond fudge). I sit where Amy sat. I eat my ice cream before it melts, and I do not cry at all.

Finally, I go home, plant myself on the curb, and wait for the mail.

If our mailman, Jim, is at all curious about why I have been waiting for him lately, he does not say. Instead, he stops his boxy little truck and bypasses my outstretched hand to put the mail into the box. He will not alter his methods simply because I happen to be standing there.

I can respect that.

He grudgingly says, "Good day," and putters away.

I wait until he's a few houses down the street and then I pull the stack of envelopes out of the mailbox. One particular corner, vanilla-hued with dark blue print, catches my eye. I slide it carefully from the pile, like I'm choosing a magician's playing card.

Yes.

The return of Gerald?

No one is home, but I open and close the front door quietly anyway, then sprint up the stairs without taking off my shoes or hanging my house keys on the hooks over the hall table. Only when I hit the top step do I realize that I have gotten there without thinking of Nate, the sound of him coming into the house and my mother's reprimand. I tap Gerald's letter on Nate's bedroom door for luck—or to mark the moment—and close my own behind me.

My heart is pounding and I'm a little sweaty. I wipe my hands on my jeans before I open the envelope, ease the letter out, unfold it. Dark ink on the page, spiking and dipping like heartbeats on an EKG.

Dear Mrs. McGovern, it says. *My full name is Gerald Rackham. I wanted you to know that right away.*

A tiny twinge of guilt taps at my gut. I ignore it, as I ignore the headache forming like a thunderstorm between my temples.

Read.

> *I am so grateful for your letter. My illness and my long recovery have left me feeling quite isolated, and it is a great relief to correspond with someone whose suffering is, perhaps, like my own. I do not mean to imply that our experiences are equal. But I know loss, Mrs. McGovern. I have been quite close to death and I have returned from its precipice with a new sense of vitality and purpose.*

The irony, I think, is that Dad would probably love this guy.

> *I wonder if you might agree to continue our correspondence electronically. I have requested that the good people at Life Choice enclose with this letter the necessary forms for your*

consent, which I have already signed. My email address is
profrackham@altamail.com.

But somebody missed something, because there are no consent forms in the envelopes, and the email address, which I'm guessing was supposed to be blacked out, is completely visible.

The universe has smiled upon me.

I stroke my river scar as my computer wakes up.

It takes less than a minute to set up a new email address in my mother's name. To combat the guilt about taking forgery to a new level, I give her a username I think she would love but would never give herself: Mama2Nate. Plus, it will tug at Gerald's heartstrings when he sees it, maybe sway him in my favor when I ask for his help.

That part is quick, but then I stop, frozen in place.

What do I say?

Think, I tell myself. *This is the puzzle.* Nate's treasure hunts always seemed impossible at first, with their coded messages. *If the house had no walls and you were a crow,* one began, *how would you fly and where would you go?*

But once I figured out the key—*as the crow flies* means "in a straight line"—it was surprisingly simple.

Chances are slim that Gerald knows where the other recipients are, but he might have some information about support groups, or be able to set me up on a message board somewhere. I gather from my online research that these people spend quite a bit of time finding each other and comparing experiences. Although it doesn't sound like Gerald is at the top of his game, technology-wise. He talked about being isolated and I could practically hear him stumbling over the word *email* in his letter.

Still, he's my only direct link to Nate. And there's got to be a way to find the others. I have to trust that something, someone, will show me how. I take a deep breath, put my mother's sadness over me like a cloak, and start typing.

Dear Gerald,
I am so touched by your kind words, and I do feel that we are truly connected now.

In my mother's voice, I ask questions about his family, tell him a few things about ours (omitting the tendency toward forgery and deception). I ask if he has found "a community of people like yourself."

At the end, I wish him well.

Our brief correspondence has already meant so much to me, I tell him. *I am eager to hear more about your journey.*

My brother's ashes live in an urn, which is inside a box. The box is in my father's closet. My father's closet is perfectly organized, shirts neatly folded in stacks on wire shelves, shoes lined up like soldiers on racks below. Sometimes, when my parents are not home, I walk quietly into their room and open my father's closet doors, because seeing everything so arranged is like looking at a museum exhibit. It is not the messy, thrown-about stuff of actual life. It calms me down. Everything has a place of its own. Everything is always the same.

Which is why I noticed the box as soon as it took up residence there. It was sitting on the very top shelf, angled ever so slightly like it had been set up there quickly. Like my father couldn't wait to stop touching it.

I always knew that my brother had been cremated. There was a casket at the funeral, closed tight, keeping its secrets. I sat in the church, between my parents, and stared at the casket. I tried to picture Nate inside and couldn't. Then I tried to picture myself inside and got so freaked out that I had to count panes in the stained-glass windows until I could breathe again.

After the service, we all walked outside and watched the casket slide into the back of the black car from the funeral home. No one said anything. But I remember that now and think, *They knew then. They knew that all these parts of him were missing already and they watched him go away and they didn't say a word.*

In a weird way, I admire my parents for having secrets.

It makes them a lot more interesting.

The funeral car, I guess, took what was left of Nate and delivered him back to the funeral home, where he was burned to ashes, and those ashes were put in the box, and the box was given to my parents. It's just a cardboard box, smaller than a shoebox but bigger than a book. When I first saw it, I thought how odd it was that a whole person could be reduced to that size.

Now I know better.

And when I come downstairs after emailing Gerald, the box is not in my father's closet anymore. It is on the kitchen table. And my parents are sitting with it, their hands folded, looking at it with a kind of stunned sadness. I heard them come in, I knew they were here. But this tableau is not what I expected.

"What's that?" I ask, feigning ignorance. It feels cruel, but necessary.

"It's . . . ," my mother starts, and then turns her hands over as if she has suddenly forgotten the answer.

"Tallie," my father says gently. It's so weird to hear my name in his voice that I almost want to interrupt, tell him to forget it, stop talking. I don't need to know. "We think it's time to inter your brother's ashes." He taps the box with one careful finger.

"Now?" I ask.

"Tomorrow," Mom whispers. "Tomorrow morning?"

Her hands are still turned on the table, palms up and vulnerable. She has soft hands, my mother. I used to pet them when I was little, stroke them with my fingers like they were feathered birds. Those are the hands that would have held Gerald's letter and trembled as she read it. Those are the hands that would have written her reply.

Except I did it first.

I speak to those hands when I say, "Okay." Then I go up to my room and listen to Matty for a while. I scroll through the list of artists, looking for one that will stir something up. A memory, an idea. Something I can do. Nate's yearbook and his shirt are bundled in my closet, laid to rest, but Matty still has stories to tell me. I pick Elliott Smith.

Wish I could call you today, just to hear a voice.

I got a long way to go, I'm getting further away.

I concentrate on the words, the individual syllables, not what they mean. I focus on the sounds. I do not think about the box downstairs, or the fact that we are about to put what little we have left of Nate into a wall somewhere. I push my eyes closed and then open them the tiniest bit, so everything I see is blurred and kind of jumpy, like a really old movie.

"Nate," I whisper. My eyes are starting to water. I don't know if it's from squinting or crying. I press my river scar against my face, wipe my eyes. My hand feels warm. I press harder, so there is no border between what my hand feels like and what my face feels like. Parts of Nate are still warm like this. Other people's bodies are sustaining them, but they are his. They are made of him, and I want so much to find them, and when Elliott Smith sings *Wish I knew what you were doing and why you want to do it this way,* there is no mistaking my tears for anything else.

TWENTY-ONE

GOODNIGHT, GOODNIGHT

saturday 10/4

Everything in here is cold. I guess marble is supposed to impress people, make them think they're preserving their loved ones in a rich, reliable medium. But it's just so slick and unrelenting.

Nate was a summer guy. He loved heat and sun and being outside. He was the first kid at the town pool on summer mornings and the last one to leave, always begging my mother for five more minutes even as the sun-reddened lifeguards were glaring at her and pointing to the clock.

But I will not say this, of course, because it would upset my parents. And anyway, I know as well as they do that only a percentage of Nate is inside the urn that my mother is clutching like it's a grenade that will explode if she lets it drop. And maybe if we can just get this over with, she will stop crying in the middle of the night and when she's in the bathroom and all the other times she thinks I'm not listening. Maybe she can go back to work full-time and lose herself in fabrics and couch-sized paintings and knickknacks. She will remember that there are other people in the world and she will remember that she likes at least a few of those people, and there will be brunches and cocktail parties and orchestra concerts, and life, for once, really will *go on*.

Except in here.

This place will stay exactly the same, cold and opaque and hard. It's a time capsule. It's a glacier. It's the opposite of alive in every way. Nate would hate it here.

The four of us walk into the building. My mother's purse slides down her arm and I take it from her, the way I used to when she was carrying too many things. The weight of it feels good in my hands, across my shoulder when I put it on. Each of us fidgets mildly while we wait for . . . something. Instead, we get a someone. The tallest man I have ever seen emerges from around a corner at the end of the hallway and lopes toward us stiffly, as if he is walking on stilts. He folds himself at the waist and leans down to shake my father's hand.

"Eben Dolmeyer," he says. "I am very sorry for your loss."

This, of course, is a phrase that all of us have heard many, many times in the last four months. But this man sounds like he truly means it, and I wonder how he manages to sound that way when he probably has to say it every day of his life. If he actually feels as sorry as he sounds, he must be the saddest man in the world.

"Let me show you to your niche," Eben Dolmeyer says.

My mother compulsively compliments people when she is nervous. "You have a lovely mausoleum."

Eben Dolmeyer dips his head a bit. "Thank you. Although this is not a mausoleum."

"It's not?" Mom clutches the urn a little tighter, like maybe we have brought it to the wrong place entirely.

"This is a columbarium," Eben Dolmeyer informs us. "From the Latin *columba*, meaning 'dove.' The term referred originally to compartmentalized housing for doves and pigeons."

My father coughs. "Pigeons?"

Eben Dolmeyer chuckles dryly. "Of course, we don't keep pigeons here. But you will notice that we have incorporated a dove motif in our wall carvings and much of our artwork."

I have a sudden urge to grab the urn from my mother. *Urn*, I think, seeing the word swim into the air in front of me. Then the *u* and the *r* switch places, making the word *run*. It's tempting.

"Here we are," says Eben Dolmeyer. Our slow procession has stopped in front of a wall that looks like every other wall here. It is a grid, the entire surface covered with marble squares. Most are engraved with names and dates, but some are still smooth and blank. One open square awaits us, a tiny cubby that will hold the urn and whatever portion of my brother is inside. The cubby is flanked by blank plaques. My stomach flips, and I ask the question even though I'm pretty sure of what the answer will be.

"Who are those for?"

My father shuffles his feet uncomfortably. "Well, er . . . us, honey. Your mother and I will be in one, and the other one . . ."

This is too much. They have brought me to look at my own grave.

"I'm getting out of here," I announce.

"Tallie," my father says, a warning in his voice. *Do not disrupt things,* it says. *This is important to your mother.*

"It's okay," Mom tells him. She is staring into the dark open cubby. "Let her go."

"There is a waiting area at the front of the building," Eben Dolmeyer offers. "There are magazines."

"We'll meet you there," my father calls after me, because I am already walking away from them, my rapid footsteps echoing in the glossy marble halls, my mother's purse knocking against my hip.

My heart is beating just as fast, and there is a needle point of pain in my left temple, which distracts me enough that I am quickly lost in the winding maze of the columbarium. I can still hear my parents' voices, distant and small, and the low hum of Eben Dolmeyer comforting them. I do not want to go back to where they are, admit that I couldn't find my way out.

The pain digs into my head and I rub at it. I close my eyes, count to three, and open them again, expecting . . . what? To see a different hallway? I feel like Alice after falling down the rabbit hole, faced with innumerable tiny doors.

The light around one of the corners is different, so I walk to it. The irony of walking into the light is not lost on me, by the way. But it works. I find myself, finally, at the entrance to the columbarium. I have escaped my tomb, for now. This has not helped my headache much, but at least I feel like I can breathe again.

And I can think again, too, which means I can remember that Mom keeps a bottle of aspirin in her purse. I pop the cap and let a few tablets roll into the palm of my hand. The bitter, powdery taste when I chew them is like the taste of disappointment. I force myself to swallow.

My teeth are gritty.

Ashes, ashes. We all fall down. And then my parents are standing beside me, silent and statuesque. Empty-handed. The task is done, and I'm half wrecked with guilt for running away, half weak with relief that they did it without me. It was their goodbye, not mine.

We could all ask each other if we feel better. But we don't.

I check my phone as we're walking back to the car. There's a text from Chase:

call me

I slow my steps, let my parents gain ground in front of me. My father glances back but I just point to my phone and he nods and keeps walking.

Chase picks up right away.

"I found something," he tells me. And then there's a long pause.

"Yes?" I say.

"Are you sure you want to do it this way?"

"What way?"

"All, like, cloak-and-dagger. I know you don't want to involve your parents, I get that. But it seems like it would be a lot simpler that way."

They're getting farther and farther ahead of me. They're almost to the car.

"I'm sure," I say. "Tell me what you found." Then I add, "Please."

"There was an exchange with a doctor named Samira Fikri at

Brigham and Women's. She's doing a study with a bunch of organ recipients and she asked my dad for contacts at the procurement agencies."

"What kind of study?" I ask. "Like, to see if they live or die?"

"No, she's a psychiatrist. I think she's trying to see . . . how they deal with it."

"With what?"

"Doesn't say, exactly. Having part of someone else's body inside them, maybe?"

I imagine a room full of these people, wandering around and trying to match themselves up like a human jigsaw puzzle. I do not actually care how they are coping or how they feel. But if some of them have parts of Nate . . .

"What can I do, though? Pretend I'm one of them?"

"No," Chase says. "That would never work. You're not going to be able to get into the study itself. But if I can get Dr. Fikri to share some of the data with my dad, maybe we can match up the surgery dates with your brother's—"

"She would do that?"

"She might. If I can pretend I'm him and offer to consult on the study. Convince her it's purely professional."

Now we're both posing as our parents. It's like some weird parallel universe, a world of deceit and decent intentions. I feel myself luring Chase slowly and steadily away from the benchmark of his honesty, like I'm pulling him underwater. "Do you have a lot of experience deceiving surgeons?"

"I have a lot of experience eavesdropping on my parents' cocktail parties. Excruciating. But I know how they talk to each other."

"So how are you going to ask for the info on the study?"

"Simple," he says. "I send an email from my dad's account and bounce his email forward to mine so I can catch the reply."

"But what if he sees it first?"

"He has his assistant filter through everything before he looks at it. And unlike surgeons, assistants don't work weekends. I'll send it right now and I'm betting we hear back from Dr. Fikri before morning."

"Thank you," I tell him. It sounds like any other phrase, too short to carry the hope and relief I want it to.

"Don't thank me yet," he says. "This may not work."

"Thank you anyway."

There's another a long pause. Then, "Tallie?"

"Yes."

"Rosabelle, believe."

"What?"

"That's what Houdini was supposed to say to his wife if he could get a message to her after he died."

"Oh." My parents are waiting by the car now, looking at me as if they're surprised to see me. "I have to go."

"Okay," Chase says. "I just thought you'd like to know."

"A message from beyond the grave," I say. "Imagine that."

Except that Houdini's message never came through, I think. But the psychic on the show I used to watch delivered hundreds of messages, maybe thousands. Even Absalom seemed to believe with absolute conviction that he was capable of channeling some kind of communication from another realm. If they can do that, why can't I? Not every message is made of words. I can follow these bread crumbs, find Nate's pieces and make things right. It doesn't have to ruin my chances of being normal again. It might even be part of the plan.

It has to be *worth* something, all of this aching and sadness and remembering, the broken glass and stitches and scars on my arms and hands. It cannot be for nothing.

If I can do this for Nate, then maybe we can both move on.

TWENTY-TWO

ALL I NEED

We get home from the columbarium and the three of us stand in the kitchen, none of us sure what to do next. It feels like there should be a statement of some kind, an announcement, a declaration. But my parents probably already said something after I fled the scene, and now whatever there was in that box, whatever was transferred into the urn and then into the marble cubby under the watchful gaze of Eben Dolmeyer, has been very officially laid to rest. There really is no more of Nate's body in this house.

"Well," my mother finally says to no one in particular. She seizes a pen from the decorative cup on the counter and scrawls out a grocery list. "I should get to the store," she says, and waves her list as evidence of this. *Life goes on,* the paper tells us. *People have to eat.*

My father nods. The paper is right.

"I'll be in my study," he says.

I stand very still as my mother and her list retreat through the door to the garage and my father slinks silently away, and then I am alone again. *If this was a movie,* I wonder, *would the director yell "Cut!" at this point or would the scene continue? Should I keep going? What's my line?*

I picture a page, the screenplay. Stage directions. *Tallie goes to the refrigerator,* it says. *Tallie selects a yogurt smoothie. Tallie drinks the smoothie thoughtfully.*

I do these things. I await further instructions.

My phone buzzes.

Mel has texted this:

drv arnd? need rdkl

Her name looks strange on the screen, like when you've been staring at a word for so long that you start to think it's misspelled, or not a word at all. It's been days since I actually talked to her, but she did sign me into school yesterday, so I feel like I owe her something. And there is nothing quite as effectively distracting as watching Mel, in coveralls and goggles, gathering roadkill. I usually stay in the car while she works and try not to catch any accidental glimpses of maimed and bloody animals. Although part of me feels like I should make myself look this time, after chickening out at the columbarium. Face the music, so to speak.

I reply:

ok

Molton produces a wide variety of roadkill. It may simply be the combination of plentiful woodland creatures and reckless drivers, but whatever the reason, there is probably no better place for an aspiring taxidermist to reside. That may well be the reason so many members of Mel's family have lived here, and explain why the only ones who move away are those who don't participate in the family hobby. Mel's mother is always looking for jobs on the

West Coast, for instance. But so far she hasn't gotten an offer good enough to take them away.

According to Mel, she doesn't love most of Mel's interests (especially not the projects that bring the police to their house), but I guess she figures that they're better than not knowing what Mel is doing. A girl like Mel could get into just about any kind of trouble that a paranoid mother could dream up.

So could a girl like me. But no one seems to have caught on to that yet.

Mel drives slightly more carefully than usual, for scouting purposes. I am the lookout, watching for circling turkey vultures, signs of unfortunate creatures up ahead. Molton is a small town but sometimes it seems like there is an infinite maze of side streets and cul-de-sacs, like we could drive for days and keep finding new turns to take. We wander, like Odysseus. Searching.

I am normally attentive to my job but today I find I am distracted by the brilliant leaves on all the trees. There are so many trees and the sun blinks rapidly between them as we drive. It's like someone is pointing a giant flashlight at me and turning it on and off, like Morse code. Nate used to do that every summer, try to learn Morse code, and he would practice with a pen in his room, tapping on his desk. He wanted me to learn, too, so we could tap messages to each other through the walls, but I never really got it, especially not the first year. He kept testing me, trying not to get totally exasperated when I got it wrong.

"Okay," he would say, "I'll do it really slowly this time."

I listened as hard as I could, until I thought my ears would burst, but I got lost about halfway through his tapping and scraping, and in the end, every answer was a guess. The only words I learned that first summer were our names.

The car stops suddenly and I almost scream at the sound of the brakes screeching. I'm still bracing myself for the crunch of metal when I hear Mel's voice instead, saying, "Be right back."

She leaves the car running while she walks around to the trunk to get her shovel and a bag. I force my breathing back into a normal rhythm and crane my neck to see over the hood of the car. Looks like we've stopped to retrieve a raccoon. Or what used to be a raccoon.

I imagine the raccoon's family watching from the woods as Mel lifts their loved one from the asphalt and shimmies it into her garbage bag. I imagine them patting each other with their little paws and silently mourning their fallen relative. They cannot know what will become of him, that Mel will, in a matter of days, have done unspeakable things to his body and transformed him into a raccoon version of Zorro, galloping to new adventure on the back of a cat. Or, what used to be a cat.

Mel deposits the bag into a cooler in her trunk, gets back in the car, and announces that we need to stop for ice.

Which means going to the Y Not.

Y Not Convenience.

Y Not Convenience?

It bothers me that there isn't an actual question mark on the store, just the *implication* of a question mark. I sit in the car, glaring at the space where a question mark should be, while Mel goes inside. After a couple of minutes, I am tired of glaring and desperate for a beverage, so I head inside.

Y Not inspires many questions, like *Why not clean this place once in a while?* and *Why not hire someone other than Jason Rice to work here?* Jason possesses an unfortunate combination of qualities that seem set in stone, even at the age of seventeen, and make him less than ideal for a job that involves human interaction. He is both ill tempered and overly confident, which has given him a superiority complex that seems all wrong on a cashier in a convenience store. Like a tuxedo on a sloth. He treats Y Not like a cave of treasures that he must guard, dragon-like. He insults customers openly, judges what they buy, and examines anything they put on the counter in front of him as if it is up to him whether or not they are allowed to purchase it.

Also, for reasons that I never understood, Jason was Nate's best friend. A fact that makes my trips to Y Not more complicated than either of us enjoys.

The bell over the door announces me, and Jason looks up. A kind of grimace rolls over his face and he does not correct it. Not many people are happy to see you when you walk around draped in the stench of tragedy, but Jason openly dreads my appearances here. Which is why I'm willing to come in when Mel brings us here, despite my feelings about the store's punctuation. Or lack thereof. Jason and Nate used to tease me when we were younger, because Nate became *that* kind of brother when Jason was around, and now I get to provide a bit of my own torture.

"Hello, Jason," I say, putting on a maudlin tone. "How *are* you?"

He is still wearing a pained expression as he says, "Good. I mean, fine. I guess."

He does not ask how I am. He never does.

Mel emerges from the back of the store, where (judging from the tint of her lips) she has been stealing cherry slushie samples. She slaps a couple of dollar bills on the counter.

"Two bags of ice," she announces.

Jason slides the money toward himself but does not touch the cash register. We all know he will pocket the money after we leave. We stand there in silence, all of us caught in supreme discomfort, knowing what comes next but hoping, as we always do, for a different outcome.

I want to grab Jason around the neck and scream, *Why can't you be a better person?*

He coughs. "Anything else?"

I remember then that I wanted something to drink, so I reach into the fridge by the counter and grab a bottle. Only when I hold it up do I see that it is that half-lemonade, half-iced-tea stuff that Nate loved. I wave it at Jason spitefully. To shame him. To remind him of my brother, who was good and is gone, and to make him see how unjust that is when he—Jason Rice, unkind purveyor of snacks and cigarettes—sits here alive and well. Anger rises up like an underwater missile, threatening to break the surface, and I am very close to throwing the bottle at Jason's head when Mel pulls me out the door and calls "Put it on her tab" over her shoulder.

"Get in the car," she says, and I do. I hold the cold, wet bottle of half-and-half like my mother held that urn, and I watch Mel haul two bags of ice out of the huge freezer in front of the store. She marches them to the trunk and it sounds like thunder when she dumps them into the cooler. She stuffs the empty plastic bags into a pocket in her door when she gets in, and then she turns to me.

"Why are you two always so *weird* with each other?"

I could say, *Because we hate each other for still being here.* Or *Because we remind each other of Nate.* I could say, *Because we both know that the best person who will ever care about us is gone.*

Instead, I say, "Why do *you* always bring me here?"

She rolls her eyes. "Oh, right. It's *my* fault."

There is no point in trying to pick a fight with Mel. It's like trying to plant a tree on an iceberg. It just won't take. I stare at the *Y* on the store sign, a coward with its arms in the air.

"What's the opposite of convenience?" I ask her.

"Wisdom," she says.

And we drive.

My father is waiting for me at the kitchen table when I get home. Either I just walked through a wormhole and it's Friday again, or I'm in for a talk.

"Tallie," he says. "Sweetheart."

I am in trouble. Someone else died. Mom left us. My mind is racing with possibilities.

"Sweetheart," Dad says again. "I owe you an apology."

I haven't checked his browser history in a few days. I wonder if Dad has replaced his home-improvement videos with self-help tips from the grief group.

"I have been . . . emotionally . . . absent since . . . the accident." The words fall from his mouth like stones he's spitting out because they taste bad. "You deserve better than that. You . . . you lost him, too."

You didn't lose him, I think. *You gave him away.*

And maybe honesty is contagious, like yawning—or maybe I don't want Dad suffering the delusion that things are so easily resolved—because another thought pushes itself through. *Tell him you know.*

My uncle taught me and Nate to play poker when we were younger, because he thought it would be funny, but we both turned out to be weirdly good at it, even though Nate took forever to play his cards. "There's no game if you don't lay something down," my uncle told him.

I don't know what was more annoying: the fact that Nate always won, or the way he yelled "Yahtzee!" when he did.

I decide I can't tell Dad about the letters from Life Choice and Gerald. Not yet. But I can play one of the cards I'm holding.

"I know about Nate's"—now it's my turn to spit out a word—"*organs*. That you *donated* them. And I know one of the *people* wants to write to Mom."

This, obviously, is one version of the truth. There are always many to choose from.

My father reddens, like a time-lapse movie of a tomato ripening. "How?" he asks hoarsely. "How do you know?"

"I heard you arguing in the kitchen. Mom wants to talk to the person and you don't want her to."

"It's not that I don't want her to. It's just—I don't really see the point. We need to move forward with our life as a family."

"But aren't you curious about them?"

"Who?"

"The *recipients*." The worst-tasting word of all.

"No. I'm really not." Dad rubs an edge of the table, testing its ability to give him splinters. "They have their own problems. My problem—my *concern*—is this family and getting this family up and running again."

A project. That's what we have become. Like an old furnace that just needs a new filter, or a leaky roof to be patched. He thinks this is something he knows how to do, but it isn't.

"What about Mom?"

"Today was harder than she expected. I think she may need some time before she decides what to do."

So I'm safe. As far as anyone knows, there have not been any letters yet from Life Choice. And there won't be any more coming from Gerald now that we're emailing, so unless other recipients suddenly start writing, I can keep this under control.

Dad sighs. "Sometimes the things you think will make you feel better . . . just aren't the things you need."

I reach over and pat my father's hand. "Thanks, Dad. I'm glad we talked."

And I wonder, as I walk up to my room, if he knew I was doing my best impression of him.

I run my hand across Nate's door as I walk by, letting my fingers feel the gritty texture of the paint Dad used to cover up the marks left by Ninja Turtle stickers and taped signs that told all of us to stay out. Nate would make those when he was in a bad mood and then take them down an hour later. He could never stand to be alone for longer than that. He could never stay mad as long as I could when we had a fight, and then he'd do all kinds of goofy things to make me laugh so we could be friends again, like lip-synching some old song by the Pixies with his underwear on his head.

They'll never understand—these people, these *recipients*— that whatever his parts gave them, it will never, ever equal what was taken away from me.

And I can stay angry as long as it takes.

I pull up the bookmarked transplant site on my computer and find the email for the Boston support-group coordinator.

Dear Ms. Goldman, I type, my fingers jabbing the keys. *My name is Sarah McGovern.* I'm about to tell her that I lost my son, that I'm seeking the recipients of his organs, but then I stop. I don't know this woman, but if she's someone who devotes her time to leading a support group for transplant patients, she's probably a really nice person. And really nice people tend to follow the rules, and in this case, the rules say that she can't go off and ask everyone she knows if their new organs came from a seventeen-year-old boy named Nathaniel McGovern from Molton, Massachusetts.

I'm a freelance journalist, and I'm researching a story about post-transplant life for people in the Boston area. If you happen to know anyone from your group who might be willing to speak with me about their experiences, please feel free to give them my email address.

I read it over, then add: *Stories from recent recipients would be best. Anyone who underwent surgery in late May or early June would be ideal.*

I send the email, then spend the rest of the afternoon listening to songs on Matty in alphabetical order. Like a pharaoh on a sarcophagus, I lie on my bed with my hands folded on my stomach, feeling it rise and fall as I breathe, hovering between sleep and consciousness for as long as I can.

TWENTY-THREE

CONCRETE SKY

sunday 10/5

People talk about how if someone loses one sense, their other senses become heightened. Like if someone becomes blind in an accident or something, they suddenly hear better. I used to think that was just their imagination but now I think it's true. I understand that term *stream of consciousness,* because it feels that way when I lie in bed and let my mind wander, like water in a stream, flowing around rocks and debris and pushing stuff out of the way. I free Matty from his tin and I listen to him as much as I can—I'm not afraid anymore of wearing him out. I immerse myself in the only messages I have from Nate, in the songs he chose and the way he put them together, the way that "Come as You Are" leads into "Where Is My Mind?" It's like speaking a new dialect. The other day I listened to the same Elliott Smith song all the way home, over and over.

And I notice, when I do that, how much the singers he liked sound like *him.* I can hear him in every song. I don't mean that the songs remind me of him. I mean that if I let myself follow certain threads of the song, I can actually hear him because I am really listening now, more than I was before. Or in a new way, maybe. It's hard to sustain, though. Sometimes I pull back when it feels like I'm at the edge of something that I can't quite see.

I wonder if *they* feel him, too. The organ recipients. The ones who divided Nate's body into pieces and claimed them as their own. I killed him, but they took him. They owe their lives to me. They owe me their lives.

I try to imagine meeting them face to face but I can't picture what they'll look like. They will probably appear completely normal, but with my new vision, I will see through them, see underneath. See their scars, Nate's organs glowing from under their skin, showing through like a flashlight held under a sheet. Gruesome and beautiful.

My hair looks crazy in the mirror but I don't feel like brushing it, so I just smooth it back into a messy bunch and loop a ponytail holder around it a few times. With my hair off my face, I look more like Dad.

"My concern," I say to myself in a deep voice, "is this family."

I know Dad wants to start over somewhere else, but how far will he go? Sign us up for family counseling? Join a grief cult somewhere? He should have made his move while Mom was still in her state of mental exile. Now she seems to be gaining strength. She's been going to work regularly and even suggested having someone over for brunch next weekend. Everything will be okay if I can just solve the puzzle Nate has set out for me before they find out that I've been using Mom's name, staging Internet deceptions. That would, I suspect, be immediate grounds for something drastic.

I check for new emails, but there's nothing from Gerald or from Sandra Goldman. I open the messages I sent them, put them in windows side by side, checking for anything that might have tipped them off. It's like an out-of-body moment, reading the words I typed but hearing my mother's voice in them instead of my own.

Vrrrt. My phone vibrates, scurrying on my dresser like an errant insect.

It's Mel.

ride along to the barn? leaving in 5

I am tempting fate if I accept, tempting my own tongue to betray me with guilty secrets, but staying home means risking a full-on intervention with Dad. I text back a simple yes and head downstairs to grab some breakfast and a jacket. I can tell it's cold outside by the foggy landscapes that have formed at the bottoms of the windows. Mom and Dad are talking in low voices that snake under the closed door of Dad's study. Maybe he's campaigning, showing her online listings for perfect Victorian houses far away from here. Real estate porn. I press my ear to the door but can't make out distinct words. Not the right ones anyway.

There's coffee left in the pot on the counter, so I pour some into a travel mug, dump some sugar into it, and scrawl a note for the kitchen table: *Gone to barn with Mel. Back later.*

Under normal circumstances, my parents might actually ask me why I would want to spend my time at Mel's uncle's haven of taxidermy. I guess if Dad's project takes shape, I might have to get used to answering those questions again.

For now, I'm on my own.

I take Mom's bottle of aspirin out of my pocket, shake a few into my hand, and chew them to bitter powder. A penance. My grandfather used to take aspirin every day to prevent a heart attack . . . and then died of cancer. The last time I saw him, he slapped me on the knee as I sat on his hospital bed and said, "They always get you somehow, Tallie." I don't know who "they" are, but I got the message. I wonder if Chase's binder contains any mundane deaths like my grandfather's, or if he's mostly drawn to flashy disasters and crime. I picture my own contributions, the obituaries I printed for him in the library, filed among other, more violent pages.

Speaking of death, I think when Mel rockets into the driveway.

"Hi-ho, Silver!" she calls to me when I come outside.

"What?"

"Zorro reference," she says.

I buckle my seat belt. "I think that was the Lone Ranger, actually."

"Oh." She drums her fingers on the steering wheel. "Is that your dad?"

"Where?" But I see him, too, peeking out of the break between the curtains in the living room. He pulls one to the side, revealing himself, and waves. I hold my hand up as Mel whisks me away.

"That was weird," she remarks.

"He's trying to put us back together," I say.

"Humpty Dumpty," Mel says. "That one didn't work out so well." Then, abruptly: "How come you've been walking to school?"

Heat flashes across my face. "I . . ."

"Never mind," she says.

"No, it's okay, I—"

"I said, never *mind*."

It's as if whatever momentary impulse she had to actually talk about something departed as quickly as it appeared. I could insist. I could tell her that I just like walking, or that I need time to myself, or that it scares me to be in a car. All of those things are partly true, although none of them are the truth. I'm not scared of being in a car. I'm scared of the sound of a car crashing into a tree. And I don't need time to myself. I need someone—Gerald or Sandra or Dr. Fikri—to play one of *their* cards and keep this poker game going.

Mel reaches forward and turns the radio on. "You pick," she says, without looking at me. It's as close as she'll get to a peace offering, letting me choose the music. I accept, even though the radio stations within range of Molton are limited, at best. The choices are pretty much country, alt-rock, Christian, or NPR. I go with option number two. It's a Neko Case track, one that's on Matty, too. I want to listen to the lyrics, in case I can detect a message, but Mel is over the weirdness of the moment and talking again, telling me about her plans for the taxidermy show. Raccoon Zorro.

Not a bad band name, I think, and I let her voice wash over me, blend with the music, while the world blurs outside the window. By the time we arrive at the barn, my brain is pleasantly numb.

I follow Mel inside. The barn is empty. The cows are outside, I guess, wandering around the fields and doing whatever they do all day, but they have left the faint odor of animal warmth behind. It makes me wonder what the inside of the pig truck smelled like. Unpleasant, probably, not like this. Not like comfort. More like fear.

Something flutters in an upper corner and I don't know how long I've been standing here looking at the empty half darkness. Mel is in the workshop and I step to the doorway, watch her rifling through the box of forms until she makes her choice. A medium-sized thing with stumps for paws, hairless arms raised like it's being held up at gunpoint. "Raccoon," she announces.

"Is that for the one we found yesterday?"

"Yes, and he is . . ." She searches through a pile of pelts on the table. "Right here!" She holds up the raccoon, waves it around. Its empty eye sockets stare at me accusingly, and I can almost see it dressed as Saint Lucy, a halo of light around its head, eyes on a platter like tiny hors d'oeuvres. If Mel was open to suggestions, I would tell her about this idea. She could put together a whole cast of saints, like her Nativity scene, and enact the litany. We did it every year on All Saints' Day at the church: *Saint Lucy, pray for us. Saint John, pray for us. Saint Agnes. Saint Thérèse.* A parade of gruesome endings. People who became something more than people, who gave themselves over in the name of something greater.

But it feels wrong to think about them now. I haven't prayed since the accident and I hardly did before it happened either. I never knew what to say, what to ask for. And the things I want now are surely against God's better judgment.

My phone buzzes. Signals are spotty out here but something has gotten through. It's a text from Chase:

no word from fikri

I reply:

patience is a virtue

A few seconds later he writes:

are you the virtuous type?

This strikes me as something that allows for a flirty response, and I'm not sure if I know how to speak that language.

i used to be

When I look up, Mel is staring at me, one eyebrow arched into a question mark. "Chase," I tell her. There's no point in lying.

"Did he finally experience a tragedy?" she asks.

"Not that I've heard."

She cocks her head. "Too bad," she says. "He isn't very interesting otherwise."

It's a challenge, this statement. She wants to see if I will agree or argue. She stands there, with her strange tools and her collection of expectant animal skins, and she waits.

Is she right? Is Chase anything more than a pair of chocolate eyes and a morbid interest in the tragedies of others? More than a fancy house and strange, estranged parents? The hypocrisy of reducing him this way, when all I want is for everyone to forget my circumstances, is very clear. But the rest of my brain is swirling, images of stained-glass windows, of the columbarium, all of those boxes in the wall, all of those little doors. *Pick a door, any door.* So many people stored there like artifacts, unaware of their own fate, and none of us knowing what they became after they died.

"Well, we all end up the same," I say.

Mel blinks, then grins. She likes me dark.

"I'm going to make you a promise," she tells me. "If you go first, I will preserve your body for all eternity. How would you like to be displayed?"

Sawed in half, like a magic trick gone wrong. Split open like a biology lab frog. Standing upright like Saint Lucy, holding my eyes on a platter. I don't know anymore which trail of bread crumbs to follow.

"You decide," I tell her. "After you know the whole story, you can decide."

TWENTY-FOUR

LOSING MY RELIGION

monday 10/6

It's dark on Monday morning, and cold, so I ride to school with Mel. It turns out that having extra time to think makes waiting to hear from Gerald, Sandra, and Dr. Fikri even more excruciating, so I let Mel provide distractions. She talks incessantly about song ideas for Scud, band politics, and the best ways to torment Amy, Fiona, and Zoey. And about the upcoming taxidermy show at the town hall on Saturday. She is certain, she says, that her raccoon-and-cat tableau will take first prize in the high school category. I think I hear something else in her voice, though. A wavering. I ignore it. I can't witness anyone falling apart right now. I can't save anyone else from going over a cliff when I may be nearing the edge of my own.

Dad waves to us from the window as we drive away. I have been finding notes in his study, lists of books about healing your family and overcoming personal tragedy and installing radiant heating in your floors. I guess he's still thinking about improving the house, as well as fixing us. Or is he making plans for a new house? Mom talks in her journal about being back at work, about feeling ready—almost—to see clients and spend time in other people's houses. But she doesn't say *in Molton*. She doesn't say *with Susan and Michelle*. She has also mentioned the argument she had with my father about the letters from the recipients, and hints at possibly pursuing things on her own.

So we are all moving forward in our own ways. And we are all keeping secrets, too.

When I get to school, Principal Hunter and Ms. Doberskiff are huddled in the foyer together, their faces masked in earnest concern. Hunter waves me over. They have been waiting for me. Mel quickly exits down a side hallway, in case she is in danger of being roped into whatever is about to happen.

"Can you come into my office for a minute, Tallie?" Hunter says. Ms. Doberskiff glares at him, a fleeting condemnation.

"Good morning," she says to me pointedly. "Did you have a good weekend?"

The emotional minefield of my weekend—interring Nate's ashes, facing Jason Rice, Dad's parental intervention—would probably send her into a complete seizure of joy. I don't think Ms. Doberskiff wishes our misfortunes upon us, but they keep her busy. And employed.

"Lovely," I tell her.

"Shall we?" Hunter sweeps his hand toward his office like I've just won a prize on a game show. As he and Ms. Doberskiff move away from the Star Students display, something makes me turn my head, almost as if someone has put a hand to my face and moved it. And then I see what their bodies had concealed: that the Star Students are gone, that Nate's picture has been replaced.

So. This remembrance has run its course. I am suddenly and strangely grateful that Chase has Nate in his binder—even if I think his mission is misguided and naive, it's a relief to know that if mine doesn't succeed, there's a kind of consolation prize.

I follow Principal Hunter dutifully, and he takes his usual seat behind his desk. This leaves me and Ms. Doberskiff on the other side, sitting next to each other as if we're some kind of team.

"I'll get right to the point," Hunter says. "I have had some troubling information from another student about some . . . erratic behavior from you, Tallie. Behavior that borders on harassment."

"Who said that?" I thought I was keeping most of my erratic ways inside my own head, and I've hardly spoken to anyone other than Chase and Mel.

"Well, I'm not at liberty to—"

"You and Amy used to be such good friends," Ms. Doberskiff chirps. "I'm sure I could help you work this out."

Amy. I can't blame her for not wanting to talk about Nate. I avoided it for months. But I didn't think she'd go to Hunter, if only to avoid being seen entering or leaving his office and tagged as a suck-up.

He ignores Ms. Doberskiff. "An altercation at the carnival was mentioned, as well as a brief incident at the ice cream stand. We all understand what you've been through, of course, but it's important that *all* students adhere to the school conduct code and respect one another's boundaries."

I guess sending her the playlist is out.

Ms. Doberskiff offers, "And you missed the Bridges meeting last week."

This is a fact. I make no excuses.

Principal Hunter clears his throat. "You will remember, Tallie, that you and your parents and I spoke at the beginning of the year and agreed that attending Bridges was a pivotal part of the plan for your . . ." He pauses, searching for the perfect administrative term. "Reentry."

"And your *healing*," Ms. Doberskiff adds. Hunter nods reluctantly.

"To that end," he says, "we wanted to catch you first thing this morning and make sure that you will be at today's meeting."

"I won't be, actually." I wasn't aware that I had made this decision until I say it out loud. Ms. Doberskiff immediately starts stammering, "But—but . . ." Hunter simply raises one bushy eyebrow and then crosses his arms over his chest. Or tries to.

"I see," he says. "And why is that?"

Yes, why is that? I ask myself. I could try to appeal to Hunter's logical sensibilities, or Ms. Doberskiff's hyperemotional ones, but the real answer is more straightforward. "Because I don't want to," I tell him.

I am testing the limits of their sympathy. I've been a fascination, a project for all of them, since the accident. My teachers, my parents, my former friends—they all think they know me better than I do. What happens when the project pushes back?

"You understand that I will have to inform your parents of your decision," Principal Hunter says.

"I do," I tell him. "I understand very well." And then I stand up and ask if I can go to homeroom. Hunter nods. Ms. Doberskiff is apparently still reeling from my announcement.

"Don't worry," I assure her. "Something terrible will happen to someone else any day now."

My heart has been beating more quickly all day, it feels like, since my meeting with Hunter and Ms. Doberskiff. I wonder how long Hunter waited before calling my parents, whether he called Mom or Dad, what they said. I wonder if I've just pushed myself a giant step closer to being sent on some kind of therapeutic wilderness retreat. I didn't see Chase in school today, so I'm still stuck waiting for a verdict on the Great Hacking Project and whether it's going to get us anywhere.

Mel has band practice after school—she was oddly thrilled when I gave her my playlist of songs for Scud to cover, which I titled "How to Be Unoriginal," and it has had the added benefit of steering her away from everything I'm not telling her. I'm living dangerously. I'm tempting fate. Adrenaline and impatience are a nasty combination.

Red Circle Day glares at me from the calendar. Nine more days before the verdict is handed down. I duck into Dad's study and use his computer to check the email account I set up in Mom's name. Gerald has written back, finally. He gives no reason for not having replied more quickly, which seems a bit rude, but at least I know now that I didn't scare him away. He shares that he lives in rural Pennsylvania, which is too far away for me to see him in person. But it tells me that at least one of Nate's organs was flown out of Boston to another hospital. Probably more, based on what Dr. Abbott told me.

It has been hard to restrain myself from just asking straight out whether Gerald knows where the other recipients are. I thought my question about finding a "community" was pretty subtle, but his response makes it clear that he has seen right through it.

Sarah, he writes. We are on a first-name basis now.

Naturally, you must be curious about the other fortunate recipients of your son's gift. As I'm sure you can understand, there are many levels of confidentiality in place to prevent any breach of protocol.

If only he knew that our entire correspondence is based on such a breach.

We are ostensibly prevented from knowing whether any of us share the same donor, but from time to time, our thirst for knowledge exceeds our respect. We do compare notes. Many of us have written to the families of our donors. If you might be willing to share with me the sources of any other letters you have received, I could confirm whether they were sent by anyone of my acquaintance.

But I don't have any other letters. Which means that Gerald's buddies have written to other families. Which means that none of the people the good professor is talking about have Nate's parts. Or they do, but they're not interested in finding out who he was.

Dammit.

The sensible, logical thing to do would be to send letters through the agency to the other recipients, right? But it could take weeks or even months for those people to write back, if they decided to at all, and I do not have that kind of time. And I would have to forge every word.

Plus, every day feels like a new chance to get caught. If my mother gets tired of waiting for a letter and calls Life Choice, or my father quits waiting for Red Circle Day and makes a preemptive declaration that we are moving, my chance to track down the recipients will vanish. This whole time, ever since the end of before, their parental instincts to nurture and protect and be responsible have been doing battle with their misery. Grief has made them selfish, weary. Complacent. But the clouds are parting, the lights are coming on again, and pretty soon my freedom will be crushed under the weight of their good intentions.

I am not the same. And I will not be cured of this, because if I am, Nate will disappear all over again.

Just when I'm nearly overtaken by the urge to hurl the computer out the window of Dad's study, I have a thought. I hit reply.

Gerald,

You are very perceptive. But I fear that my hopes of learning more about the destiny of my son's earthly body may come to nothing. I have not received any correspondence from Life Choice except for yours. I can tell you, however, that Nathaniel was airlifted to Boston after his accident, and it is likely that a few of his recipients reside there. If you could perhaps explore this possibility in your interactions with other transplant patients, I would be eternally in your debt.

Sincerely,

Sarah

I read it over. I think it hits the right tone, deferential but not too desperate. If he only knew.

Maybe someday I will get the chance to confess my sins. I will drive the many hours to Pennsylvania when I am old enough, and am not afraid. I will knock on Professor Gerald Rackham's door and tell him only what is true. I will apologize for misleading him and explain why I needed to do so.

I will know what to say by then.

I will speak in my own voice.

And he will forgive me everything.

The house is too quiet, pressing its silence against me, wrapping around me like a straitjacket. No one knows I came home, no one will know if I leave again, so I throw myself back outside and get on my bike and start pedaling. Without choosing a direction or a destination. I just go.

The air is edged with cold and the cloudless sky arcs above me. The sound of the leaves crunching under my wheels is like hands crushing paper, and after a few minutes I stop to pull Matty out of my back pocket and use him to drown out the noise. My earbuds won't stay in my ears if I put him back in my jeans and I don't have any pockets in the sweater I'm wearing, so I tuck him into my bra, next to my heart, to keep him safe.

I ride as the crisp leaves flee their branches and the blue sky swallows the world. I ride and I ride and then I stop, because without knowing where I wanted to go, I found it.

The doors to St. Anne's are like the doors to every church, heavy and carved, with enormous handles that make my hands look impossibly small and fragile. Oversized things are inconsiderate this way, shrinking us with their power. This is why, I think, little kids like dollhouses so much. They get to feel huge for once. Not like I do when I walk into the church and am overtaken by dark wood and the height of pillars, and the light through the stained glass somehow seems brighter than the sun outside. I take my earbuds out, wind the cord into a nest, and tuck it into my shirt before I get all the way inside. Another secret to carry.

The church is almost empty, except for a few small old ladies who appear to be as permanently fixed in their places as the pews or the pillars. They run their rosary beads through their fingers, their whispers echoing through the dusty air. I almost want to touch one to make sure they're real, but I'm afraid I'll find they are ghosts, that none of this is real. I lower myself into one of the pews at the side of the church, far away from where we sit every Sunday. The wood warms immediately underneath my body.

"Tallie?"

The hairs rise up on the back of my neck when I hear my name. It's Father Paul.

"It's very nice to see you, Father." My voice, the words are mechanical. What my mother would say.

"And you, my child." He is gripping the back of the pew in front of me, and the wiry black hairs on his knuckles look like hundreds of spider legs. "What brings you here this afternoon? Not our busiest day, you can see."

I may not be exactly devoted to the church, but I can't quite bring myself to lie to a priest. Or look him in the eye. I raise my face and stare at a spot just to the side of his head, hoping the shadows will help hide my evasion. "Nothing in particular, Father. I just . . . I miss the windows."

He smiles. I can see it in my peripheral vision. "You always did love the windows, didn't you?"

"I did."

"We've been praying for you, Tallie, and for your parents."

"Thank you, Father."

"Perhaps coming here today could be a kind of first step for you? A step toward coming back to our flock?"

My hand hurts all of a sudden, and when I look down at my

lap, I see that I've been digging my fingernails into my palm. Tiny red crescents are lined up like angry smiles.

Father Paul takes my silence as a chance to keep talking. "Sometimes, when something very difficult happens, we find ourselves resisting God and his work in our lives. It's important, Tallie, that you remain open to the message that God is sending you. He has great plans for you."

Between the words he is saying, I can hear something else. Almost like when my father is tuning his ancient radio and the needle falls between stations and two different voices overlap in the static. Father Paul's words are doing that, separating, and the echoing whispers of the old women are smoothing the edges but I can hear something anyway. Both of my hands are clenched into fists now, the points of pain from my nails waking me up, tuning me in like the radio needle.

"It does us no good to be angry at God, Tallie," Father Paul says. And beneath his words, I hear:

good Tallie

"We cannot wait for life to become what we expect."

wait

"We will all find peace in our own time, but we must be patient and listen."

find time

listen

"Tallie? Are you all right?" Father Paul's voice has changed. He sounds alarmed, and it is only then that I realize I have closed my eyes, squeezed them shut with the effort of listening to the words I am hearing.

I clear my throat. "Fine, Father. I have to go. Thank you."

I don't even feel the stone floor under my shoes as I walk back outside.

Nine days is an eternity. I see it now. Anything can happen in nine days. But that could help me, or hurt me. Nine days is long enough for a breakthrough, for finding a whole new set of clues, but it's also plenty of time for my father to convince my mother to sell our house, pack our things, flee the scene of the crime, and start over.

Nine days can change everything.

Just look at how much happened in a few minutes in May.

And the words I heard in the in-between of Father Paul's advice—*good, wait, listen*—are the words I've been hearing all along from well-meaning adults like Principal Hunter and Ms. Doberskiff. *Be* good. *It will get better, just* wait. Listen *to us, we know what's best for you.*

I'm done listening. I'm done being good.

I've been chanting *Get back to normal* all this time, like a litany, like a mantra. But maybe there's no going back. Maybe there's just pushing forward.

When I get home, the house is still empty. I go upstairs, into Nate's room, and I take a ballpoint pen from the cup on his desk. Pull up my sleeve and write on the inside of my arm, just above the crook of my elbow: *Nate.*

TWENTY-FIVE

MESSAGE IN A BOTTLE

tuesday 10/7

Chase is absent again.

I manage to avoid both Principal Hunter and Ms. Doberskiff by hiding in the library for most of the day. I've convinced my teachers to give me independent assignments for the rest of the semester, playing the I'm-just-a-little-overwhelmed card. I think they were relieved to send me off on my own, given that the alternative was an in-class meltdown that would probably involve a lot of administrative paperwork. My self-imposed social separation meant that I was one of the last people to hear the news that Jackson's mother died over the weekend.

At first I felt relieved to have been replaced as the object of everyone's pitying glances. Then I realized that this could mean an expiration date on the preferential treatment I've been getting.

I'm not proud of either response.

I make a mental note to compile Jackson's favorite movie themes into a playlist for him, and then I check my mother's dummy email account. Gerald is waiting in the in-box.

It must be so difficult, the desire to know where every part of Nathaniel now resides. I wish I could do more. Perhaps we could arrange to meet? Perhaps seeing me in person—seeing the effect of his gifts—would put your heart at ease.

Those words—*his gifts*—bring a wave of heat across my neck. As if Nate took his organs out himself, wrapped them like Christmas presents, and gave them to other people.

I write back to Gerald quickly, a terse note. *It is too soon,* I tell him. *It would be too much right now. I need more time. I will write again when I am stronger.*

I feel a little cruel, having encouraged him to write to me and used him for information, but also relieved because now I will not have to explain to him why I am not my mother.

I close the email and go back to the in-box. There's a new message from someone called SparkleCat76. At first I think it's spam because the subject line just says *Hello,* but I open it anyway and then I see that it's from someone named Jennifer. She's writing because Sandra Goldman told her that I'm looking for transplant patients in the Boston area.

Sandra is kind of pushy, IMO, but she kind of made me promise to write to you because she thinks I need to talk to someone other than her about myself. IDK, maybe she's just sick of me calling her. Anyway. I had my surgery at the end of May and I'm doing pretty well. I'm tired a lot. I had to quit my job at the record store, which sucks, but I'm all caught up on every season of Breaking Bad so I've got that going for me. ☺

I'm torn between excitement at potentially having a new lead and disappointment that whatever part of Nate may have ended up in this woman missed its chance to spend all day in a record store. He would have loved that. I skim the rest of her email for anything that might be a clue about whether that is the case, but there's nothing but inane clichés, references to second chances and gratitude.

Then I remember that she thinks I'm a reporter. So she's going to get some questions.

I thank her for writing and express my deepest sympathies for everything she's gone through. I tell her that I'd like my article to help people understand her experience, both physical and emotional. She didn't say which organ she had replaced and I wonder if it's rude to ask—too personal, according to some spectrum of medical inquiries—but I figure I can find out later, if she's even one of Nate's recipients. I ask her what she knows about her donor, if anything, and whether she thinks about that person. Hidden behind my mother's name and the story I've made up about who she is, I tell myself that these questions are necessary.

And I pray that the answers are what I need.

I ride my bike home from school. My parents aren't there, and I wonder if Hunter has notified them yet of my insubordination. If he called yesterday, or today, they have opted not to say anything. At least, not right away. Maybe they are sitting on the information like a cat with a mouse, waiting to see what the mouse does next.

With Matty threading songs into my head, I get myself an apple from the bowl on the kitchen table and rub it against my jeans until it's shiny, reflecting light I didn't see before. I hold it in front of me all the way up the stairs like a beacon and drop my backpack on my bed. I'm about to bite into the apple when I hear a noise behind the music. At first I think it's part of the song, but when I take out one of the earbuds, it's still there, separate from all the other sounds. Short taps like staccato beats, mixed with quick little scrapes. It's coming from my closet. Still holding the apple, I open the door. The tapping stops, then starts again. It sounds like it's coming from the other side of the wall. From Nate's room. It's probably an animal, a squirrel or something, that climbed in through the attic. But it sounds so familiar, almost like—

Morse code.

Nate and I used to ask for our rooms to be connected. We wanted my dad to cut a hole through our shared wall so we could crawl back and forth and visit each other, but we always got one of those noncommittal parentisms like "Oh, that would be fun, wouldn't it?"

Eventually we stopped asking and tried to send each other messages in Morse code instead. Nate got a book from the library with a chart of the Morse version of the alphabet, and he eventually taught me how it worked, how the taps were measured. A dot is the quickest, one short beat, and a dash equals three dots. A one-dot pause between the parts of a single letter, a three-dot pause between letters, and a seven-dot pause between words. On a telegraph, someone could hold the signal longer for the dashes, but we had to figure out another way. Nate came up with scrapes for dashes, mixed with taps for the dots. I could never think quickly enough to understand his messages as he tapped and scraped but I got better at recognizing the patterns, and by the time I was ten or eleven, if I listened closely enough, I could write the "words" down and then look up the translation. Which was usually a lot less exciting than what I expected. THE CROW FLIES AT MIDNIGHT. SMELLS LIKE TEEN SPIRIT. MEAT LOAF FOR DINNER.

I step into the hallway and listen for signs of life from downstairs, but it seems that I am still alone in the house. Or at least that my parents aren't here. Nate's door swings wide without noise or resistance, just like any other door. I have been in his room plenty of times since the accident, but only when my parents were sleeping or gone. A few rules were established after it happened, rules we never discussed but that were somehow understood between us, and staying out of his room was one of them.

The first time I snuck in, I thought maybe the door would be stuck like the sword in the stone, locked under some mystical spell. I was almost disappointed when it was so easily opened.

Now I close it behind me, just in case my parents come home.

Everything in Nate's room looks the way it did before, like a museum exhibit preserved behind glass. When I took things after the accident, I was careful not to move his stuff around too much so Mom and Dad wouldn't know anything was missing. Not that they ever spend any time in here. The room smells stale. I flip the latch on the window and slide it open a few inches. Dust bunnies emerge from the corners and dance across the floor, animated by the breeze. My mother would be appalled. I gather them up with my fingers, and when I bend down to tuck them into the little trash can next to Nate's desk, something catches my eye.

There's a kind of pocket stapled to the back of the desk. Nate must have swiped one of Mom's fabric swatches and her staple gun to attach it. I reach inside and pull out a book.

I recognize the red cover. I turn it sideways and see a white tag at the base of the spine. Little black numbers.

It's the codebook from the library.

He was so sure that we'd learn Morse code, that we'd be able to communicate with it someday, and he never got impatient when I couldn't figure it out. But we hadn't talked about it in a long time, so I thought he'd given up.

I sit down on Nate's bed and open the book's cover. There are notes written in his careful capital letters, a list of words he used a lot and their Morse translations: *and, with, music, everyone.* My name is at the top. I close my eyes against the sight of it and flip to the back of the book instead, then let the pages flip forward past my thumb until I feel them skip. I open my eyes and see a folded piece of paper tucked into the middle of the book.

Nate is written on it in rounded print, the letters of his name huddled close together.

I've seen this print before, on notes passed to me in classes every year of middle school. On birthday cards and silly drawings and lists of boys' names at sleepovers.

I open the note fold by fold, my breath catching on the edges.

Dear Nate,

I don't know how to tell you this in person. I mean, I've tried, but I just feel bad and I can't get all the words out. So I'm really sorry to be doing it this way, but I think we need to break up. I really do like you. You're a great guy. But I can't lie about my feelings anymore.

I'm sorry,
Amy

My head is spinning. I lie down, without even thinking about it. I lie down and put my head on his pillow and even with the fresh air coming through the window it all smells as dusty and stale as a tomb. Everything whirs through my mind like a lightning-fast slide show: the playlist he made for her, the kiss I wasn't supposed to see, this note, Amy crying at the Sip'N'Dip, going to Principal Hunter, yelling at the carnival. All this time, I've been trying to help her, trying to make up for what I took away from her.

And she'd already thrown it in the garbage.

TWENTY-SIX

HELP

wednesday 10/8

All I can think about is Amy's note, how much there was that I didn't know. That Nate hadn't told me. *How many other secrets did he keep from me? What did I keep from him?* I ask myself over and over on the walk to school, desperate to remember, to keep score.

"Who doesn't have secrets?" I say aloud.

"Who doesn't what?" Chase says from behind me.

I whip around. "Taking this Houdini thing a little far, aren't you? What's with the disappearing act this week?"

"I have bad news and good news." He doesn't ask which I want first.

"Hit me," I tell him.

"The bad news is that I am the worst hacker in history. I have obviously watched too many movies on the subject, and I grossly overestimated my skills."

"What happened?"

"I got caught. Completely and totally busted. I'm probably

grounded until after I graduate from college. My dad was so pissed that he wouldn't even let me come to school until today."

"So what's the good news?" My ears wait for words I want to hear. *We found the rest of Nate. We know where he is.*

"My dad is a lot smarter than I thought."

"That's good news?"

Chase shrugs one shoulder. "If you need surgery when he's on call, yeah. Very good."

I give him what feels like a grim look. "I hope never to be in that situation, thank you."

He looks sheepish. "I confirmed that Dr. Fikri is doing a study with organ recipients. She meets with them every Monday at four o'clock. And I have her email address. Maybe you can interview her for your 'article.'" He puts heavy finger quotes around that last word. Which is only fair.

"Chase, I'm . . ." I'm a lot of things. *Sorry. Grateful. Furious. Confused.*

He studies me for a long moment, and I wonder what he sees. The girl who caught his eye at the coffee shop? The girl who ambushed him with this whole crazy plan? Or something else? I can't read his face. He just looks like a picture of himself.

Finally, he pulls his phone out of his pocket. "I'm sending you her email," he says.

"You still have your phone?" Mine is the first thing my parents take away when I'm being punished for anything. When I used to be punished for things.

"Just so he can check up on me. I'm not allowed to turn off my GPS. He claims to be checking on me at all times."

"It's like you're some kind of supervillain," I say.

He arches an eyebrow, smiles a little. "Maybe I can finally perfect the art of mind control and get him to give up on this. But until then, I better lay low."

My phone pings and Chase's name flashes at me from the corner of the screen. "Thank you," I tell him.

We let those thoroughly inadequate words hover between us for a moment.

"Could Houdini do mind control?" I ask.

"In a way," Chase says. "He was very good at getting people to think what he wanted them to. But I think that alienated him from everyone, in the end."

"Why?"

"Because when you know you're deceiving someone, you can't be happy when you're with them. Even if you don't feel guilty, there's part of you that knows it's all based on tricks and lies and it's not . . . it's not real. Too many secrets kill the joy, y'know?"

I do. Without knowing it, Chase has just articulated my current existence, and I suddenly feel unspeakably sad. And so, of course, I start crying.

I hate crying. I hate that it ever happens anywhere, but I especially hate when it happens in public, in front of other people. Real crying isn't pretty like gentle soap-opera tears with a soft-focus lens. Real crying is ugly, it's messy, it's your nose running and your eyes getting red and swelling up and your ragged voice choking you as you try uselessly to pull yourself together.

To his credit, Chase does not freak out or run away, even though by all appearances I have been reduced to a blubbering mess at the thought of Harry Houdini's loneliness.

"It's okay," he tells me quietly. "He was happily married. He didn't die alone or anything."

Clapping my hand over my mouth to silence myself, I nod and take a few deep breaths. I wipe my nose on my arm. I am neck-deep in humiliation, so what difference does a little sleeve-snot make?

"Okay?" Chase asks.

I nod again. "Sorry," I manage to say. "I don't know what that was all about."

"Yes, you do," he replies. "But you don't have to tell me."

"Another hole in the story," I say.

He shrugs. "As long as I'm not going to fall into it."

We're not supposed to have our phones out in class, and that rule I will follow because if mine gets confiscated, it goes straight to Principal Hunter. So I have to wait until after biology to write to Dr. Fikri. Then I decide I don't want her to see that I've sent the email from my phone, in case it makes me seem less serious as an aspiring journalist, so I decide to skip gym and use my school laptop. I sit at the same desk in the library where I told Chase the truth about Nate and hope it brings me luck again this time. *Best to keep it simple*, I think. *Don't jump the gun and sound desperate.*

We were taught to pray when we were young, and taught to write business letters, and the two always seemed very much the same to me. Begin with a greeting, introduce yourself, state your problem and supporting arguments, sign off. Be polite. Be concise.

Dear Dr. Fikri,

My name is Taliesin McGovern. I am a high school student, and I am researching organ donation protocols for a newspaper article.

I pause, debating whether to use Dr. Abbott's name, then realize that I don't know his first name. But how many Dr. Abbotts can there be?

> Dr. Abbott kindly offered to put me in touch with you and suggested that your current research study might be of interest to my readership.

I have unintentionally lapsed into writing like my mother. Which is maybe not a bad thing, since my mother almost always gets people to do what she wants.

> If you would be willing to answer a few questions, I would be deeply grateful. Please reply at your earliest convenience.
> Yours sincerely,
> Tallie

I end on a friendly, casual note to appeal to her humanity. I read it over, checking for mistakes but also because the pit of my stomach feels fluttery and weird, and I wonder if this entire thing is just completely hopeless. To make myself feel better, I pick a Kinks song—"Superman"—on Matty and listen with my eyes closed. And then a memory floats into focus, like the rituals reviving themselves.

Nate's basketball friends used to come over all the time after practice, and even though I was only a year younger than them, they would always treat me like a little kid. They liked to make me play a game called Doorknob. Whenever one of them yelled "Doorknob!" I had to run as fast as I could and touch a doorknob before they caught me. If I didn't make it, they all stood in line to punch me in the arm. Nate felt bad, I think, but he wanted his friends to keep coming over and I refused to let them see how much the punches hurt, so he probably thought it was no big deal. But then the game changed. They started yelling things like "Toilet," and "Top step!" and chasing me all over the place.

One day Jason Rice yelled "Ceiling!" and I took off running as fast as I could, desperately trying to think of something I could climb to reach the ceiling, but there was nothing and they were getting closer and they were just about to catch me when Nate jumped in front of me in the hallway. I stopped cold and stood there, waiting to see what he was going to do. And just as Jason reached for me, just before his fingers latched on to whatever part of me he could grab first, Nate swung his hands out, caught me under the arms, and lifted me up as high as he could. And the sound of my hand smacking the ceiling was the most beautiful thing I'd ever heard.

When I open my eyes, my stomach feels better. Everything feels better, even my head. No new mail in my account, so I check the one I set up for Mom.

There's a message from SparkleCat76. *Thank you, lucky desk.* But my elation withers as I read.

The main thing is that I don't want anyone to feel sorry for me, so make sure that whatever you write about me doesn't make me sound sad or pathetic or anything, okay? I'm also not really sure I want everyone to know that I have part of a guy now, so maybe you could leave that out. Anyway, all I know is that he was young—like, seventeen—and I feel shitty about that even though it wasn't my fault he died. He was in a car accident. Oh, and they told me his blood type. O-negative. They call that "the universal donor." Isn't that cool?

No gratitude, none of Gerald's optimism or deference. The facts point to Nate as her donor, but I can see now how little of the story those facts actually tell. She doesn't understand how it happened, that someone else was in the car, that the roads were wet, that I bullied my way into the driver's seat. And it doesn't matter, because she can build any story onto those flimsy details, can tell herself anything at all, any version of Nate's death that will make her feel the most okay. They all can.

Heart, liver, lungs, kidneys, corneas.

There's more.

Do you ever come to Boston? We could talk or get coffee or something. I'm not really supposed to drink coffee anymore but sometimes I cheat. Here's my cell number.

The digits swim on the screen like tadpoles I can't catch. I hit reply, more out of habit than anything else, but I can't think and my fingers are shaking, so I save a draft. I'll send it from my phone later, I tell myself, after I calm down.

And then Amy walks into the library.

By the time she sees me, I've positioned myself between her and the door. Ms. Huff is tucked away behind the glass wall of her office—she's used to me being here and she leaves me alone. She thinks I won't cause trouble, but Amy obviously has a different expectation.

"I wasn't looking for you," she says, as if I might just have the wrong idea.

"I wasn't looking for you either. But here we are." My hands are steadier now, adrenaline pulsing through me. "And we have so much to talk about."

Amy twirls her hair and tries to look unaffected. "No, we don't."

"Okay," I tell her. "Then I'll do the talking. I know you told Principal Hunter I was harassing you. I know you broke up with Nate. And I know you regret it because I saw you crying into your ice cream. Vanilla fudge dip." Those three words have probably never been used as an accusation before, but I fire them at top speed. And wait for blood.

Instead, I get laughter.

"You don't know *anything*." Amy's voice is shrill, like a bird out of tune. "Principal Hunter came to *me* because your father has been checking up on you and Hunter is helping him. And I wasn't crying because I miss your brother. I was crying because no one knows I broke up with him, and now I can't tell anyone without them thinking I'm a total bitch. And no one else will date me because I'm, like, socially mummified now. The dead kid's girlfriend."

"The accident was my fault," I say. "I was driving."

Amy rolls her eyes. "So what? You were driving because he let you drive. That was his choice. So why don't you blame him?"

"Because . . ." It's always been so clear in my mind, but now it feels like I'm underwater and I can't quite make it out. "I talked him into it."

"No. Because after someone dies, we can't blame them for

anything anymore. You think you're remembering him as he was? You're not. He wasn't perfect. He could be a total jerk sometimes. He had terrible taste in music. He was smart, yes, and cute and fun. But he wasn't perfect."

"You broke up with him." It's already been said, but now I'm saying it with a question underneath. *How could you? Was he okay?*

"Yep. I did. And he would have been fine. He would have moved on, but now he can't move on. And neither can I."

Maybe Amy's the one who should move, start over. Maybe my parents could adopt her and leave town and I could stay here.

"Doesn't sound to me like you're having any trouble," I tell her. I'm angry now. The comment about Nate's taste in music was below the belt. "Maybe you *are* a horrible person."

"Maybe I am."

"Aren't you sad? Don't you miss him at all?"

A shadow passes over her face, a specter of the old Amy.

"I was. I did. But I didn't . . . I didn't love him. He was a nice guy. I was sorry when it happened. But he's gone, Tallie. Remembering him doesn't mean we have to act like we're dead, too."

She sounds so calm, so sensible. Like she's already finished the entire process, figured everything out, put it to rest. Moved on. It should have been harder for her. He should have meant more.

"He was my *brother*. We were best friends, and he was my brother."

"I know."

I was going to tell her about the recipients, about Boston, about finding him. But it's clear to me now that she doesn't deserve to know. Or maybe just that she wouldn't care enough to listen.

■ ■ ■

Before I fall asleep that night, I look again at the Life Choice letter, at the page where they list how many lucky recipients benefited from the donations of a single person. Nate's heart, his lungs, his kidneys and liver and eyes. So many parts to claim. All those pieces taken, missing from the urn. The universal donor. The one who can give to everyone, but can only receive from his own blood type. More cosmic imbalance.

You'll never find them all, I tell myself. So I focus on the heart. The essential thing, the part that keeps all of the other parts alive. *Cross my heart,* he said, whenever he wanted me to know he meant what he was saying.

I press my hand over my own, picture it: a fist inside my chest. Picture Nate's: a fist inside someone else's. Both of them keeping us alive, drawing us toward each other with every pounding beat. *That's the treasure,* I think. *The heart is the one to find.*

And when I fall asleep, I do not dream about anything.

TWENTY-SEVEN

SYNCHRONICITY

thursday 10/9

Now that I know SparkleCat76 lives in Boston and most likely has some part of Nate (whether or not she deserves it), I stash that info in my back pocket and wait to hear from Dr. Fikri, imagining what she might tell me, *if* she tells me anything at all. Waiting makes me distracted, and being distracted makes me careless. I don't even see Ms. Doberskiff approaching until it's too late and she's got me cornered in the hallway. Wordlessly she tugs my elbow ever so slightly and I follow her into an empty classroom.

"Are you . . . Is everything okay, Tallie?" she asks. Her hair is pulled into a high ponytail because she has just come from cheerleading practice, and her face is flushed, and she looks like a sweaty movie star.

"I am *fine*." I very much want this to be true. "How are *you*?"

"You look like you've been crying. Have you been crying?"

This is one of Ms. Doberskiff's rules. She will not articulate your problems for you. She makes you do it yourself. And no matter how hard you try, you sound like a guilty child every time. Or a robot.

"No, I have not been crying."

"Do you want to talk about it?"

"No, I do not want to talk about it."

"You might feel better if you talk about it."

"I don't think so."

Ms. Doberskiff sounds a wee bit exasperated when she says, "I am here to help you, Tallie."

I am tired of people telling me that I need their help. As if I can't decide for myself. As if I must just accept their aid, swallow it like medicine that burns going down. Did the saints have to endure such interference?

I smile at her pretty, sweaty face.

"Tallie," Ms. Doberskiff says. "I was hoping I could change your mind about coming to Bridges next week?"

"I need some time off," I tell her gently. "I have some things to figure out."

"You don't have to do this alone, Tallie. There are so many people who care about you. . . ."

She continues but she is fading, as if she is a radio and someone is turning down the volume so I can let my attention wander. We're in Mr. Gennari's history room and there are maps all over the walls, maps with stars marking important places, dark lines in all colors showing how to get from one place to another. A huge map of the state of Massachusetts, with pins and strings between them to trace the routes of past settlers, from Boston to . . .

"I have to go," I say, and I start to edge out of the room, tiptoeing backward, as if any sudden movement might somehow upset the certainty that I feel right now, the conviction that I know what to do. And who to tell about it.

But I have to pass my creative-writing classroom to get to the cafeteria, and Mel is waiting in the doorway. She seizes my arm before I can duck out of her way. I do a quick pros-and-cons analysis and decide that it's not worth trying to evade her. Instead, I let her lead me to our usual seats. I sit in front of her so she can use me as a human shield and take naps while hidden behind my body.

"So, little stranger," she says. "Where ya been?"

"Communing with the dead," I tell her. Maybe the truth is so absurd that I don't have to lie to her after all.

"No fair," she replies.

The class starts, as it often does, with a writing exercise. Something about what our characters would carry around in their backpacks. Mrs. Cohen gives us five minutes to write. The room is completely quiet at first, and then everyone starts writing at once. The soft shushing of pens on paper gets layered, amplified, until it sounds like a chorus of whispers. I cover one ear, then the other, and close my eyes, trying to keep myself together.

Mel taps me on the shoulder. I lower one hand so I can hear her say, "Are you coming to Battle of the Bands? Our set list is finally free of alt-country atrocities."

I am almost touched by her invitation until I notice that she is holding her phone and aiming it at me, ready to take a picture, and suddenly I feel sure that I will end up in one of her taxidermy tableaus or on fake HAVE YOU SEEN THIS GIRL? posters or worse. She is smiling in that way she smiles, full of twisted hidden plans, and I hate her—for just a second—for making me like her. Untrustworthy. Draped with secrets and lies.

"No," I growl.

She retracts her phone, still smiling.

The whispers are louder now and I want to look around to see if everyone is talking to themselves, but Mel will notice. So I just listen and I hear the words start to form and they are all in my own voice. They are in my head. *Tallie,* they tell me, *you don't have time for this. You have to go. Go now. Go.*

I risk a glance at Mel over my shoulder. She is writing, everyone is writing, pens singing on paper. No one else hears it. It's only me, like I am trapped, in limbo all over again and no one knows and no one is coming to get me. I put my fingers up my sleeve to where Nate's name is written, press against it, and feel my pulse racing.

"Tallie?" Mrs. Cohen is staring at me from the front of the room. "Is everything all right?"

"Yes," I manage to croak, but it's not all right because the whispers are drowning me now and I can't breathe in this room, I can't breathe, I have to—

I lurch toward the door.

"Tallie!" Mrs. Cohen calls, alarmed. "Do you need a hall pass?"

I leave her behind with all the others in the whispering room.

Mrs. Cohen is still calling my name from the room of whispers but I ignore her and run down the shining corridor. The locker doors line the walls and they are just like the little doors in the columbarium, standing at attention, ready to receive our offerings. I turn the corner and duck into the library. Ms. Huff is in her glass box, a fish in a tank, and I manage to hide myself in the stacks without detection. I can almost breathe again, running my fingertips across the books that are lined up like the vertebrae of some huge creature. The spines in this section are black with gold letters, thick with pages.

Black, like Chase's binder.

Chase.

I need to find Chase.

I will tell him what I decided, what I'm going to do, and he will tell me I'm right and it will solve everything and it cannot fail. I am jubilant, I can almost breathe again, my heart is racing, alive.

I look at the clock. The numbers seem to shudder at my gaze, but I can read them well enough.

Then I am in the cafeteria, where Chase is sitting with a few of the guys from the photography club. He looks up as I approach, there's a camera in his hands and he raises it slowly—to show me? to take my picture?—and just as I start to tell him that I know what to do, everything

goes
black.

My mother comes to pick me up from school.

The school nurse tells her that I had a panic attack or maybe just a "syncopal episode." At first I think she is saying *sinkable*, as if fainting proves that I am somehow less buoyant than other students, but then I see where she has written it down on the incident report she's filling out for the school office. Another memento for Hunter's TALIESIN MCGOVERN scrapbook.

More evidence that will end up on Dr. Blankenbaker's tally sheet. Tallie sheet. I keep my hand on my chest all the way to the car, to see if I can detect disruptions in my heartbeat, get some warning that it's about to happen again.

Mom turns the car on and buckles her seat belt and fiddles with the radio for a minute. Then she turns the car off again, and the radio, too.

"I need to tell you something," she says, and then sighs, as if she is tired of hearing her own voice.

"Okay." I pull down my sleeve, as if it will leap up and reveal Nate's name written on my arm. Ballpoint wears off too quickly, so this morning I wrote it in Sharpie. I admit to scoffing a little at the word *permanent*. How naive.

Mom's hands are folded around each other, knuckles straining. "I'm going to clean out his room this weekend."

She still won't say his name, but she'll put his ashes in a wall and give his stuff away to whoever wants it. Objections line up in my head but I can't start an argument. Anger makes us make mistakes, say things we regret later, and I have too many secrets now to risk it.

"Okay," I say again.

"Is there anything you want? Before I box it all up?"

"No."

"Are you sure? I know this is hard. It's hard for me, too, but Dr. Blankenbaker thinks I'm ready. . . ."

As long as you're *ready,* I think. Maybe I should have kept going to Dr. B. Actually talked to her. At least then I'd have a say.

Why didn't you tell me that you donated Nate's body? But I ask this only in my head. Maybe Dad has already told her that I know the truth, but even if she knows, I don't want to have that conversation just in case Professor Gerald Rackham—and, by association, my layers of lies and deception—comes up. Aloud I say, "It's okay. I don't need anything from his room."

"Well, I'm listening. If you want to share your feelings," she says. Therapyspeak. She's picking up Dad's habits.

"I'm fine," I tell her just as a swarm of blackbirds take off from the trees next to the school, all at once, the way they do. They fill the sky like shattered pieces of nighttime. I am spellbound.

"What are you looking at?" my mother asks.

"What?" I turn to her then, and notice how many new lines are etched on her face. When I look back at the sky, the birds are gone.

"Nothing," I say. "Let's go home. I think I just need to lie down for a little while."

Mom does not drive the way Mel does, either in terms of speed or direction. She takes the same route she has always taken, since Nate's first year in the middle school, which is right behind the high school. She used to pick me up from fourth grade and then we'd come to get him, and she still goes the same way even though new roads have been built that she could use as shortcuts to our house. It is only now that I realize her route takes us down Sycamore Street, past the legendary Victorian with the wrong color blue trim. And I can feel her slow the car slightly as we pass it, so I look at it, too.

The house is massive compared to ours, with its peaked roof and high windows and porch that wraps all the way around it. The trim is painted in layers, blue on gray on white, and for once I agree with Mom. The blue is garish, Cookie Monster bright. It makes the house look like a woman wearing the wrong necklace with her dress.

I crane my neck as we drive by.

"Do you like that house?" Mom asks hopefully.

Something flares in me then. Frustration that I have to protect her. Anger that she has been coveting this house, that she is just like Dad, that she wants to forget the place where Nate was and leave it behind.

I will not forget. I will not move on without him. There is no back to normal anymore. There is only this.

I will find him.

"Not really," I say. And I close my eyes so we won't have to talk anymore. And we don't, and then we are home.

I really do just want to lie down, but something makes me check my email and there's a message from Dr. Fikri. I stare at her name in my in-box, savoring the excitement that's gathering in my gut. I am ready for her to bring me the answers. I will not forget. I will find him.

But when I open the email, I only have to read a few words before my excitement curdles like milk.

Dear Tallie,

I regret to say that Dr. Abbott has informed me of your personal history and what he feels are questionable intentions. He has also made me aware that you incited his son to make some very poor choices and break his father's trust in him. For these reasons, I must decline your request for an interview. I wish you the best of luck in whatever pursuits you deem worthy of your future.

Sincerely,

Dr. Samira Fikri

My *personal history?* *Questionable intentions?*

My throat is burning as I dial Chase's number. I am too angry to text, and the letters on the keyboard refuse to hold still anymore.

He answers on the second ring. "Hey, I—"

"What the *hell?*" I sputter.

"Tallie? What's wrong?"

"Your father told Dr. Fikri some kind of stuff about me,

personal stuff and about my intentions, and she's not going to help me, so *what the hell* did you say to him?"

"Nothing, Tallie, I swear. I didn't tell him anything."

"Then how would he know? How would he know what I really wanted to ask her?"

Chase makes a noise like *uh* or *huh* but doesn't say anything.

"What?" I ask.

"He must have looked it up," Chase says. "He found out about Nate through the hospital. He must have. Because I swear to you, I didn't say a thing."

"And I'm just supposed to believe what you're saying?"

"You don't have to. But you know my policy."

"Honest emotional exchange," I say. "And don't tell you anything that isn't true."

"Right. And I follow my own rules."

I want to believe him. I want to, because it means I can still like him and also that somewhere out there, in the informational ether, my answers are findable. *He is my ally,* I tell myself. *We are connected. We share a mission.*

"Okay," I tell him.

"Okay," he says.

And we both sound like we mean it.

After we hang up, it comes back to me, like a flower opening in slow motion. My plan, the one I was going to tell Chase about when I fainted in the cafeteria. And I know now that I was right, because Nate is telling me exactly what to do.

Dr. Fikri is going to help me, whether she knows it or not.

Time to play another card.

I sneak out the back door and ride my bike to the package store on the corner, the one with an ATM inside. I know Nate's PIN because he used the same four digits for everything: 1171, the month and year of my mother's birthday. I feel a twinge of irritation at how *good* he was. I withdraw a hundred dollars from his bank account—I can't take it all at once because there's a daily limit, so I will do this each day, a new ritual. I feel like I'm committing a crime. Technically I guess I am, but my uncle did say that my parents should give me this money, and even though I have some of my own saved up from working at Common Grounds, it feels right to use Nate's money for this mission. He was saving up for a car, I'm going to get myself a train ticket. It's practically the same thing. It's all transport.

I take my phone out of my pocket to make room for the cash. There's a text from Chase:

r u ok?

I text back, trying to pin the letters down like butterflies.

rosabelle, believe

TWENTY-EIGHT

DRIVE ALL NIGHT

friday 10/10

Sometimes, when someone has died, one of the survivors says, "I'd give anything just to hear him say my name one more time" or "I just want one more day." This is absurd. Nobody wants *one* more day, *one* more sentence, or *one* more anything else. We want all of the days, as many as we can get. We are greedy in our unhappiness. We feel we've been robbed and we want back what we've lost, and then some.

I think if I was a ghost or a spirit or whatever and I heard someone say they wanted just one more day with me, I'd be really disappointed in them. I would think they didn't really want me back, and I'd also think they were showing very little imagination.

If you're going to ask for the impossible, why not ask for as much as you can? Why not say, *I want him back here now and I want us both to become immortal rock stars!* Or *I want ten thousand more days and a Mustang convertible so we can drive cross-country over and over again and see all of America's kitschiest tourist attractions.*

Nate would make the world's longest playlist and I would pack a cooler full of tuna sandwiches and potato chips and root beer. We would have burping contests and he would let me win. We would call Mom and Dad every night to tell them we were okay and we would roll our eyes when Mom said "I love you" at the end, but we'd say it back before we hung up. We'd stay at motels and watch terrible late-night movies and make fun of them. We'd each get one arm really tan from driving with the windows down, sitting in the same spots the whole way because I wouldn't ever ask Nate to let me drive.

He would drive, just him, and I would ride along, and we'd keep our eyes on the horizon and we would have all the days we ever wanted.

Maybe I am only remembering the good things now. Maybe I am idealizing him, like Amy said. But isn't that how memory works? Our bodies go into shock so we can't feel the pain when we get hurt, really hurt, and so we can't remember it later. We protect ourselves. When I did the rituals, I tried to remember bad things, too, because I thought it meant that I was being honest with myself. But I'm the one who should have been in that passenger seat. It should have been me, and I like to think that if Nate was here, if he was the one doing the remembering, he'd make me better than I really was.

When I wake up, it's still dark outside. The days are getting shorter—there's frost on the windows in the mornings and dusted across the grass like glitter. I wonder about Thanksgiving, about Christmas morning, if we will even acknowledge the days or if we will cocoon ourselves in denial. I wonder where Red Circle Day will take us. Five days away. Principal Hunter and Ms. Doberskiff aren't on my side anymore. I have a mission, but that will not matter if Dr. Blankenbaker gathers all of this evidence—what if she knows Dr. Abbott? What if she finds out about what Dr. Fikri wrote to me? A new school might not be enough for them then. They might just go ahead and commit me. Dad has been going to therapy again, and I have heard him trying to convince Mom to go with him. And now she doesn't argue about it. She listens to what he says, lets him lay down his reasons like stepping-stones to somewhere better than where they are.

I won't follow that path. I am making my own.

But the time to make my own choices may be running out.

Last night I compiled as much information on Dr. Fikri as I could find in the webiverse. Her bio from the hospital website, various references from bygone medical conferences, articles she wrote on organ donation protocols and the psychological effects of transplants on living donors and recipients. Her current study, I learned, is the first she has done with people whose donors are deceased.

I stared at the words—*recipients, donors, deceased*—until the letters swam like tiny fish, rearranged themselves on the screen. *Ripened. Dirt. Sores.*

I printed out Dr. Fikri's picture from the hospital site and slid it into the codebook, which I stashed behind my computer monitor. Now, sitting down at my desk, I can see a corner of the red cover peeking out, teasing me with its secrets. Reminding me that I never could understand its language like Nate wanted me to, that I failed him even before I killed him. I push the book so I can't see it anymore and check Mom's dummy email account.

Just one new message, from Jennifer. I managed to put together a fairly coherent email, striking a balance between enthusiasm ("universal donor, how amazing, I never knew") and subtle requests for personal information ("I don't get to Boston as much as I'd like but I love it there—what neighborhood do you live in?"). But her response ignores all of that, focusing instead on a recent support-group meeting.

> It's just so frustrating. They all act like they're so much more important than me because they were sicker than I was or because they got a bigger organ. Those heart transplant people are such snobs. Like the heart is SO much better than everything else. It's like they don't even want to know what I went through.

I can't even formulate a response to this through my aching disappointment. She doesn't have his heart. She has something else. Is it even worth pursuing her now? Do I even want to know? But this group that she's a part of—the person with Nate's heart could be there. It could even be Dr. Fikri's group at Brigham and Women's.

I close her message and stare at the screen, at Gerald's name on the emails I've already read, and remember when I first saw it, when I opened that first letter and realized what it meant. I was so sure that he could help me, and I guess, in a way, he did. The spark that started the fire.

There may be reliable laws of this universe, but the rules are not so clear when it comes to those of us who inhabit it. There is no law of physics that will tell me how to feel, no mathematical formula for right and wrong. I've been looking for exceptions to the rules, stretching and pulling at my conscience so it expands to fit the choices I'm about to make. So I can tell myself that what I'm doing is okay. Even if it's not.

I turn the monitor off so I can't see his name anymore, then get ready for school.

I keep myself calm while I'm walking in the hallways by focusing on the bland vanilla floor, which is blessedly the same throughout the school. The library being the one exception, with carpet that is cruelly patterned and bright and is almost enough to give me vertigo. I walk to my lucky desk with my eyes closed. If Ms. Huff notices, I don't see it and she doesn't interrupt me. She, like all the other adults, just leaves me to my stricken self.

We learned about this in health last year. It's called the bystander effect. When there's an accident or a crime happening, everyone who sees it assumes that someone else in the crowd will call for help and then no one actually does. It's why they told us that if we're ever attacked, we should yell "Fire!" instead of "Help!" because a fire is a threat to everyone else, too. And people will help themselves even if they won't help you. Even if they think they *would* help you, they won't. Because they figure that someone else will.

It doesn't mean they're bad people. It means they think other people are just as good as, or even better than, they are.

In a twisted way, it's a sign of their faith in humanity.

When my hand touches down on the desk and I finally open my eyes, I can see through my haze that Chase is lurking behind the encyclopedias. I am tempted to yell "Fire!" to see what he does, but I'm not sure Ms. Huff could handle the excitement.

I make my way over to the shelves, trying to keep my eyes from moving too much. He has one of the volumes open and appears to be reading it. His bag is on the table, the edge of the black binder peeking out like a curious pet. "*H* for Houdini?" I ask.

He smiles without looking up. "I already know everything about him," he says. "I've moved on to *T* for Tesla."

"Another magician?"

"Sort of." Chase marks a spot on the page with his finger and fixes his eyes on me. "He was an electrical engineer. He invented the alternating-current induction motor and some of the earliest components for radio transmission."

This sounds incredibly dull, and I am about to tell him so when he says, "He also had some kind of mental condition that made him see things."

I trace my scar, try not to sound too interested. "What kinds of things?"

"Um . . ." Chase checks the encyclopedia. "I don't know. It just says he had 'visions' about problems he was trying to solve. Supposedly he got trapped under a dock when he was a kid and saw a way out in his mind. There's a story like that about Houdini getting trapped under the ice in the Detroit River, too."

Some of my favorite saints had visions, but I keep this to myself because I don't want to talk about religion right now. "You seem to have a fascination with people who escape from places," I say.

He closes the book, slides it carefully back into its slot on the shelf. "I guess so," he says. His eyes are lit up by the sun coming through the window, like orbs of stained glass.

"I've been working on an escape plan of my own." The words come out quickly, before I can think about holding them back.

"Am I invited?"

"Don't you want to ask where I'm going first?"

He shakes his head. "Escape isn't about where you're going. It's about what you're getting away from."

"You make a lot of definitive statements about things," I tell him.

"I find that most people won't argue with you if you sound really sure of yourself."

And I guess he's right, because I don't feel like contradicting him even though I know that my escape is absolutely about where I'm going. So maybe I chose the wrong word. Maybe I should be calling it a *quest,* or a *journey,* a word that speaks of pulling me toward something instead of driving me away. Suddenly my brain feels like a Scrabble board and I'm trying to find the right letters to put on the tiny squares. I close my eyes, try to clear the picture. And either Chase steps closer to me or I step closer to him or both—because when I open them, we are inhabiting the same few inches of space. Our faces align, mirror images of sad and sweet.

"So, am I invited?" he asks again softly.

I study him—dark hair, eyes reflecting all the light they can gather—and I think of my mother gazing at that Victorian, imagining a whole new set of chances. Maybe I could fall in love with him and feel it happening, and let him fall in love with me. But this is like the Chinese finger trap, the two of us stuck in either end and pulling in different directions. I don't want to do this alone. But I know how he feels about keeping secrets, and if I have to tell him everything, then there's no protecting him if I end up doing something really awful. Carefully I say, "I'll get back to you on that."

"Is there an application I can fill out?"

It's another one of those moments, a question that could kick off a volley of flirtation. If only I could peel another version of myself away and set her aside, give her the guilt and the sadness and the quest so I could just talk to a cute boy, play this game again.

His eyes are liquid, muddy pools. There could be hundreds of secrets under the surface. Or there could just be water.

I say a silent prayer that he will still look at me this way when this is over.

"I have all the information I need," I assure him. "You'll be hearing from me shortly."

And since a statement like that requires an exit, exit is what I do.

All the way home, Mel rails against the hypocrisy of a school that claims to support freedom of speech but has forbidden Scud from performing a song called "Hung Like Jesus" at Battle of the Bands. Mel and her fellow band members are, apparently, the latest population of the disenfranchised and misunderstood.

"I'm going to get online and mobilize our fans," Mel huffs. "The world needs to know our art!"

It turns out that Chase is right. Mel sounds one-hundred-percent sure of herself, and there is no arguing with her. I make a note to practice sounding inarguable.

She turns into my driveway smoothly, which is surprisingly considerate, given her mood. Just as I close my hand around the door handle to let myself out, Mel locks all of the doors. "You're coming tomorrow, right?"

"Where?"

"The taxidermy show," she says, stung.

"Oh. Well . . ."

"You said you would be there. C'mon, you have to see Raccoon Zorro in all of his glory!"

My choices may be morally questionable these days, but I keep my promises. I can still claim that much. "I'll be there."

"Great," she says, and the doors click once more. I'm free to go.

I gather the mail (nothing from Life Choice, another kick in the gut) and make my way into the house. Dad's car is in the driveway, so I know he's around here somewhere, and I'd like to spare us both the how-was-your-day talk or, worse, another series of self-help platitudes designed to jump-start our healing. Mostly because everything still seems to be moving, almost vibrating, and I am not entirely sure of my ability to act normal. I set the mail silently on the hall table and am about to tiptoe up the stairs when the quiet is shattered.

"Tallie."

It isn't his kinder, gentler, make-things-better voice. It is his you-are-in-serious-trouble-young-lady voice. Weirdly, my first response is to smile. I haven't heard this voice in so long. But my smile is dashed when he says it again, even more forcefully. *"Tallie."*

I drop my bag and step into the kitchen. Dad is sitting at the table with his back to me.

"Dad?"

"Sit down." No *sweetheart*. No *please*.

I sit across from him, and I can see the red circle peering at me over his shoulder, pulsing like a heart.

"I was getting your laundry today," he says. "Giving Mom a break. And I noticed you hadn't turned your computer off. So I thought I'd shut it down for you. And when I saw what was on the screen . . ." His voice cracks, steadies, and his eyes find me. "How could you *do* this?"

He found it. The email account in Mom's name. Every email between me and Gerald—and SparkleCat76, and the others—left right there for Dad to see.

I forgot to log out. Shit.

And there's nothing I can say. This is one of those conversations parents start, with questions that aren't questions, disguised as a search for answers when, really, they do not want to listen. They only want to speak, to lecture and rant. So there's nothing I can say, but I have to say something. Something that's not the entire truth, but something that isn't a lie either.

"I found a letter in the mail. That's how I knew about Nate."

"You said you heard us arguing—"

"I did hear you. So I knew something was going on." I can't get my voice above a whisper. I sound contrite, at least. "But I didn't know what it was until the letter came from Life Choice."

Dad pushes air from his throat, a backward gasp. "And you've been writing to these people? You've been pretending to be your mother and lying to all of us?" He doesn't sound as angry as he first did. Now he sounds sad, which is worse.

That about sums it up, I think. "Yes," I say.

I know how these conversations go: The crime is verified, disappointment is expressed, punishment is issued. I grip the table to keep it still, and wait.

"This is . . ."

Disappointing, I think. *Unbelievable. Very troubling.*

". . . an important moment for all of us."

Oh no.

"Obviously, I'm not happy that you would deceive us this way, or that you would mislead someone like Gerald. Or this Sparkle-Cat woman. They have probably been through a great deal already and they don't deserve to be lied to. But we have an opportunity here, to move forward as a family. I just have to figure out how to tell your mother, because she may not see it quite the way I do. . . ."

He goes on, about how he has finally embraced the chance to communicate with the recipients, how we could use this to learn to communicate with each other again, we've all been so isolated, et cetera. Now he sounds excited, which is even worse than sad. The worst. Because I've just given him the last piece of the puzzle he's been trying to complete. It is all I can do to keep my eyes in one place. It's like I'm on a carousel, with the red circle passing my vision over and over again. It's reminding me, chanting *Time to go* over and over again. All this time I've been dreading October fifteenth, but now it looks like the finish line for a race I've been running for weeks. If I can just get across it, I will be free of the dread, the fear of it, the terrible anticipation.

It's not my parents' circle anymore.

It's mine.

TWENTY-NINE

TALK OF THE TOWN

saturday 10/11

After I assure her several times that I will seek medical attention if I start feeling sinkable, my mother says that I can go to Mel's taxidermy show at the town hall. My father says nothing to contradict her, but insists on driving me instead of letting me ride my bike.

"And you can text me when you're ready for me to pick you up, okay?"

Again, the question mark is pure formality, tacked onto the end of Dad's statement so it sounds like I have the option of objecting when we both know that I don't.

Walking around a room full of eviscerated animals is absolutely the last thing I feel like doing, but dammit, I promised. I wish Chase could come with me but he is still under house arrest. And I doubt he could convince Dr. Abbott that attending a taxidermy competition was a required school assignment.

Dad informs me that he will drop me off on his way to Lowe's.

"Big project?" I ask.

"Just a few things for the house," he says. There's a list sticking out of his shirt pocket of items that would need to be fixed or replaced before the house could be sold. "If that's what we decide to do," I heard him say to my mother before we left. "Just want to be ready."

If she said anything in return, I didn't hear. Only the sound of cardboard boxes bumping against each other as she climbed the stairs to Nate's room. I tell myself that it doesn't matter if she puts his things in boxes, that I have Matty and the codebook and the rest is hollow. But it feels like there are rocks in my stomach anyway.

"Thanks for driving me," I say. My voice sounds strange. I think of the cold night when I saw the banana moon, before the séance. Before all of this.

"Yep," he says. It's curt, but he looks relieved, to utter such regular things. To know what's coming.

We don't talk much the rest of the way, but the weight of all that we're not saying fills the car like water, making it hard to breathe. When he stops to let me out, Dad offers, "See you later, alligator." Which is something he used to say when I was little, and now it seems so out of place, a phrase in the wrong language. The world is not the same. But I pretend, I play along and reply, "In a while, crocodile."

He is smiling as he drives away, and I know I did a good thing because the wind kicks up and the trees wave their branches, rubbing their leaves into whispers.

Walking into the taxidermy show feels like a dream in which I have forgotten how to walk and I have to think through the steps one by one. There is a surprisingly large crowd, probably because there isn't much else going on in Molton on a Saturday morning.

Small children cower behind their mothers, hiding from the foxes and possums and squirrels that appear to be preparing to leap at them.

I see Mel before she sees me. She is standing to the side of her display at the far end of the hall, her eyebrows squinched together in a worried way. There is a crowd in front of her but she is looking over their heads, toward the door.

Looking for her parents. Knowing they won't appear.

Some families don't work even when everyone's still around.

I stop next to a huge falcon mounted on a tree branch and holding a snake in its beak. I watch Mel for a minute, my eyes locked on her, and hers on the entrance.

The man standing behind the table—the creator of this entry, I assume—coughs.

"Is that snake poisonous?" I ask him.

He grins eagerly. "Not anymore!"

"Thank you," I say, and head for Mel, passing through the rows of installations. Most are small and straightforward, animals as they looked before they were dead, doing normal animal things in normal animal ways.

Mel's contribution is very, very different.

The raccoon we retrieved from the side of the road is mounted on a huge cat, brandishing a sword, his furry mask the perfect complement to the black hat on his head and the cape flying out from behind him as the cat rears up and prepares to run. Chipmunks and moles dressed as tiny townspeople stand reverently before him, and a Spanish village is painted on the backdrop behind them, model houses with tile roofs peppering the landscape.

When Mel sees me, she smiles a smile that I can't quite read.

Relief, I guess, mixed with pride. Before I can say anything, she hugs me and then seizes my hand. Her fingers are like a clamp.

"Can you stay until the judging?" she asks brightly. She looks amped, almost deranged with glee.

"Are you okay?"

"What? Of course, I'm just—it's just *exciting,* y'know, to be here!" She sounds utterly insane, and I'm just about to ask her if she took some of her mother's pharmaceuticals when she tucks her arm around my shoulders and drops her voice into my ear. "The judges are, like, undercover this year. So I'm trying to sound enthusiastic. Too much?"

"A little," I tell her. Honesty. It helps, in small doses.

"What is *she* doing here?"

I turn and see Amy pushing a cart loaded with baked goods and some very familiar-looking coffee dispensers across the room. She is wearing a pink-and-green apron and a huge smile, one that is much less complex than Mel's. And Cranky Andy is right behind her.

"Great," Mel says. "Common Grounds is ruined forever."

"I'll be right back," I tell her, and march back between the display tables so swiftly that Amy actually takes a step backward when she sees me coming. She looks away, looks behind me, searching for some way out of the conversation that's about to happen. I can feel her fear like crackling rays shooting out of her body, leaping to mine, and I receive it without flinching.

"Don't," she says.

"Don't what?" I ask innocently. "Don't buy a cookie?"

Cranky Andy turns from the table where he's arranging the little placards that identify the different kinds of coffee. They are hand-lettered with fancy calligraphy. Either Martha has talents I never suspected, or Andy's been expanding his skill set. "Oh, hey," he says. "We're not quite set up yet."

The way he says this, as if I'm nothing more than any other customer, is far more infuriating to me than the fact that Amy is working with him. But not as infuriating as what happens next.

Amy places her hand on Cranky Andy's arm gently, as if it's something valuable, and says, "I think Tallie wanted to talk to me. But"—she glares at me—"I don't think we have anything else to say to each other."

"Huh." Cranky Andy looks like he couldn't care less.

"We used to be friends," Amy tells him.

"Oh," I say, "but it was so much more than that, wasn't it, Amy?" I have adopted some of Mel's false cheer, and it echoes in my voice like an off-key instrument. "We might have become *family*."

Her face gets pale as a full moon.

"Amy and my brother were *in love*," I announce. "High school sweethearts, until—well, you know."

"Stop it," Amy hisses.

"It's hard for her to talk about it," I tell Andy.

He is frozen in place, a huge tray of croissants shielding him from whatever is about to happen. The blood is singing in my ears, rising like a crescendo, and before she can get away, I lock Amy's arms with my hands and hold her there. I make her stand there so she can never say she didn't hear what I say next.

"Maybe I did make him out to be better than he was. Maybe I'm remembering him all wrong. But on his worst day, he deserved way more than you."

She's trying not to flinch, she's looking right at me, and I see it, an almost invisible flick of her eyes that tells me she knows I'm right. I take my hands off of her, and in that one motion I say good-bye to the friend I thought she was.

Maybe we're all wrong about each other, I think as I walk back to Mel's Zorro. Maybe all we have is our own version of the stories we wrote, the things we said to each other, the fights we had, the jokes, the sleepovers, the ballet recitals, the day we met. All of it. Maybe we never would have agreed on how any of it happened.

Mel is waiting expectantly, a thousand questions written on her face.

So I ask, "What's the opposite of scud?"

Mel thinks for a moment. "Darling," she says. And then she goes back to stand next to her raccoon Zorro, and I take what few steps there are between me and the back exit.

The house is quiet when Dad and I get home. The driveway is empty, which means that Mom either went somewhere on her own—a sign, perhaps, that Dad's family-repair project is working—or sold her car and is hiding out somewhere. Probably the former. I hope she's not parked in front of that Victorian again. She's in danger of getting arrested for stalking a house.

Dad explains that he has some work to do in the basement. I assure him that I can handle his absence, trying to keep a straight face. I count his footsteps, match them to the number of stairs, and when I know he's at the bottom, I do a browser check in the study. All of the home-improvement tutorials have been replaced with searches about "talking to your teen" and "grieving" and "heal-ing" and "how your marriage can survive the loss of a child." Dad is in full-on research mode. I can feel my freedom dwindling. He's preparing his case for Red Circle Day, and he knows too much. In four days we are supposed to walk into Dr. Blankenbaker's office for the verdict to be handed down. Dr. B. has become like an oracle, the one with the magic answer. Will Mom be on my side? Does she want to stay anymore or has Dad convinced her that I need to be saved?

Her journal doesn't offer much new material at first, just some weakly written statements about how she appreciates Dad's efforts but she isn't ready to let go yet. But then there's this.

I feel betrayed by a stranger. This person, whoever he is, asked to make contact with me and never did. How could he do that? Is he just toying with me? Is he flaunting the fact that he is alive and my little boy isn't? I am going to call Life Choice tomorrow and file a complaint.

So Dad hasn't told her yet about my unsanctioned activities, about Gerald. Makes sense—he didn't want her getting in touch with Life Choice in the first place. He likes controlling the variables, holding on to my secret until just the right moment. But if Dad read Mom's journal like I do, he would realize that all this time he's taking to formulate his plan is only making it harder to begin. Or maybe he knows that the plan is the only perfect part of the process. Once you set the plan in motion, things get messy, full of holes and unexpected trouble.

Maybe that's why I haven't left town yet.

Maybe Dad and I have more in common than either one of us wants to admit.

But I can't give up now. I owe this to Nate, to see this through, to find as much of him as I can. It seemed so simple at first. The revelation that Nate had not really left after all, that he had just been redistributed, like jigsaw pieces separated from the puzzle box. That I could find him. That the barriers—death and guilt and the whole stupid world—would vaporize and fade. It all seemed possible. And I don't want to give up.

He found a way to get me to the ceiling, once.

So I prepare. I write a note to my parents explaining that I have to leave for a little while and that they should not worry but I know they will anyway and I'm sorry for that.

For that, I will say I am sorry now.

For the rest, Nate deserves the first apology. My parents can wait their turn.

After my note is written and folded and sealed, I fire up my computer and send an email to SparkleCat76. Dad took my computer but I have my school laptop—I'm not supposed to bring it home but the rules are getting easier to break. My shaking hands make it difficult to type, but I manage to tell her that I will be in Boston this week and I would be so honored if she would allow me to share her story. An in-depth profile, *all* about her. She won't be able to resist.

I give her my phone number.

Text me your address, I tell her, *and I'll come to you.*

I refuse to worry about how I will explain that I am not my mother. Maybe someone who calls herself SparkleCat76 lacks a firm enough grip on reality to notice. Or maybe she'll have just enough kindness to talk to me about the boy who allowed her to stay alive.

After I send the message, I think about what else I should do before I leave. I've withdrawn most of the money from Nate's bank account, enough for the bus from Molton to Worcester and the train from there to Boston, enough for some meals and some cab rides. I will buy a map of Boston so I don't have to use my phone to find my way around. I will ply Jennifer with flattery and the promise of sympathy from strangers, which is its own kind of currency for people like her. Like Margaret, the legendary liar. But not like me.

And I will find his heart.

I do not let myself think about all of the other possibilities. That Nate's heart went somewhere else. That whoever got it isn't even alive anymore. That Dr. Fikri's group of patients will not be where they are supposed to be. That I will be caught and dragged back home before I even get to Boston to find out.

I do not let myself think these things, but they are all around me anyway. I wander through the house, feeling it tilt and rock like an unmoored boat. In the kitchen, the red circle on the calendar shouts at me and I have to look at it. Four days away.

On Monday, when my parents leave for work, I will watch them go. I will gather my things and walk to the door and step out toward something new, my own escape, a girl Houdini. I have called it a plan but even I know (though I suppress the words) that it's not a plan—it's the pushing of a rock down a steep hill, and once the rock is tumbling, it will go where it likes.

I just hope I can keep it in sight.

I hope I don't disappear.

Suddenly the risk of running away without anyone knowing why seems like it could erase me altogether.

I text Chase:

meet me @ atm next to cg tmrw 10 am

THIRTY

STOLEN CAR

sunday 10/12

The next morning Dad knocks quietly on my door and invites me to come to church with them—part of his repair work on the family—but at the risk of it being used against me later I tell him that I'd rather not. He doesn't argue.

I have at least an hour, more if Mom and Dad go to the parish hall after Mass for coffee and cookies. I picture them there, standing in a corner together, hands huddled around the chipped, ancient mugs that the church offers every week. Then I draw them out into the crowd, paint smiles on their faces, give them things to say.

There, I tell them. *You're okay.*

The wind tickles my cheeks on the ride to the bank, and rattles the leaves on the trees. The sun fights the chill in the air but there is no denying it. Fall cannot hold the battleground for long. Chase is standing outside the bank, shoulders hunched against the cold, a skateboard tucked under one arm.

"New wheels?" I ask, leaning my bike against the bank's brick wall.

"Old ones," he says. "I think my dad forgot I had this. Not ideal for the weather, but he won't let me drive. So."

Dr. Abbott has Chase on his own version of parole. He calls at random times and Chase has to answer his phone or Dr. Abbott adds two weeks to his sentence. If he brings home any grade lower than an A−, he gets two more weeks. Misses his eight o'clock curfew? Two more weeks.

"Doesn't he care what you do before eight o'clock?" I asked when Chase told me the terms of his punishment.

Chase shrugged. "I think this is more about asserting his control, y'know? Twisting these particular screws. And it's not as if he's ever home before then. Who's going to keep me out of trouble? My mother?"

It makes me sad that Chase knows already that he can't depend on his parents. I mean, I can't depend on mine either, at the moment. But I could before. And some part of me assumes that I will again, someday. After this is all over.

I use Nate's card to unlock the door into the ATM, and Chase follows me inside to get warm. The flourescent lights are giving me a headache but I finish the transaction and stuff the cash and the receipt in the front pocket of my backpack. Chase and I head back outside.

"There's thirty-four dollars left," he says. He must have been peeking over my shoulder at the screen. "Want to come back tomorrow and get the rest?"

I shake my head. "I should leave a little something."

I feel a bit like I did before I fainted in school, so I try to glide smoothly over to the bench in front of the bank, but I trip on the uneven pavement and lurch to it instead.

"Are you okay?" Chase asks.

"I'm fine!" I snap.

He puts his hands up like I'm pointing a gun at him. "Okay, okay. Just asking."

"I'm sorry," I tell him. "I'm just . . . That question. I'm sick of it."

"Understandable."

I laugh, even though it makes my head hurt more. "Why are you so reasonable all the time?"

"Fear of conflict."

"C'mon."

"Are you afraid there's a Mr. Hyde behind my Dr. Jekyll?"

I'm afraid of all kinds of things. All the words I want to say pour into my mind like water into an empty bowl. *You don't know me. I'm a mess. Why haven't you tried to kiss me?* But the words just float, and my mouth can't shape them.

"What do you want to hear?" he asks.

"Did you look for me?" I ask him. "Because of who I am? The girl whose brother died?"

"No. I've never looked for anyone from the binder. Most people aren't as interesting as you expect them to be." He touches his fingers to his hair, and my heart twists, and he says, "But I found you anyway."

Through the front window of Common Grounds, I see Martha and Andy behind the counter. A world I used to inhabit, preserved behind the glass. "Did you feel sorry for me?"

Chase puts his hands in his pockets—they want to get out, I

can see them struggling, but he keeps them trapped. "I talked to you because it seemed like a sign, like there was some message I was supposed to understand. And then I kept talking to you because . . . because you're you."

We both watch his feet take one step toward me and then our faces lift, line up, dare each other to touch. Something inflates in my chest, pressing against my heart, something slippery and fragile that will explode if we continue poking it, and then all our secrets will come flying out.

"Okay," I tell him.

And we could leave it at that. But we don't.

"What are you going to do with the money?" Chase asks.

"I'm going to Boston." The wind tries to steal the words, drown them out. But I've said them and now they're true.

"Why Boston?" He asks the question, but his voice is flat. The question is a formality. He knows why.

"I want to see where they took Nate. Retrace his steps."

And he knows this isn't exactly the truth—not the whole truth, but the hole truth—but he doesn't call me out. Instead, he says, "I'm coming with you."

"What about your father?"

He pulls his phone out of his pocket and waves it in the air. "As long as there's cell reception, we should be okay."

"And the GPS?"

He wakes the phone up, makes a few screen trails with his finger, and puts it away again. "Taken care of. I don't think my dad actually knows how to use it anyway. But I can always tell him it got turned off by accident."

"He won't believe you," I point out.

Chase shrugs. "What's another two weeks on my sentence? There are thousands of biographies just waiting to be read."

"Okay," I say again.

And I say, "Thank you."

And I say, "We leave tomorrow."

The clouds dip and swirl above us, and I watch Chase get smaller as he rolls away, and I pray for enough time to finish this.

THIRTY-ONE

TIME TO RUN

monday 10/13

I don't wake up because I never fell asleep. I lay in my room all night, listening to the sounds in the house, holding my anticipation like a bird in a cage. Paying attention. Not wanting to miss anything.

I get up before my parents, shower, and get dressed—I laid out clothes last night but change my mind at the last minute and put on Nate's green flannel shirt. It doesn't smell like anything anymore but it still feels good, soft from hundreds of days on his body, and it feels like the right thing to wear.

And then I wait, still listening, for Mom and Dad to make their coffee and eat their toast and put on their armor for the day. I hear their cars cough and growl in the driveway, then roll away, cutting through the cold air like knives. I count to one hundred, to make sure they are gone, and that feels good, too. I send Mel a text:

sign me in

Time to go, I tell myself. I say it again, out loud, and my voice bounces against everything in the house, every object throwing the sound back to me as if it's saying goodbye. I tuck the note for my parents under the bright yellow sugar bowl on the kitchen table, touch it once for luck. Pull my jacket on and my backpack over it, buckle my helmet, unbuckle my helmet and set it down gently on the floor. Climb onto my bike, and go.

The air thrums in my ears as I pedal faster and faster, then slow for the stop sign at the corner, and I'm just about to turn toward the bus station when Mel pulls up next to me in her car.

"Get in," she says.

"Did you get my text?"

"Yep. No deal." She reaches down and pulls the lever to open the trunk, then stares at me, waiting.

"Mel, I—"

She slams her hand against the steering wheel, a slap like a gunshot. *"Get in."* Then she takes a deep breath and says, "I will do whatever you need, I will cover for you, I will lie and cheat and steal, but before you do whatever it is that you're about to do, you need to come with me."

Underneath her promise, there's a threat.

I lay my bike carefully in the trunk, but it doesn't entirely fit. The back wheel sticks up into the air and will not submit to my pushing at it.

"Leave it," Mel hollers. She's leaning out her window, watching me. "It'll be fine."

It's only a few silent blocks to school. Mel pulls into the parking lot at her usual speed, whirling into her assigned space so quickly that the trunk lid thumps against my unfortunate bicycle. The only good thing about not having been able to close it is that I can take the bike out again without needing to ask Mel to pop the trunk, without saying a single word as I walk it to the rack and lock it up.

"Be right back," I whisper, even though I don't know why Mel insisted that I come here or how long it will be until she lets me go. I check my phone while we're walking to the front door.

I'm supposed to meet Chase at the bus station in half an hour.

All I can hear as we navigate the hallways is the ticking of clocks.

Ms. Pace's room is empty except for us. There's a flock of plaster skulls lined up along the shelves, casts of students' faces painted for Halloween. They will fill the case in the front hall when they're dry, empty eyes greeting us in the morning and watching as we walk to class, our footsteps echoing in their hollow cavities.

Mel beckons me to the back of the room, where a row of easels stand waiting, covered with drop cloths.

"What are we doing here?" I ask her.

"Okay, okay," she says. "Keep your pants on."

She walks behind the easels, gathering the ends of the drop cloths together like a bouquet. "Ready?"

The sound of the cloths sweeping through the air is like a flock of birds lifting into the sky and then I am looking at something both familiar and completely strange.

Each easel holds a square canvas. Each canvas bears a close-up black-and-white image, a section of a photograph. An eye and the curve of a nose. Half of a mouth and chin, a cheekbone and an ear. The pieces are out of sequence, so it takes me a minute to realize what I'm looking at.

Nate.

"Do you like it?" Mel asks quietly.

"What . . ." My voice is hoarse, the way it was the night of the séance.

"I made them. For you. I took his yearbook picture and blew it up and cut it into a grid, and then I mounted each square onto its own canvas. It was pretty simple, actually."

My brain is reeling, trying to make sense of what my eyes are seeing. I look at Mel. Is she crazy? Is she messing with me? "Is this a joke?"

The pride on Mel's face begins to slip into something else. "No. It's . . . I saw your father in town a few days ago and he told me about your brother. What you found out. At first I was mad that you didn't tell me, but then I thought of this project and—"

"This is not a project," I say. "This is not like your fake band or your farm sculptures or your art installations."

"N-no, of course, this is d-different," she stammers. "I did this for *you*. To help you."

"Help me what?"

"Face the truth. He's dead, Tallie."

"No, I know, but—"

"Your brother is dead."

"He's *not*. I mean, he is, technically. But in another way, he's not."

"Do you know how crazy that sounds?"

"Since when have you cared how anything sounds? You love crazy. You collect dead animals and stuff them and dress them up. How is anything I'm doing weirder than what you do?"

"Because," she hisses, "what I do, I've been doing for years. I've always been this way. But you . . . you were so normal before. Even when I first came to see you and it was right after the accident, you were totally normal. And now . . ."

I ask calmly, "What?"

"You're . . . different."

I smile.

"Of course I'm different," I say. "What kind of person would I be if my brother died and I stayed exactly the same as I was before?"

"I thought we were friends. So why didn't you tell me about . . ." She glances at the pictures, Nate's face divided. "Why didn't you tell me?"

I hurt her, I realize. But I can't linger, there's no time. So I have to hurt her a little more.

"It's none of your business," I tell her. "I have to go."

I turn to leave, but Mel runs across the room and grabs my arm. Her fingers are like iron. She pulls me until I'm looking at her. I expect her to look angry but she doesn't. She looks hurt, frantic. "I bet you told Chase, though, didn't you? I bet he knows all about this."

"Again," I tell her, keeping my voice even, "none of your business."

"Why not?" she asks. "I was the first one to come see you after it happened. I was your only friend all summer and when school started. I took you to the séance and let you in the barn and I told you things about my parents."

"I know," I tell her. "And I'm sorry. But I have to do this on my own."

"Bullshit," she snaps. Then her tone shifts, becomes a furious creature. "I looked at your phone, y'know. I saw all the texts to Chase, I saw the playlist for Amy. *For Amy.* She doesn't even *like* you anymore, but I *love*—" She claps her hands over her mouth.

The stairwell. The pictures she took. I thought I was a novelty to her, a fascination. But it was something else. A story she wrote and I misread, and maybe this is one of those chances another Tallie could have taken but that I—at least for now—will waste.

I can't explain everything now, make her feel better, walk her through how I decided to do what I did, or whether it was even a decision. Retracing the steps of how we got here would be like running backward through an obstacle course. Life isn't designed for rewinding.

Ms. Pace's clock gazes down on us. I'm going to be late.

"I'm sorry," I tell her again, and I am. So I make a small concession.

"I'm going to Boston. I don't know when I'll be back. You want to be part of this? Text me if my parents are looking for me. I'm sure my dad will call you first, since he confides in you now."

"Okay, but . . ."

I pull my phone out of my pocket and take a picture of the canvases. Then I hold it up and show it to Mel.

"But if you tell them where I am, I will send this to everyone in school, and your whole wacky-girl-who-doesn't-care-about-anyone thing will be completely blown. Got it?"

She nods. I don't feel good about making threats, but I need the insurance.

Nate's eye watches me leave. I run through the maze of hallways that I know so well, relishing the pace of my feet hitting the floor, the sting in my lungs. My bike is waiting for me on the rack outside, an obedient pet, and I'm sure that if I looked up at Ms. Pace's window, I would see Mel, but I don't look up because it's time to leave. And there's just enough doubt in my heart that the sight of her might convince me not to.

. . .

We catch a bus from Molton to Worcester. No one tries to stop us. And it's the same thing at the train station—even though I feel like there's a searchlight shooting up into the air from the back of my head, giving me away, no one even notices that we're there. It's like we're cloaked by something invisible.

I talk to Nate inside my head, replaying conversations we had before he died.

Will you go to UCLA if you get in?

Probably.

But it's so far away.

I'll pack you in a suitcase and take you with me. You can clean my dorm room and write papers for me.

I pretend he's along for the ride, to distract myself from all of the questions that I should be asking myself. Doubts slice at my gut like razor-sharp butterflies and I pray, almost, that I will get through the day without another sinkable episode.

It's nearly noon by the time we get on the train, and my nervous edges are dulled by the steady bumping motion of the seats and the rattling of the windows and the occasional hiss of the heating vents. A kind of fog brushes over everything in front of my eyes. When I look at Chase, slumped and dozing in the seat next to me, it's like I'm watching a movie of him.

I think about what he said outside the bank, how backward everything has become. He wasn't looking for me, but he found me. A treasure hunt without intention, an *X* across both our hearts.

But I don't have a map for this, and there are so many reasons this will not work. We are running away, we are trying to fulfill an impossible mission, we are completely unprepared, and we might not be anywhere near as smart as we think we are. Doubts are scratching at the door.

I look out the window. The trees are dressed in their bright colors and all of the cars coming into Molton are full of people seeking the beauty of this change, but I can see it better. I see it for what it is: the slow, unstoppable death of innumerable leaves.

Storm clouds are gathering and they darken the landscape, changing the shapes outside into more menacing things. The metal towers that connect the high-tension wires look like giant dressmakers' dummies. Water towers become alien ships landing among the trees, and the trees themselves blur and merge into one continuous mass. The train holding me and Chase and strangers hurtles past unseen details, toward everything that awaits us. My mind lifts, lightens, hovers. Time is suspended. There is only this, only us, only the crosshatched track on which we ride.

I hear tapping nearby and I close my eyes to hear it better.

"What's that?" Chase asks. "Morse code?"

Oh my god, I think. *He hears it, too.* For a moment I am elated, and then I realize that the tapping is my own finger on the metal arm of the train seat.

"You know Morse code?" I ask him, tucking my blabbermouth finger and all the others under my leg.

"A little, just enough to recognize the patterns. Houdini used it to transmit fake messages from the dead to their relatives at his séances."

"I thought he hated séances. Didn't he spend years discrediting fake mediums and spiritualists?"

Chase grins. "Someone's been doing her research."

I free my fingers and scratch at my neck, which is prickling.

"Just a bit of browsing online." *To pass the time while I was waiting for inspiration to strike.*

He sits up straighter, eager to share this tiny piece of his own weird history. "It's true that Houdini wanted to expose the spiritualists who were scamming people, but he actually really wanted to believe that some of them could contact the dead because he wanted to speak to his mother's spirit. He was just so disappointed over and over again that his hope was——"

"Shattered," I whisper.

Chase nods. "It ruined his friendship with Arthur Conan Doyle, because Houdini just couldn't go along with what he was seeing. He knew all the tricks. And then it got worse because other people couldn't understand Houdini's tricks, so they started saying *he* was a spiritualist, that he vaporized himself to escape from things."

"But he must have still believed, right?" I say. "Because he worked out that message with his wife and told her to contact him after he died."

"I think he was just desperate. He couldn't let go. He couldn't accept that the door between here and there was something that could hold him back."

"Maybe he'd used up all of his escapes while he was still alive," I say. Threads of rain are covering the windows now. "Or maybe whatever was over there was better than he thought it would be, so he decided just to stay."

Maybe Nate is happy where he is. Maybe he imagined this, in his last moments, parts of him being given to other people. Maybe he wasn't afraid at all. Maybe . . .

Chase reaches over, pulls my hand away from where it's

scratching at my neck, and gathers it into his own. "Maybe he wanted his wife to move on with her life."

I will do that, I tell myself. *As soon as this work is done, I will go home to the after and figure out what's next.* But a little part of me, behind that thought, says, *There is no after. Not for you. You've lied, stolen, run away. You've already gone too far.*

I set my head on Chase's shoulder, and it dips under the weight of me, but it stays where it is.

THIRTY-TWO

BORROWING TIME

When I wake up, it is only the waking up that tells me I slept. I have no recollection of any dreams or evidence of sleep, except for a sore neck and a small wet spot on my shirt where, apparently, I drooled on myself. I dab at it and then notice that Chase is awake, watching me.

"Morning, sunshine," he says, even though it is early afternoon, only three hours since we left Molton. "We're here."

We shuffle off the train with everyone else and make our way down the long platform to the station. The lights seem to flicker and brighten as we pass underneath them, and inside the station, it's like the sun itself is burning. Impossibly high ceilings, webbed with angled ironwork, pull our voices upward when we enter, and the smooth stone walls remind me of the columbarium. I have to touch one then. I stride across the room and Chase follows.

"Hold up!" he calls behind me.

The wall is cool when I press my hand to it, and I can't resist putting my forehead against it, too. Chase looks worried. "Are you okay?"

Of course not, I say in my head. But it's amazing how easy that question has become to answer with a simple lie. "Fine," I tell him. And before he can ask me anything else, my phone pings. I thought I'd turned it off. My confusion is causing mistakes. I need to be more careful, or just go ahead and throw the phone in a trash can somewhere. But that will have to wait until Chase isn't looking—he's my ally, but he's also made himself my keeper.

The phone's been keeping its own secret. A text from Jennifer:

hi sarah. let me know when you get to town

Seeing my mother's name there—I drag my eyes up the walls, climb with them to the ceiling, breathe and breathe.

"Everything copacetic?" Chase asks.

"Not now," I snap.

"What?"

"Can you just— I have to think for a minute."

He snorts. "Look, you wanted me to come along for this—"

"No!" I yell. "I didn't! You *told* me that you were coming along for this. And really, this has nothing to do with you. So maybe you should get right back on the train and go home."

"And let you wander around the city like this? I don't think so."

My hands are slick with sweat now, and I'm shaking so hard that I have to clutch my phone to keep it from falling on the floor. "I am not a damsel in distress, okay? So whatever weirdo reason you have for following me here—"

"Is everything all right, miss?"

A police officer has appeared next to us. His badge and his

shoes and the handle of his gun are so shiny, reflecting the light like lasers in my eyes, that I have to look away. But this, of course, makes me look even more suspicious. I pull my sunglasses out of my backpack and slip them on.

"Everything is fine, Officer," Chase tells him. "We were just rehearsing for a play. Was it convincing, do you think? Did we sound genuinely angry with each other?"

The man looks at me. "Is that true, miss? You were rehearsing?"

I cannot think straight because the paths in my brain are all full of sand. But I can imagine what Mel would say. "Well, life is a kind of rehearsal, isn't it? Is anything really real?"

The police officer slaps his hand to his nightstick and says, "Keep it down over here." As he walks away, I hear him mutter, "Goddamn kids."

I hope he doesn't have any of Nate's parts.

The thought makes me look around the station, wondering. All of these people. What are they made of?

"Tallie," Chase whispers. "I'm sorry. But I'm worried about you. You're panicking or something. You need to calm down."

I bat my eyes at him from behind my sunglasses. "You sure know how to sweet-talk a girl." Then I hold up my phone. "I have to send a message to this woman."

"Who is she?"

"I don't know. Jennifer something. I think she has Nate's—I think she has some information for me."

"*What* about Nate?"

"Hmm?"

"You said 'she has Nate's.' Has his what?"

"His doctor. The one who—worked on him. She might be able to introduce me."

Chase's eyes narrow. "Do you think she has one of his organs? Is that why we're here?"

"Maybe." My voice is loud again, and the police officer looks in our direction. More quietly I say, "Just give me a minute, please?"

Chase sighs. "Okay." His own phone is cradled in his hand, a key ready to open the escape hatch.

I rub my temples. I need to keep the message short, to keep anything from sounding suspicious. And I'll have to find a way to explain myself when the time comes. I also don't want Chase to know that I've been deceiving these people, what with his whole-truth policy and everything, so I can't give anything away to him either.

I lean against the cool stone wall and keep my hands steady.

have just arrived @ south station. are you available to talk? let me know when possible. with gratitude

I leave out my mother's name this time.

"Done?" Chase asks. His voice is hard, and when I look at him, even through my sunglasses, I can see that his eyes are, too.

"Yes. Thank you."

"Now can we talk about what we're really doing here?"

"I will make you a deal," I tell him. "You just follow my lead and do what I ask you to do, just while we're here, and when we're done, it's your turn to be in charge. You can take me home, you can throw me in the harbor, you can do whatever you want. Okay?"

"Why would I—"

"*Okay?*"

He takes a deep breath. "Okay." Then he adds, "I'm giving you twenty-four hours."

I hear a fluttering sound above me. Two tiny brown birds are coasting and dipping through the air inside the station. I watch their unplanned ballet, shielding my eyes against the glare of the fluorescent bulbs.

"Ceiling!" I call to them.

"What?" Chase asks.

"Should be plenty of time," I say.

We both can admit, at least, to being really hungry, so we find a diner and order cheeseburgers and milk shakes. I keep my sunglasses on even though we're inside, and the waitress looks at me strangely, but I know that she could never imagine why I'm here, could never write this story like I can, and I smile as she walks away.

Chase doesn't even bother to ask what's funny. He just keeps glancing up from his plate with a worried expression.

His phone does not ring, and neither does mine.

I wonder how long it will be before my parents find my note, if they'll see it right away or go about their business and assume that I'm with Mel somewhere. I haven't heard from her since I left her standing in Ms. Pace's room with her failed offering. But I am not anxious. I know she will do what I asked, now that she has revealed herself.

I do not really want to hear from any of them, though, so I block their cell numbers and our home phone, just to be safe. I do this robotically. I feel like a spy.

"I feel like a spy," I whisper to Chase.

He nods, poking at his food with his fork as if he is expecting it to start moving around.

After we finish our burgers, we move on to coffee and pie. I am ravenous, like I have never eaten before. Like I will never eat again. I wonder how prisoners feel about their last meal, if they are ever satisfied with their choice, or if after they've eaten it, they immediately think of something that would have tasted better.

"What would you want your last meal to be?" I ask Chase. The silence is making me itchy.

He drums his fingers on the table. "That depends. Would I know it was my last meal? Or would this be, like, the last meal I eat before I am unexpectedly crushed by a bus?"

"I think the term *last meal* implies that you know the end is coming."

He swirls a spoon in his coffee, leaving trails of cream. "Then I don't think I'd be hungry."

This seems like a cop-out, and I tell him so.

"Fine, then." He drops the spoon on the table. The metal sings out, shrieking, and I feel my heart jump in my chest. "I would have grilled cheese with avocado and tomato. But the tomato would have to be perfectly ripe. None of that crap that's forcibly ripened with ethylene."

He goes on about genetically modified wheat for a few minutes and then excuses himself. I watch him walk between the tables and disappear into the bathroom. It makes me anxious not to have him in sight, as if he might vaporize like Houdini was accused of doing. I look around for something to focus on and see the corner of Chase's phone sticking out of his bag.

Watching my hand pull the phone out is like watching someone make a bad choice in a movie, my brain yelling, *No! You'll get caught! You'll ruin everything!* But my hand doesn't stop. And just like every bad choice, this one carries a consequence.

He texted Mel. He told her that he was worried about me, that I was acting weird. He asked what he should do.

My feelings battle like competing voices. *How could he do this? You can hardly blame him for trying to help you. I had things under control. You are falling apart in front of him.*

And then Chase is there and he sees that I am holding the phone, and he is saying something but I am having trouble listening because I'm there all over again, at the beginning of after, where everyone thinks they know what to do for me and everyone gets it wrong. I am not myself, I am a butterfly waiting to be pinned into a box and kept safe.

Chase is still talking, I can hear his voice outside my ears. I feel like I'm going to be sick, and it's bad enough that Chase has seen me cry but I'll be damned if he's going to see me throw up. I grip the table, lifting myself up and out of the booth, and the phone clatters to the floor and I try to say that I'll be right back but I'm not even sure if it comes out right and then I'm running to the door, through the door, hearing the door close behind me as the frigid air outside slaps me on both cheeks and tells me to pull myself together.

Chase is calling my name and I see him banging on the window when I look up and his face looks better but I can't watch that happen again and I don't even know if he's real anymore.

Run, Nate says in my head. *Run or he is going to catch you.*

I don't know where I'm going but I can see where we came from, so I head away from South Station, deeper into the city. I move quickly. I follow the cobblestone street like Hansel and Gretel followed their little white pebbles.

I left my backpack in the diner.

But I have my phone.

Which is ringing.

I see Chase's name on the screen. *No no no,* I tell myself, and it becomes like a refrain I am singing as I walk swiftly through the streets, and there is no one who can catch me now.

The trees are monsters slipping in and out of themselves, and I watch them.

All the colors are moving, melting, slurring their words.

The air presses against me.

I am made of paper now. I can almost fly.

The trees begin to whisper their sinister sounds, their whipping branches humming a dark tune.

You belong to us, they tell me.

We will swallow you in browning gold and hide you.

"Yes," I whisper.

And I run.

THIRTY-THREE

PUTTING THE DAMAGE ON

I run until I am out of breath and my throat is raw with cold, and then I hide myself in a doorway and try to think. I do not remember which way I came to get here. I also do not remember turning my phone off but I must have done it. I'm tempted to leave it off, to hide that way, too, but I need to know how to find Jennifer, so I turn it back on. I watch it come back to life and wait to feel something. But I am feelingless. Again.

There are several missed calls from Chase. Seeing his name is mildly fascinating, and I almost want to call him back to see how he will explain his betrayal. But there is also one from a number I don't recognize and the trees remind me that there is work to be done. I dial into my voice mail and delete each of Chase's increasingly desperate-sounding messages, and I am scrolling through so quickly that I almost accidentally delete the one message that isn't his.

It's from earlier this afternoon.

A woman's voice.

"Hi," she says. "This is Jennifer Martin. I got your message and I'm, well, I'm actually home today, so, I don't know, if you wanted to come by, I guess that'd be okay. Just, um, call me back? This is my home number."

She doesn't sound very smart, I think. *But beggars can't be choosers.*

She answers on the second ring.

"Hello?"

Her voice is reedy, weak-sounding. I wonder if she is shy. If she was shy before her transplant or if having part of someone else's—

"Hello?" she says again.

"Oh, s-s-sorry," I stammer. "Hi. You called me. About getting together."

"Is this Sarah McGovern?"

"Not exactly."

"I don't understand."

"Sorry," I say again, and I try to sound jovial but I am still feeling pretty much entirely flat, so it comes out forced. "I think there's been a little mix-up. My name's Tallie, um, Nathaniel? I'm writing an article for my school paper. Sarah McGovern suggested I talk to you. She didn't tell you I'd be in touch?"

"No," Jennifer says warily.

"Sorry!" I say brightly. "Do you have some time to talk to me today?"

"I'm really confused." Jennifer pauses and I sink deeper into the shadow of the doorway while I wait for her, just in case Chase is walking around looking for me. Finally, she says, "You're not Sarah McGovern?"

"Nope," I say. "But she told me all about you, and it sure would help me out to talk to you." Then I add, "My editor thinks this story is going to be huge." Now I definitely sound overeager. But she seems to accept it.

"Okay. I guess. I live in Back Bay, on Dartmouth Street. Do you know where that is?"

I don't, really, but I want to save my questions for the important stuff. "No problem. I'll be there in an hour."

And before she can object to anything, I hang up and start walking.

It's only about a mile to Dartmouth Street, and I am still full from what I ate at the diner before things fell apart with Chase. I can think those words to myself and they don't even sound strange. *Things fell apart with Chase.*

I am standing on the bridge in the Public Garden. I remember coming here with Mom and Dad and Nate when I was five, to ride the swan boats and see the statues of the ducklings, their heads polished bright by countless tiny hands. It was one of the memories I used to reach for when I did the rituals, the taste of the ice cream we bought from the truck at the corner outside the park, the feel of Nate's hand at the back of my head, giving me rabbit ears while my mother took our picture on a bench.

Now I look down, and next to my reflection I see a looser shape that darkens and then fades like a shadow on the water.

I see you, I tell him. *I know you're here.*

I stagger over to the other side of the bridge and follow the footpath out of the park. Jennifer's street is three blocks away. When I think I've gone far enough, I stop on a corner and try to focus my eyes on the street sign above me but the letters are swimming like alphabet soup. *Stop it,* I scold them, and just for a second, they fall into place. DARTMOUTH.

I giggle. What a weird word.

This is it.

I step onto the street and realize that I don't know what number Jennifer lives at. I fumble for my phone and turn it on to call her. But before I can dial, I hear a tiny voice coming out. *Nate is in my phone,* I think. And then I realize that it's Chase.

I put the phone to my ear.

"Tallie? Hello? Tallie, are you there?"

"I think so," I say quietly.

"Oh my god, are you okay? Where are you? I'm coming to get you."

"No, you're not," I tell him, and I hope that my saying it makes it true.

"Tallie, listen, I called my father and . . ."

"Okay."

"I didn't know what else to do. I'm in massive trouble and I didn't want to tell him anything, but you ran off—"

I hang up on him. He probably thinks that I'm angry, and normally I would be, but right now I can only deal with one ghost at a time and also there's a woman walking up to me. She walks slowly, uncertainly, as if she's old, but her face is young and I'm reasonably sure she's real and she says, "Tallie? I'm Jennifer."

THIRTY-FOUR

CLOUD ON MY TONGUE

Jennifer has an Elliott Smith poster in her living room. Well, her mother's living room. She has lived with her mother since the surgery, she tells me, and she is hoping to go back to work at some point but she's not really in any rush. She drops onto the couch as she says this, and though she doesn't look heavy, the cushion sinks low as if it's resigned to holding her. As if it's been expecting her.

Jennifer strikes me as someone who is not going to accomplish very much.

She starts to tell me about the record store she used to work at, how the manager was always hitting on her. I think briefly of Cranky Andy, grateful that he spared me that kind of attention.

"What about you?" Jennifer asks. "Got a boyfriend?"

I think we probably do not have much time, because Chase is, well, chasing me and I am really not feeling very well. So I ignore her question and stick to my own. Since I left my backpack in the diner with Chase, I had to borrow a pen and a pad of paper from Jennifer. She is still willing to believe I am a high school reporter, despite my unpreparedness and the fact that I am twitchy and exhausted. She must be really desperate for social interaction.

"How are you feeling?" I ask her.

"Good, really good," she says.

Without looking up from my notes, I ask, "And your surgery was when?"

"I told Sarah that already. End of May."

"But the exact date was . . . ?"

"Why do you need to know that?"

I glance at her. I am having trouble not staring at her, searching for some sign of Nate, but I force myself to look away. "For my timeline," I tell her. "I need to be precise. Journalistic accuracy."

"Oh," she says. "The twenty-sixth."

That lines up nicely, doesn't it? Within twenty-four hours of the accident.

"And what kind of transplant was it?" I ask. And then I brace myself because though I think I know already that she doesn't have his heart, maybe I misunderstood her before, and maybe she does, and the idea of *this* woman having it . . .

"Liver," she replies.

Relief and disappointment tumble all over me.

"Do you know whose . . . I mean, do you ever think about the person whose liver you got?" I ask her.

She nods. "Of course I do," she says. "Like, I wonder exactly how he died, like, if he was a bad driver or if his accident was somebody else's fault."

Something swells up in me then, but I push it down, reach for another thought. I wonder why Jennifer needed a liver transplant in the first place. She's not that old. Maybe she drank too much in college.

"Does it matter?" I ask.

Jennifer shrugs. "I guess not. But it would sort of be better if it was something tragic, y'know? Like, it would be a better story."

I could answer all of her questions. I could satisfy her curiosity, give her all the gory details, the sound of the car hitting the tree, the feeling of being pulled from the car, of seeing my brother taken away. Except I don't actually remember those things, and even if I did, I wouldn't give them to her.

I cough, dislodge the words I *really* want to say. "Okay, next question: If the donor's family wanted to meet you, would you be open to it?"

She looks confused. "Why would they want to meet me?"

"Well," I say, "part of their, um, loved one has become a part of you."

"So?"

"You don't think that's important?"

She takes a long sip from her can of diet soda. Is she supposed to be drinking that? "Of course I think it's important. I'm alive, aren't I? But I don't see what his family would get out of seeing me. I mean, it's not like I got the *face* of their loved one. I got the liver. You can't see the liver."

"That's true," I tell her. "But it might help the family cope with their loss to see how the donor's contribution has changed your life. It has, hasn't it?"

She stares at me. "Of course it has. I'm not dead."

I feel my optimism draining away, emptying all of the moisture from my body. Specifically, my mouth. "Can I have a glass of water?"

"Sure." Jennifer stands up and walks into the kitchen. I seize her absence to push my sleeve up, trace Nate's faded name with

Jennifer's pen, watch the ink feather into the tiny channels on my skin. When she comes back from the kitchen and hands me the water, I quickly pull my sleeve back down and say, "I see you have an Elliott Smith poster."

Jennifer looks over her shoulder as if she'd forgotten the poster was there. "Oh, yeah," she says. "I love him."

"It was so sad when he died," I say.

"I know," she says. "He was really cute." Then she adds, "But no one ever knowing exactly what happened? *That's* pretty hard-core."

I ask her what her favorite song was.

"Oh, you know," says Jennifer, "the one about the little house and the mayor named Fear? I can't remember what it was called. I used to listen to it all the time."

"Memory Lane," I think. It's on Matty. But I won't answer that for her either.

"Okay, well, I guess that'll do it," I tell her. After an awkward handshake, I remind her I have her email address in case I want to follow up, even though I would rather eat glass than have another conversation with this girl. Virtual or otherwise. Also, she looks extremely relieved that I am leaving her apartment. Her mother's apartment.

She closes the door behind me but I don't leave. I sit on the top step in the stairwell and look at all the other steps below me, all the dependable straight lines and perfect right angles.

Nate loved that song and he can't listen to it anymore. She can listen to it whenever she wants but she can't even remember what it's called.

Now what? I ask myself. My fake interview with Jennifer didn't tell me anything. She may or may not have Nate's liver. I almost hope she doesn't, because knowing that part of him will be trapped in that apartment for all time makes me furious. Or it will, when I no longer feel like I'm wrapped in emotional insulation.

Just then the door flies open and Jennifer is standing there, pointing at me. "You're his *sister*," she spits.

"What?" The step I'm sitting on suddenly feels a lot less dependable, like the stairs have turned into an escalator.

"Some kid named Chase just emailed me," she hisses. "He says you're hunting down your brother's organs."

"I'm not 'hunting' anyone," I say, and then I stop because I've just confirmed her suspicions and, in the same moment, realized how he did it. My laptop. It was in my backpack, in the diner.

He got into my email because I was stupid enough to choose a password he gave me. *Rosabelle.*

Jennifer crosses her arms and sighs dramatically. "I'm not happy that you lied to me."

I don't care about your happiness. Oh, I want so much to say it.

"How old are you, anyway? Do your parents know what you're up to?"

"What do you care?"

She tilts her head. "Well, I don't, really. But it seemed like the responsible thing to ask."

I let myself stare at her then—her smug expression, her ratty cardigan, the shadowed circles under her eyes—and I hate her for being the one who lived. One of many who lived. Just like me.

"I have to go," I tell her, and I follow the unsteady lines of the stairs.

She calls after me, "Wait! Tell me about your brother! Tell me the story!" All the way down she calls after me, her voice echoing through the stairwell, and I can still hear her as I walk outside.

I look at my phone. More missed calls from Chase. I delete the notifications and check the time.

It's almost four o'clock.

It's Monday.

I throw my arm in the air, like Mom does, and a white car with red writing on it comes whipping around the corner like a dog running to its owner.

"Brigham and Women's," I tell the driver.

THIRTY-FIVE

HOW TO FIGHT LONELINESS

I'm in a boat. The water is dark as night, rolling toward me, rippling like the skin of a predator ready to strike. The boat is so small and I am rocking, rocking, starting to tip, falling over—

I wake up screaming. "Nate!"

"Miss?" The cabdriver is peering at me over his shoulder, one elbow hooked over the back of the seat. "You okay?"

I don't remember falling asleep, but I can see through the car window that we are here. Brigham and Women's Hospital.

"Yes," I gasp. "I'm fine."

"You're not fine," he says gently. "Do I need to get somebody out here?"

I shake my head, take the last of my cash from the pocket of my jeans, and hold it out. My hands are trembling and he's just staring at me now, so I thrust the money into the front seat and bolt out of the car.

Somewhere along the way, I dropped my sunglasses, maybe in Jennifer's apartment or in the taxi, but it doesn't matter anymore because the sun is crawling down the sides of the buildings and I am here and I will find him. *I will find him.*

I say it, again and again, make it the rhythm I walk to as I enter the hospital.

The swooshing automatic doors sound like an air lock opening on a spaceship and everything is so clean and shiny and white. Everyone is walking crisply and looking straight ahead and no one even sees me as I speed-walk from the door to the bank of elevators. There's a list on the wall, but there are so many names and my whole body is humming with adrenaline, making it hard to focus. The letters are all so tiny and they are swirling like paint in one of those spinning toys that make dizzying artwork for kids. I wish this was one of those old-fashioned elevators with a man that rode up and down all day and I could tell him who I wanted to see and he'd take me to the right place.

I press my hand against the wall to feel something solid, to calm myself down.

Pull yourself together, I imagine Nate telling me. *Don't fall apart on me now.*

That's what he said after we saw the jumper.

We were driving down to Washington, D.C., for spring vacation, one of those educational family field trips. My parents filled the front seat with talk about monuments and museums and bickered about whether a visit to the FBI building was worthwhile. Nate and I stared out our respective windows, occasionally turning to look out the other side in case we were missing something good. I had the right, he had the left. We had just crossed over the George Washington Bridge into New Jersey when I noticed a man standing on the edge of the cliff next to the northbound lanes. I was about to say something like "Hey!" or "Look!" when the man jumped.

He did not look scared. He held his arms out like wings, and it almost seemed like the most natural thing in the world, for a man to leap from a high place like that.

But I knew it was not.

I looked to my brother's window and he was already looking through mine.

"Did you see that?" I whispered.

He nodded. He held my hand.

"See what?" my mother chirped from the front seat. She did not turn around.

"Nothing," my brother said. "It was nothing."

And we kept our secret, through the nightmares we both had afterward, through our parents constantly trying to figure out what we weren't telling them, because we didn't want them to imagine what we had seen. I went to his room in the middle of the night, shaking, and he told me, again and again, *Don't fall apart on me now. We can't tell them. It's our secret, you and me.* We saw it, really saw it, and nothing they could picture in their minds would have been even close to what we saw.

It was our moment, ours together. Ours alone.

"Help me," I whisper to him now.

And then, like the Ouija board, like magic, I feel a push against my hand—not the one that's holding me up but the one that's dangling at my side—and it lifts to the squirming list of names and guides my fingers slowly up, over, up a little more. There. FIKRI, SAMIRA, MD. 8TH FLOOR.

I think I hear my name just as the elevator doors close, but I am hearing so many other things, too. Nate's voice, my own echoing thoughts, and something else, something like doubt tapping out its own warning. I still have Matty in my pocket. I tuck his earbuds into my ears and turn the music on, keeping it low. Just loud enough to cut the noise.

I watch the numbers light up one by one.

6

7

8

I can hear the doors when they open, and then I hear voices. New voices. Familiar voices.

Chase and Dr. Abbott are here, waiting for me.

I fold into the corner of the elevator car and let the doors close again.

The elevator is already sinking to the lobby when I think of the directory. Other floors, other offices. And the elevator isn't the only way to get to them.

The doors open, then close, and I press 9. All of this rising and falling is hellish for me, but at least the inside of the elevator is not too brightly lit, and the metal walls feel like ice against my body, lovely and cold. I watch the numbers until the doors open again.

Just around the corner from the elevator is the door to the stairwell. I test the door from the inside before I let it close behind me, to see if it will lock. It doesn't, so I trust that the other doors are the same way. One door wouldn't be different from the others, would it? Mr. Cunningham says that conformity is much more likely than chaos in the natural world, and I'm not sure if stairwells count as part of the natural world but they were designed by people, so . . .

. . . I wonder if I'll ever see Mr. Cunningham again. I wonder if he and Ms. Pace will get married. I wonder if I would have been invited to the wedding, if they would have asked Mel to design a little taxidermied bride and groom out of field mice, if she would have asked me to help her pick the flowers for the mouse bride's bouquet. . . .

I see then that I have sat down on the steps and I'm not sure how long I have been here. I stop the music and tuck Matty away, so I can think.

Get up, I tell myself. *You're so close.*

But doubt drowns my thoughts. Doubt, and terror that my mission will fail, that I'll have to keep carrying all the words I have wanted to say, the message I have for what's left of my brother in the world. I pull my sleeve up, to see his name, but the letters are smeared across my arm. Just another mess I've made.

"It's all my fault," I whisper, practicing, trying to get it right. "I shouldn't have been driving. I didn't know how yet, I told you I knew how and you believed me, and I . . . I killed you, Nate." I am sobbing, the stairwell amplifying my misery. I am crying for him, for myself, for our family of four that will always be three. For all the stories that will never be told. Nate going to college, falling in love with someone who loves him back, getting married. Being there when I get married. The possibilities that will never become anything more. The promises that will never be kept.

Cross my heart, he said.

His heart. His heart is here. *Get up.*

"Okay," I say. And I launch myself like an uncertain rocket, I reach the door and pull the handle.

THIRTY-SIX

SAY HELLO TO THE ANGELS

Mr. Cunningham is right. Conformity reigns. I come out on the eighth floor, around the corner from the elevator, just like on the ninth. I can still hear them talking, even over the sound of my own ragged breath.

"We need to call her parents," Dr. Abbott is saying.

"I already did," Chase replies quietly.

"Well, it wasn't your place to do that, son."

"What *difference* does it make *who* called them?" Chase snaps. "The outcome is the same. They have been called. They are on their way."

Dr. Abbott clears his throat. "What makes you so sure she's coming here?"

"I just know."

Then a woman's voice, slightly accented, takes a turn. "My group is waiting for me. I cannot make them wait forever."

"You go, Samira," Dr. Abbott tells her. "Chase and I will wait here in case Tallie shows up. And in the meantime"—he clears his throat again—"we can have a long talk about boundaries and expectations."

"Terrific," Chase mutters.

"Very well," Dr. Fikri says. "I'll come back when my meeting is finished." I hear the *click-clack* of her shoes coming toward me. Moving quickly, I manage to roll myself along the wall and through the stairwell door just before she turns the corner. Through the tiny window, I catch a glimpse of her passing by.

Follow her. This is it.

I ease the door open, hold it with my foot, and slip my body through one piece at a time.

Dr. Fikri *click-clack*s to a door down the hall. I watch that door after it closes and I inch my way toward it, leaning against the wall, such a strong, steady wall, and my hands are sweating, slick with ambition, ready to fight, but the edges of my sight are getting black and fuzzy and I know I am sinkable, but not now, please, not now. . . .

I turn the handle.

I am in the room.

They are all in a circle in plastic chairs.

Their faces are swimming and indistinct and I can't be sure. . . .

Is that Jackson? Margaret? Bethany?

It's the wrong room.

Isn't it?

A woman stands up.

"You must be Tallie," she says calmly.

Calmly to calm me.

I giggle.

"Are you here to talk about your brother?"

All their faces, staring, expectant.

"I'm here," I rasp, "for his heart."

"Pardon me?" a man says nervously.

"One of you," I tell him, "has my brother's heart. And he needs it back. For promises."

"Tallie." Dr. Fikri steps out of the circle. "You look unwell. Will you let me help you, please?"

With all of the sound left in me, I roar, "I'm *fine*!"

But it doesn't matter. She doesn't believe me.

"Just tell me," I plead. "Just tell me who has it, I need to talk to him."

Now the other chair-sitters start shifting in their seats, but I am between them and the door and they can't get out. They can't get out without giving me what I want.

"Tallie," Dr. Fikri starts, but I yell, "Stop saying my name! I don't want to hear you say my name!" Then, because yelling makes the blackness close in, I whisper, "I just want his heart. I need it. I just need it."

"I have it," says a voice from behind me.

I spin. Wobble. Catch myself again.

Chase.

"I have it," he tells me.

"No," I say. "You shouldn't be here. I lied to you. I ruined everything."

He reaches for me with grasping fingers that I shrink to avoid.

"But I did, too," he says. "So we're even. And I'm not lying now. I know where Nate's heart is."

I want to believe him, so badly.

Chase nods, like he can hear me. "I know where it is," he says again. "It's in another room, though. Do you want to come get it?"

274

I step toward him. The energy between us is a pack of animals, scratching and sharp.

"It's okay," Chase says. "I'll show you."

And I am almost there, to him, when Dr. Abbott appears in the doorway. "Okay, now," he says to no one in particular. "I think we've had just about enough of this."

Run.

I leap, and they're not ready for it. Instinctively they both step out of the way before they remember that they're supposed to catch me.

And then they're all just yelling.

But their voices can't catch me.

Run.

I am so fast.

I run to the bathroom. Lock the door behind me.

It's cool in there, every glacial surface, but I am sweating and I can't breathe.

I open the window, lean into the air. I look down.

Remember the jumper.

Is it far enough? Can I get to him this way?

I pull Matty out of my pocket. His metal is warm, the cord of his earbuds wrapped around him like a blanket. I press him to my lips, and then I throw him out the window. I count the seconds—four of them—until I hear him hit the ground.

It doesn't tell me anything, that sound.

There is pounding at the door.

But I hold my body to the window. My hands grab the frame on either side.

Jump.

I want to, I want it to be over, but my hands won't let go.

"Please," I hear myself whisper, sobbing. Pleading with myself, whatever part of myself demands to go on living even though I don't deserve it. "I killed him," I tell my hands. "Please, let go."

But they will not obey.

Come with me, Nate says. And then his voice is drowned out by the roaring of my own, screaming, "I can't!"

The door bursts open and someone, someone strong, is pulling my hands. Someone is holding me. Before I can even turn my head to look, the world closes in and I think, *I failed,* and it all goes black again.

THIRTY-SEVEN

BELLS FOR HER

I wake up in white.

"You're going to be fine," the doctor says.

I try to speak but I can't. My tongue is thick in my mouth, glued in place.

"You need to rest. We gave you something to help you sleep," the doctor tells me. "But you are going to be fine. You'll be back to normal before you know it."

I want to scream, I want to say no, because I know now that there is no normal anymore, there is no back, there is no memory that can keep him. He's gone. Nate is gone. For real, this time. I want to tell the doctor this, tell him that I should have jumped, should have broken myself into pieces to give away. *My gifts.* The price to be with my brother.

But my body is a slab of wood. I cannot lift my head or my arms or anything else. I cannot speak or scream. I feel tears running down my face and I cannot wipe them away.

I still didn't get to tell him. I still didn't tell him how sorry I am.

"I know," the doctor says. "I know."

But he doesn't.

THIRTY-EIGHT

IT IS WHAT IT IS

wednesday 10/15 and so on

Mom holds my hand. She traces the bones in my wrist with her thumb.

"We have a lot to talk about," she says.

I touch her hand, too, feel her skin like paper. Like canvas for painting.

"We know everything now," my father tells me. "I got a notice in the mail. A collection notice, for an unpaid ambulance bill. Four months overdue. And at first I thought that I must have just forgotten to pay it. But then—"

"We went through your room," my mother blurts out. "I'm sorry, honey, but we had to do it. And we found—"

My father jumps in again. They're ping-ponging the conversation, like they used to do. Before. "Nate's mail. And some of his clothes. And things from his room."

"I'm sorry," I tell them.

They both shake their heads, mirror images. "You don't need to say that," my father says. "What's done is done. We're just grateful you're . . ."

Alive. The word hooks into the air between us.

I want them to be angry, I want them to ask me how I could do what I did, stand in a window and think about jumping. Ask what stopped me. Ask me anything.

My mother makes a little sound, like a choke meeting a gasp, and her hand tightens around mine.

"Are you okay?" my father asks.

That question.

"I don't know," I say. "I thought I could make things different. I thought I could put Nate back together but—"

"Tallie," my mother interrupts. "It doesn't matter now. You are going to get better, that's the important thing."

"You said that already."

"Well." Dad shuffles uncomfortably. "We should probably let you get some rest."

I didn't get to tell Nate, but I can tell them.

"Guys," I say, so quietly that it's hardly even audible.

Dad has his arm around Mom, and pivots them both around at once. "What's that, sweetie?"

"I'm . . ." My throat is tightening, trying to stop the words. But this has to happen, doesn't it? The doorway out of limbo opens with the words that have been drowning in my crazed imagination. This is the hardest part, prying them out of my scarred, wasted, reborn body. I push, I push hard, and then, finally, the dam is shattered.

But instead of a river, only a trickling stream comes through.

"I should have let him drive." I hear myself say the words, but they don't feel like anything. And I remember Dad telling me that sometimes what you think you need isn't what you need.

I thought it was all my fault, and I thought my guilt was keeping me from becoming myself again. Now I know I will never be myself, not the way I was before. I will carry this, the memory of the accident, the sound of the crash echoing in my ears. Maybe forever. It's part of me. The *after* me.

I look at my parents, and they look like they were asleep for a long time and just woke up and are confused about where they are. They have heard me name the thing that I regret the most, that I will always regret more than anything else, and they tell me, "It's okay, sweetheart," but they don't know everything else, and I don't think I need to tell them. It's the jumper all over again, a story I can't quite explain, something they would wish I hadn't seen. Something they can't fix.

Bad things happen, and we are not the same when they are over.

But we go on.

They sit down and we talk for a while—Mom, Dad, and I— about what to do now. They don't want to send me back to school, but I tell them (and I mean it) that school is the only place that makes me feel normal again. I need to go through those motions, do the normal things that normal kids do, even though the motions may not be smooth for a long time. Even though I will see Mel and remember our adventures like a movie I watched once. Even though Chase may not be there—and if he is, I don't know what he'll do with me if I don't need a rescue team.

Maybe we can just get coffee.

That would be nice.

Eventually I convince my parents that I will be okay. And I almost convince myself, too.

Before they leave for their hotel, Dad pulls a cardboard box from inside his jacket. For a moment I think of Nate's ashes, the box we took to the columbarium and surrendered to Eben Dolmeyer, but this box is white and a bit smaller, and I recognize the symbol on the outside of it. So I kind of know what it is. But I open it anyway.

It's an MP3 player. Green, not blue like Matty was.

"I didn't know if you'd want the same color as Nate had," Dad says. "We can exchange it, if you want a different one."

I shake my head. "No," I tell him. "This is good."

Mom says, "You were listening to his music a lot." It isn't a question.

I nod.

"Now you can listen to your own, too."

And so I am. I'm listening to some new songs that I've downloaded and I'm stroking the smooth green metal when Dr. Blankenbaker comes in a few days later. She's taller than I remember, and softer-looking. She's smiling but her eyes are serious, and when she sits down in the blue chair that's still warm from my mother's body, I see that they're the same color as mine. Carefully, I pull my earbuds out and set them in my lap. I can still hear the music threading out, tinny and distant.

"I just saw your parents in the hallway," Dr. Blankenbaker says. "They look a lot better than when I first saw them." Then she adds, "As do you."

"I feel better," I tell her. It's good to say something that is both simple and true. I make a note to do that more often from now on.

But despite what I told my parents, that I'm ready to move on, there is still a story I need to tell. There is still so much I haven't said out loud and it's not enough to say it to myself, to fill this hospital room with words and let them echo off the walls into nothing. So Dr. Blankenbaker hears it all: Gerald and Jennifer and Dr. Fikri, Mel and Amy and Chase, what I did and what I said, what I'm sorry for. She raises her eyebrows higher and higher but she lets me finish before she speaks.

"There's a lot we don't know about grief, Tallie." She looks inside the folder she's holding, as if there's a script in there that will tell her what to say next. Then she closes it and tosses it on the bed. "No one knows better than you do how it felt to lose Nate. Death is like a really confusing foreign film. Everyone in the theater has a different idea of what it means. And the subtitles are no help at all."

"I guess it's just one of the big mysteries," I say.

She nods once. "It's good to know there are still a few of those, isn't it?"

"I didn't think doctors like things they can't explain. I thought you wanted to have answers for everything."

"For every thing we can explain, there are a thousand that we can't. I can't tell you exactly how life begins, or why some people can tolerate pain that is unbearable to others, or whether death is an ending."

"Or how the pearl grows in the mollusk?" I ask.

"Sure," she says, a little uncertainly.

"And that doesn't drive you crazy?"

She smiles. "If I had all the answers already," she says, "I wouldn't have any questions left. And questions are the whole point of what I do."

"What's your favorite question?"

She thinks for a moment, her eyes fixed on something invisible across the room. *"Why."*

"*Why* is your favorite question, or why am I asking you?"

"*Why* is my favorite. Because it just keeps going, and it opens so many doors."

After she's gone, I think about *why*. About how it was the question I hated most after the accident, because there was no answer at all for the longest time. And now I see that the answer I give today might not be the one that works tomorrow, or next year, or when I get married, or when I tell my son or daughter about their uncle Nate, who they can never meet.

But maybe it's not about the answer, in the end. Maybe just being able to ask the question has to be enough sometimes. The question, the asking, my brain, my voice, my body. I am here. I am alive. I am lucky.

It sucks to be facing a life without my brother.

But it's a life, just the same.

THIRTY-NINE

SOMEONE YOU'D ADMIRE

"Tallie?"

It's a woman. She has inky dark hair and eyes and at first I think I am imagining her because her voice is so soft and gentle and hardly anyone who is real ever talks like that. She is wearing an enormous sweater that she has wrapped around herself. She is holding herself with her arms, like she is afraid she might fall apart.

I know that feeling.

Everyone else is gone now, my parents and the doctor and all the others who want to get a look at me, and I am empty as a bag from all that talking.

"Yes," I tell her. "I'm Tallie."

She steps into the room and comes almost to the side of the bed. I will not call it my room or my bed. These are not my things. At least, I know that much.

"I'm Ann," she says. "Ann Shepard."

"Hello," I say.

She steps a little bit closer, wraps her sweater even more tightly. "I think," she tells me, "that I may have your brother's heart."

I push myself up with my fists, sit straight.

Ann smiles, her mouth wobbling as it moves. She is very nervous. "Everyone is talking about you, all over the hospital. I've been participating in Dr. Fikri's study but I wasn't in the room when you— I was at another appointment down the hall, and when I heard about you, well—" She takes a deep breath. "I asked Dr. Fikri if she could find out."

Your personal history. Questionable intentions.

"And she did?"

"We compared the dates of my surgery and your brother's death. And they matched up. Your friend—Chase? He wanted to tell you right away. But we didn't know for sure, until your parents got here. And then they had to talk to Life Choice and I had to talk to them, too—" She stops, out of breath. "I'm sorry, can I sit down?"

"Of course."

She pulls the blue chair from the corner and sets it next to me. It's a bright blue, a cartoonish blue. I wonder if Mom noticed.

"It doesn't usually work out this way, but the Life Choice people decided that since we were all in the same place already, and everyone gave their consent—well, they confirmed it."

And she actually places her hand over her heart, the heart that used to be Nate's, when she says, "Thank you for sharing your brother with me. I'm so sorry you lost him, and I know it won't fix anything, but I want you to know that I am taking good care of him."

There's an invisible rope around my throat. "Thank you," I say.

Then I think of something.

"So," I ask, "Chase didn't know for sure that you had Nate's heart until after I broke into the group meeting?"

She smiles. "None of us did, not for sure. But I spoke to Chase when he and his father first got here, when they came looking for you. They thought you might try to find us, the people from the group, and well—I don't know. But they wanted to warn me."

"Chase thought I was going to hurt you?"

She shakes her head. "No, he promised you wouldn't do that. He did that thing, you know, that kids do?" And she traces her index finger across her chest, making an *X* with her finger.

"Cross my heart," I say.

"That's right. He did that, and then he told me that he thought you and I would have a lot to talk about. After you were okay again."

"But he didn't know . . ."

Anne shrugs, crosses her arms again. "Maybe he has special powers."

Chase, I think. His name has become one of those words, the ones I will have to practice until they feel okay again. Until I know if he can forgive me for everything I did.

"Thank you," I tell her. "I'm glad you came."

"I'm glad you're okay," she says. "I should let you rest."

"That's what everyone says in hospitals."

She smiles. "Yes. I remember."

"Well," I say, "I'm glad you're okay, too." I try not to look at her chest, try not to see the beating heart inside it. I look at her eyes instead. Dark, like Nate's. But not Nate's.

She stands carefully. "I wonder if . . . well . . . could I write to you sometime? I'd really like to know more about him. I've wondered, you know, what he was like. Maybe you could tell me some stories or—"

"I don't think that's a good idea."

"Oh." Ann is as surprised as I am to hear the words come out of my mouth. But as soon as I say them, I know they are true.

"I just mean . . ." *What do I mean?* "I can't try and explain him to you. He's—he was . . ."

"He was a whole person," she says. "It wouldn't be fair to summarize him."

"Right."

And she is, but it's more than that, too. I thought finding the rest of Nate would let me keep him somehow, but it wasn't him I was looking for. It wasn't a way to get him back.

It was a way to let him go.

She stands and turns to leave, and then she pivots back again. "It's the strangest thing," she says. "I never liked ice cream before, but lately I've been craving it. It's all I can think about, getting a vanilla fudge dip cone. Isn't that odd?"

She accepts my smile as an answer and a farewell. I watch her walk all the way down the hall, past all of the other doors that hold all of the other patients and visitors and doctors, and I think of the columbarium as I watch Nate's heart walk back into the world.

I reach over to the rail that runs along the side of my hospital bed, identical to the one that held me after the accident. So much has changed and yet here I am, and it's as if I've been taken back to when everything spun sideways, that day that I lost my brother and lost myself, too. The rail is cool when I wrap my hand around it, it is solid and real, and it rings like a bell as I tap and scrape my finger to the rhythm of the one word I always knew best.

Scrape tap. Tap scrape. Scrape. Tap.

Nate.

FORTY

TAKE TO THE SKY

six months later

Be back soon. I write the note and then crumple it up and throw it away.

"Be back soon," I call to my parents. Then I walk to the doorway, to make sure they heard. They are in the dining room, paint chips and fabric swatches spread across the table like a collage, debating which shade of navy blue is perfectly, absolutely right for below the chair rail. My father is putting up a fight in name only—we all know that this is my mother's domain, the choosing of colors, the application of new skins on the furniture, the arranging of it all.

He just likes to add his voice to the symphony. Another instrument in the daily soundtrack we've all gotten used to hearing again.

They look up at the same time, like expectant puppies. "Going out?" my mother asks. Her face is softer than the one I woke to at the hospital, the hollows of her cheeks filled in again, so she looks more like she did in the family pictures that have started reappearing around the house.

"Just for a drive," I say. "Maybe ice cream."

The words they do not say—*please* and *be careful,* among others—hover between us. There are still things we leave to the air, things we don't talk about. I'll never tell them about the jumper, or how close I came to following him, but some of our secrets have come back into the light of day. We are not the same, but we are okay.

The emails my mother gets from people who have read her story on message boards and organ donor forums. The meetings my father goes to. The password protection he added to his computer, and the lock on Mom's nightstand drawer. All the reminders of the sins I committed, and the apologies that I have yet to make.

Just because I learned a lesson or two doesn't mean their secrets are safe.

My car awaits me, an ancient Volvo station wagon that's too heavy to drive fast and too yellow for other cars to miss. Mel dubbed it the Mustard Missile when she saw it, when I hauled it out to the barn—uninvited—to see how her latest tableau was coming along. She let me as far as the front door and balked, said she was too superstitious to show anybody and promised me the first look as soon as she was ready. I think we both knew that was my last trip to the barn, but she did me the favor of that promise, gave me the gift of an un-goodbye.

I'll see her in school, probably.

And Amy. She and Jason Rice have been hanging out, I hear. She could do better, but I won't offer that opinion, even if she asks. And maybe someday I won't have to think about our friendship in the past tense.

I'll see Jackson and Margaret and the others, even though Bridges has all but disbanded—everyone just got tired, I guess, of talking about themselves. There are much more interesting topics. Ms. Doberskiff has bounced back nicely, though, and recently announced that she is going back to school for a degree in abnormal psychology. Maybe even she got bored with our average problems, our stories of sadness and helpless frustration.

Everyone has to move on.

The world is not the same.

I drive to Chase's house, honk the horn to announce myself, and cue up my MP3 player to the beginning of the playlist I made last night. The Mustard Missile's only modern feature is the stereo that Dad had installed, to celebrate me getting my driver's license. The license lives in my wallet, back to front with Nate's. Same little red heart in the bottom right corner.

His gifts.

I put a check mark in that little box on the RMV form. I did that. Not because I thought it was the right thing to do, but because Nate got me to the ceiling once and I know now he was a far better person than I am. He was good, and he was real. So I will copy what he did, mimic his goodness, until I figure out what mine will look like.

I pull my sleeve up to the inside of my elbow, where his name is written, tattooed in my mother's handwriting. She wrote it for me on a piece of paper, drove me to the tattoo place, and held my hand while a guy with words all over him inked *Nate* onto my arm. My mouth watered with the pain but it was worth it.

He got me to the ceiling.

I'll take him everywhere else.

The Abbotts' front door opens, and Chase comes out, blinking at the insane brightness of the sun. The sky is cloudless blue, endless and wide like an ocean above us, and he gets in the car and I think about how I will kiss him later today, so that every kiss we've already had will pale in comparison. I make that silent promise, and I reach one finger to the impatient stereo, and I press play.

And we drive.

ACKNOWLEDGMENTS

Stories are born in the hearts of their writers, but they can't become books without a whole lot of help. My boundless thanks to:

My family—especially my children, who remind me always why stories matter.

My editor, Melanie Cecka Nolan, who saw what this story could be far beneath what it was.

My agent, Linda Pratt, who found me exactly when I needed her.

My Monday-morning ladies: Jennifer Elvgren, Kathryn Erskine, Kathy May, Rosie McCormick, Anne Marie Pace, Fran Cannon Slayton, and Julie Swanson.

The Super-Secret, All-Powerful YA Binders.

The VCFA community.

And last, but most certainly not least: teachers, librarians, and independent booksellers everywhere, who work with passion and unwavering dedication to inspire readers of all ages. You open doors, you reveal worlds, you save lives. Thank you.

If you would like to learn more about organ donation, please visit organdonor.gov.